PRAISE FOR *THE LAST SISTER*

"[A] gripping novel of suspense from Elliot . . . Elliot skillfully unravels layers of intersecting stories, each one integral to the overall story of the Mills family and their small-town secrets. Readers will want to see more from this author."

—*Publishers Weekly*

"Every family has skeletons. Kendra Elliot's tale of the Mills family's dark secrets is first-rate suspense. Dark and gripping, *The Last Sister* crescendos to knock-out, edge-of-your-seat tension."
—Robert Dugoni, bestselling author of *My Sister's Grave*

"*The Last Sister* is exciting and suspenseful! Engaging characters and a complex plot kept me on the edge of my seat until the very last page."
—T.R. Ragan, bestselling author of the Jessie Cole series

PRAISE FOR KENDRA ELLIOT

"Kendra Elliot is a great suspense writer. Her characters are always solid. Her plots are always well thought out. Her pace is always just right."
—*Harlequin Junkie*

"Elliot delivers a fast-paced, tense thriller that plays up the small-town atmosphere and survivalist mentality, contrasting it against an increasingly connected world."
—*Publishers Weekly*

"Kendra Elliot goes from strength to strength in her Mercy Kilpatrick stories, and this fourth installment is a gripping, twisty, and complex narrative that will have fans rapt . . . Easily the most daring and successful book in this impressive series."

—*RT Book Reviews*

THE
SILENCE

ALSO BY KENDRA ELLIOT

COLUMBIA RIVER NOVELS

The Last Sister

MERCY KILPATRICK NOVELS

A Merciful Death

A Merciful Truth

A Merciful Secret

A Merciful Silence

A Merciful Fate

A Merciful Promise

BONE SECRETS NOVELS

Hidden

Chilled

Buried

Alone

Known

BONE SECRETS NOVELLAS

Veiled

CALLAHAN & MCLANE NOVELS
PART OF THE BONE SECRETS WORLD

Vanished

Bridged

Spiraled

Targeted

ROGUE RIVER NOVELLAS

On Her Father's Grave (Rogue River)

Her Grave Secrets (Rogue River)

Dead in Her Tracks (Rogue Winter)

Death and Her Devotion (Rogue Vows)

Truth Be Told (Rogue Justice)

WIDOW'S ISLAND NOVELLAS

Close to the Bone

Bred in the Bone

THE
SILENCE

KENDRA
ELLIOT

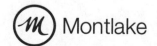 Montlake

Text copyright © 2020 by Oceanfront Press Company
All rights reserved.

Published by Montlake, Seattle

www.apub.com

Amazon, the Amazon logo, and Montlake are trademarks of Amazon.com, Inc., or its affiliates.

ISBN-13: 9781542006767 (hardcover)
ISBN-10: 1542006767 (hardcover)

ISBN-13: 9781542006743 (paperback)
ISBN-10: 1542006740 (paperback)

Cover design by Caroline Teagle Johnson

Printed in the United States of America

First edition

For my girls

1

Detective Mason Callahan stared at the severed fingers on the bathroom linoleum.

"What's the point of trying to hide the corpse's identity if he's left in his own house?" Detective Ray Lusco muttered. The burly Oregon State Police detective had been silent for nearly thirty seconds as he took in the scene. A record.

A mutilated body lay in the bloody bathtub. Arcs of blood went up the walls and across the floor. A large rubber mallet had been abandoned on his chest, the dead man's misshapen skull indicating its use. Most of his teeth had been broken off at the gumline and looked like pieces of shattered porcelain in the drying blood. Two fingers were still attached to his left hand, but the rest were scattered across the floor.

"Looks like someone was interrupted before he could finish the hands," said Mason. He scowled as he did a quick count. "I only see seven loose fingers."

Ray winced. "Aw, shit. You don't think he took one as a souvenir, do you?"

"Might be under the body."

Both men paused, and Mason steeled his stomach at the mental image of the two of them rolling the body to check. "We'll wait for the ME."

The medical examiner can have the honor.

It never got easier. Mason had seen dozens of deaths in his decades of law enforcement, and many had imprinted on his brain and cropped up in the middle of the night, ruining his sleep until he banished the images. He'd learned to compartmentalize his work. This was a job, and he was damned good at it. He was there to help and had to set aside his horror and disgust at what one human would do to another.

Even *he* hadn't been safe from a killer's wrath.

His fingertips traced the lines of rough skin around his neck. Eight months ago someone from his past had tried to hang him, fully intent on a murder of vengeance. If Ava hadn't shown up when she had . . .

He abruptly inhaled through his nose, fighting back his gag reflex, using the scent of the death in front of him to push away the memory.

The home sat on a small lot in a tiny town just outside the Portland suburbs. A local patrolman had responded when a neighbor noticed a broken window in the back of the house and saw blood on the kitchen floor. The town's police chief had taken one look at the gory scene and requested the Oregon State Police's help. The town of three thousand hadn't had a murder in more than a decade.

"Reuben Braswell. Age fifty-two. Not married. Appears to live here alone," Ray stated, checking the notes on his phone. He pointed at the pile of bloody clothing tossed by the toilet. "His wallet and driver's license were in his pants pocket. He matches the photo and stats."

"What's the tattoo say?" An American flag covered half of the victim's arm, but Mason couldn't make out the words below the flag.

"'We the people.'"

"What about the tiny print?"

"The words of the Second Amendment."

"Some people have strong feelings about it." Mason didn't have a problem with the Second Amendment, but he wasn't about to tattoo it on his body. "Any other tattoos?"

"Only if they're on his back. The ME can check."

"Was he ever married?" asked Mason.

"Doesn't look like it. I don't know how he got to that age without getting married," Ray said. "Wonder what was wrong with him."

"Maybe he simply didn't want to be married. Doesn't mean there's a problem." The marriage discussion wasn't a new one. He and Ray had broached it several times. The other detective swore marriage was the best thing that had ever happened to him and had a storybook home life. Gorgeous wife. Two great kids. Perfect home. Mason had hidden his jealousy for years. His own marriage had imploded long before.

His situation was about to change. For the better. Much better, thanks to Ava.

"It doesn't make se—"

Mason cut Ray off. "It's not for everyone. What's he do for work?" he asked to redirect his partner's train of thought.

"Works at the local Home Depot. Eight years." Ray looked up. "I wouldn't mind working there after I retire. I already know what's on every aisle."

Mason nodded, knowing they shared a fascination with the store. Between the two of them, they had enough tools to stock a new one. But he had no desire to ever work in retail.

"Immediate family?"

"Parents deceased. We're trying to find the brother and sister."

"Let's walk the rest of the house."

The crime scene tech had stood patiently in the doorway as the two detectives looked their fill, but Mason felt the impatience rolling off the tall, thin man, who shifted from foot to foot. Mason nodded as they passed, seeing relief cross the tech's face that they were leaving his crime scene.

"Are you caught up on this season of *Queer Eye*?" Ray asked as they moved down a hallway, walking tight to the walls to avoid stepping in a wide, smeared blood trail but not close enough to knock the old photos off the wall. Mason paused at a black-and-white photo of young boys in cowboy hats sitting on a pony. He owned a nearly identical one of him and his brother. Probably every family of his generation had one.

Ray continued talking. "The last episode is a real tearjerker."

"Ava had the show on the other night." Mason had stealthily watched from behind the safety of a book, pretending to read instead of watch the emotional makeover show. "I think she watched that one." As if he could forget. He'd held his face completely stiff to fight back tears as the five costars had kindly rebuilt the self-confidence of a man his own age.

Fifty wasn't far ahead in Mason's future. A humbling number that didn't match how he felt on the inside.

"Yeah, I already texted with her about it." Ray sighed. "Fucking brutal show."

It was normal that Mason's fiancée texted with his partner. When Mason couldn't help her choose between roses or peonies for their wedding flowers, Ray was stoked to share his opinion. Same with discussions about women's boots or the latest rom-com. Mason appreciated their friendship.

The men halted at the kitchen entrance, the origin of the smeared blood trail before them.

Mason looked up. More arcs of blood streaked the ceiling and one wall. The kitchen's tired wood floor was marbled with smears and small pools of blood.

"Guess the rubber mallet damage wasn't sufficient in here," said Ray. "He used it again in the bathroom."

Or he simply felt like it.

Mason could almost feel physical echoes of rage in the room. He wondered what the mallet hitting the skull had sounded like and fought back a shudder.

He spotted the broken window not far from the back door and stepped carefully around the blood, the booties covering his cowboy boots muffling the usually sharp sounds of his tread.

"Glass pieces are outside," Ray said.

"The break wasn't from someone trying to get in." Mason pointed at the arcs of blood near the window. "I think someone hit it with the mallet. Could have been accidental. Maybe not."

"I can't think of a reason to break the window from the inside," Ray said.

Mason agreed. *Why break the window when you could unlock the door to get out?*

He opened the door, which led to a small concrete patio. A large grill stood in one corner, and the faint odor of char and barbecue reached him. He inhaled deeply, hoping the smell could drive away the scent of death. The June afternoon was hot, creeping into the high nineties. Unusual for this early in the summer. The small patch of lawn had more dry, brown areas than green, and a weathered gray fence surrounded the small backyard, hiding it from the adjacent homes.

"How'd the neighbor spot the broken window?" asked Ray.

"I'd like to know too." Someone would have to deliberately peer over the tall fence to see the backside of the home. Mason had asked an officer to bring the neighbor back for an interview.

"Mason, Ray." Medical examiner Dr. Gianna Trask stood in the doorway behind them. "They told me you were here."

Both detectives had worked with the ME before. Her husband was the brother of investigative journalist Michael Brody. Mason didn't know how to label his testy relationship with Brody. Not friendship. Not acquaintanceship. *What do you call having a mutual respect but high suspicion of each other?* The reporter would be at Mason and Ava's wedding. Along with Gianna and her husband.

Hands were shaken, greetings exchanged.

"I haven't looked at the body yet," Dr. Trask said. "But judging by the green face of the patrolman who let me in and the mess in the kitchen, it's a bad one." Her voice was light, but her dark eyes were grim.

"Keep an eye out for a missing finger," Ray said.

One of her eyebrows shot up. "Noted." She stepped back inside, leaving the door open a crack.

"Back to work," said Ray. "More house to cover."

Mason sucked in a last inhalation of the faint barbecue scent, wishing he could make it last.

2

FBI special agent Ava McLane downed the last of her coffee and put the mug in the dishwasher, the new appliance triggering a smile. *When do I stop feeling giddy about appliances?* The stainless-steel dishwasher matched her new six-burner stove and wide commercial refrigerator. She and Mason had been without a kitchen for nearly four months as contractors ripped out the 1980s-style kitchen and then discovered problem after problem. The plumbing. The electrical. The dry rot.

The old Tudor home they'd purchased last year had turned into a money pit. Issues in the kitchen were just the beginning of problems found throughout the entire home. How it had passed inspection, she didn't know. Mason had wanted to hunt down the inspector, but Ava had reminded him that this was the home they'd fallen in love with and would have bought no matter what the inspection returned. He'd grumpily acquiesced and sent another payment to their contractor.

She would smile all she wanted at appliances. Remodels were hell.

Ava had worked from home that morning, finishing up reports on the case she'd closed the previous week, and had promised her supervisor, Ben, she'd be in the office by noon. She checked the time and grabbed her bag as Bingo whined. She spun to give the dog a goodbye hug and stopped. He was utterly still, his attention directed at the front door.

The doorbell rang, and Bingo uttered a low woof of warning.

"Good boy." Ava gave him a head rub. He was an excellent watchdog, knowing with no training—at least no training from her or Mason—when to sound the alarm and when to stay quiet. More than a year ago, the stray had chosen Mason as his person and become a permanent part of the household.

Ava looked through the peephole in the front door. She could have used her phone to check the front-porch camera of the high-tech security system Mason had installed, but the old-fashioned way was quicker.

The man on her porch appeared to be in his twenties. His hands were shoved in the front pockets of his cargo shorts, and he stood several feet back from the door, leaving plenty of space between himself and whoever would answer. Flip-flops and a snug T-shirt completed his look, but he didn't appear scruffy. His hair was short and his goatee neatly trimmed.

He was familiar, but she couldn't place the face.

A chill of warning went up her spine. There was a reason Mason had installed the security system. In the past, dangerous elements of their jobs in law enforcement had followed them home.

And there was always the question of Jayne.

Ava's twin sister was unpredictable. Usually for the worse.

"Can I help you?" she said loudly through the door. The man straightened, and hope filled his features.

"Are you Ava McLane?" he asked.

"Who is asking?"

"Brady Shurr. I'm looking for Jayne." His tone was desperate.

Ava's knees shook, and she pressed her hands against the door to steady herself as she looked closer through the peephole. Jayne had run off from a local drug-and-alcohol rehab facility with Brady Shurr around eight months ago. Last Ava had heard, her twin sister and Brady were in Costa Rica, using Brady's family's money to pay for a luxury rehab clinic.

At least Jayne had still been seeking help.

Ava now recognized him. The Shurr family owned a half dozen auto dealerships in the state. Brady and his siblings were often in the commercials.

Her hands icy, she undid the locks and yanked the door open. "What happened? Where'd she go?"

Brady stared at her, scanning her face. "Jesus."

Ava knew that look. She'd seen it all her life. She and Jayne were identical twins, and often the only difference between them was the current style or color of hair. People who knew only one of them were always stunned when they met the other.

"Jayne said you two looked nothing alike," he finally said, blinking hard as he continued to scrutinize her.

"She knows full well how identical we are," Ava snapped. "She's impersonated me more times than I can count." Her heart pounded. Jayne had been quiet for months, but that was part of her twin's destructive cycle. Long periods of silence followed by an abrupt tsunami of activity. Usually illegal activity. Ava had been on edge, waiting for the other shoe to drop—it always did—and now it was standing on her front porch.

The silence was over.

"She's gone," he choked out.

"What do you mean, gone? I thought the two of you were living the high life on a beach in Central America." Pretending her heart wasn't climbing up her throat, Ava leaned against the doorjamb and casually crossed her arms. "What did she do now?"

Jayne's past was full of illegal drugs, petty crimes, and stealing whatever she could from her twin. Ever since they were young, none of Ava's possessions had been off-limits, in Jayne's mind. She had helped herself to Ava's credit cards, her identity, her car, her boyfriends, and her clothing, claiming that twins shared everything. Jayne always floated from job to job and man to man, seeking excitement.

Jayne was several years older than Brady. They'd met in rehab, and somehow she'd convinced him to leave his wife, check out of the clinic, and disappear with her.

The last time Ava had heard from Jayne, she'd been upbeat, looking forward to the future with this young man and promising to stay clean.

Ava hoped for the best but always expected the worst when it came to her twin.

Brady's pleading gaze held Ava's. *He really cares about her.* How had Jayne gotten to this rich, good-looking young man?

"She vanished, and she told me in the past to find you if she ever disappeared."

Alarms went off in Ava's head. "You better come in."

3

Minutes after he'd arrived on her doorstep, Ava had Brady settled on a stool in her new kitchen, with a glass of iced tea in his hands. He sat at an island that was so big she had to stretch onto her toes to wipe its center. The contractor had measured how far Ava could reach before approving the island. He had a client who was annoyed with him that she had to climb on a chair to clean her island. He refused to make that mistake again.

Brady watched as she poured her own iced tea. "It's so weird. You walk like her and move your head the same way." He blew out a breath. "Her hair is the same color and length too."

"That's unusual," Ava said as she took the stool beside him. "In the past she's tried to keep her hair as different as possible. Blonde or purple. She's always said brown is boring."

"She was making a fresh start. We both were."

Fresh start. *How many times have I heard her say that?*

"She's a drug addict. She always will be. The same with you."

"I know that . . . We both know that."

"Who decided the two of you should leave the local clinic and go to Costa Rica?"

His shoulders slumped. "Me."

Ava doubted that. Jayne was a master of manipulation. It would have been child's play for her to convince Brady he'd come up with the idea when she'd planted it seed by seed in his brain. Ava knew Jayne had always wanted a lengthy tropical vacation. No doubt she had seen the possibility with Brady.

"You were married when you met my sister."

He slumped more. "I was. But it was over before I entered the rehab clinic. I didn't leave her for Jayne."

Maybe true. Maybe not. But either way, Brady believed it now.

"The two of you decided you'd make more progress in Costa Rica at a different rehab clinic?"

"Yeah, but we checked out of there three months ago."

Ava blinked. "Where have you been?"

"We're living not far from the clinic. It's really beautiful down there."

"Your family was providing you with money to live in a foreign country?"

"It's pretty cheap. We had a huge place with an ocean view for less than ten thousand a month."

She swallowed. Brady was serious. To him that was cheap.

"When did she leave?"

"It's been about two weeks."

"What? And you're just telling me now?" Ava tightened her grip on her glass of tea.

Not my problem. Jayne is not my problem.

Two decades of trying to help her sister had ripped holes in Ava. The scars were deep.

Jayne's suicide attempt last year had nearly destroyed her.

Ava had to build a wall and keep it between the two of them, and Mason had done everything in his power to help.

"I thought she'd be back. She would take off for a few days sometimes, but she always came back."

"Hang on." Ava pulled out her phone and opened a locator app. After Jayne's suicide attempt, she'd added her sister's phone to the app without Jayne knowing. In the hospital, she'd used the facial recognition on Jayne's phone to approve the addition.

Being a twin was good for some things.

Ava had checked the app once a month, noting that Jayne was still in Costa Rica. It'd given Ava some peace, but not much.

Right now the app couldn't find Jayne.

Her phone was off.

"Where would she go?" *This is the Jayne I know. Vanishing acts.*

Brady shrugged, keeping his gaze on his tea. "I don't know. She asked that I not talk to her about her disappearances. She was always clean when she came back. I could tell she hadn't been using or drinking."

Ava bit her tongue to stop from lecturing Brady on the characteristics of a healthy relationship. "What was she doing? Shopping? Have you checked your credit cards?" she asked bitterly. Jayne had run up huge debts with Ava's cards multiple times.

"I got her some cards in her own name." He finally met Ava's eyes. "I looked. There's no charges on hers or mine."

"What about cash?" Ava asked as she searched her email. "Did she have access to a good amount of cash?"

"Of course."

She jerked her gaze up from her phone. A deep line had formed between Brady's brows, as if her question confused him.

How do people fall for her scams over and over again?

Shaking her head, she went back to her email and found what she was looking for. "My last email from her was four months ago."

"I thought the two of you emailed every week. She always kept me up to date with what was going on with you." He frowned at her stomach. "You don't look pregnant—oh! I'm sorry!" He sat up straighter on his stool, looking stricken. "Did something happen—"

"I'm not pregnant and never have been," Ava said dryly, wondering what other stories Jayne had made up about her to entertain Brady.

13

"Give me a minute, please," she said as she hit Zander's number on her screen.

Special Agent Zander Wells was her closest friend at the Portland FBI office. If anyone could dig up information on Jayne, it would be Zander.

"Ben just asked me where you are," Zander answered as a greeting to her call.

"Something's come up."

"What happened?" His tone sharpened. "You sound like shit."

"Thanks a lot." She paused. "Jayne has happened." Her words sounded flat.

"She okay? Are you okay? It's been quite a while . . . What did she do this time? Is she back from Costa Rica?"

Zander knew everything about her sister's history.

Ava took a breath. "She's missing. Brady Shurr is here and just told me she vanished about two weeks ago."

Zander's computer keys started to rapidly click. "When did you last hear from her?"

"Four months ago."

The clicking stopped. "I'm sorry, Ava. I know how hard it is on you always waiting and wondering what will happen next."

"Well, it's finally happened, and now I can relax," she joked, feeling tears start to burn in her eyes.

They weren't tears for her sister; they were tears of release. The dark cloud of uncertainty hovering over her head since last fall had finally broken apart.

"There is no relaxing when it comes to your twin. We all know that. Let me see what I can find on her," Zander said. "Do you have an address for her in Costa Rica? Or a cell phone number?"

Ava asked Brady for the information and relayed it to Zander.

"I'll call you back in a few minutes," Zander said, and ended the call.

Ava's finger wavered over Mason's number on her cell phone. *Not yet.*

She didn't want to disturb him at work when she had essentially no information to share. He'd drop whatever he was working on. He understood better than anyone how Jayne could rip her up inside.

Ava glanced up to find Brady studying her. "I've got a coworker looking for her," she told him.

"I should have come to you sooner," he admitted. "But I honestly thought she'd be back any day."

Ava sat back on her stool and took a long sip of tea. *Now what?* "What did Jayne do in her spare time down there?"

"Paint," he answered promptly. He pointed toward Ava's formal dining room, where a painting could be seen through the wide archway. "That's hers," he stated confidently.

Ava gazed at the painting she'd bought last fall. When she'd first hung it, Mason had gently questioned whether she wanted the prominent reminder of her sister. "I'm reminded of her every time I look in the mirror," Ava had answered. He'd not brought it up again.

"I liked it right away," Ava told Brady.

"More than a dozen were sold while we were in Costa Rica," he said, looking wistfully at the picture. "She painted nearly every day. It was good therapy for her. I think it kept her brain quiet. She was always in motion, you know? Always going from one thing to the next as she tried to distract herself from the constant activity in her head. Painting helped with that."

"That's great." Ava meant it. "I met David for the first time when I bought it. He was in the shop and wanted to buy it too."

She hadn't known at the time that David Dressler was her father, but he had known Ava was his daughter. Her mother had cut off all contact with the married man after she'd become pregnant and had never told her twins their father's name. Last fall, more than thirty years later, David had tracked them down, and Ava had learned she had two

15

half siblings. She'd met them all socially a few times but still held the group at arm's length, not quite comfortable with her instant extended family. She'd been on her own for too long.

Do I ask him to give me away?

Ava shoved the question out of her head. It'd popped up a thousand times since she'd learned she had a father, and the concept of asking him to be part of her wedding was ridiculous; he'd been in her life for eight months.

But deep inside her was a little girl who'd dreamed of having a father, and that young girl arose at odd moments.

"Jayne was thrilled when she met David. She adored him instantly. He's a good guy," Brady said.

Ava simply nodded. Jayne had written an enthusiastic email about David's visit to Costa Rica, raving about finally having the father she'd always wanted. She'd jumped into the relationship with all the Dresslers with both feet. Ava had slowly waded into the shallow end and stopped, looking around with suspicion.

David, his adult kids, and their families were good people. Ava's brain knew that. But it didn't mean they all had to be best friends. Yet.

Her phone buzzed on the counter, and she snatched it up. "Zander?"

"It appears she flew from Costa Rica to San Diego two weeks ago," he answered.

Ava froze. Zander's tone wasn't normal.

She's dead.

Her vision tunneled on Jayne's painting.

"Is she okay?" Ava whispered, blood roaring in her ears.

"I don't know. I can't find any movements after that . . . but Ava." Zander paused. "I didn't find a record of Jayne on this flight."

Ava frowned.

"I found you. Someone has a passport in your name. I assume it's her."

She leaned forward and rested her elbows on the island, pressing the phone hard against her ear.

Jayne is fine. This is standard operating procedure for her.

Ava closed her eyes for a long moment. "You searched with my name?"

"When I couldn't find any results for Jayne, it seemed like a logical next step."

"I should have known . . ." She locked eyes with Brady. "Jayne used a passport with my information," she told him.

Confusion crossed his face. "She has her own passport. Why use yours?"

"That's the question I've been asking all my life."

Zander cleared his throat. "Any idea why she picked San Diego?" he asked.

"David—our father—lives there. That's the only reason I can think of." She repeated the question to Brady, who lifted one shoulder and shook his head.

"Okay. I'll look into that."

"Dammit. Sounds like I should also check my credit report."

"I thought you got alerts for new activity," said Zander.

"I do. But I'm going to check anyway. Have I traveled anywhere else in the last few months?" she asked dryly.

"Only to Denver."

"That was actually me on the plane."

"I know." A note of amusement in his voice. "Business as usual for Jayne, right?"

"It is. I'm almost relieved. But where has she been hiding for the last two weeks?"

"I'd like to know why she left me," Brady said quietly, his finger tracing a pattern on the counter.

Sympathy flowed for the young man who'd been caught up in the Jayne McLane cyclone.

17

"I suggest you go back to your family and forget my sister," Ava said kindly.

Stricken eyes met hers. "I can't. We're soul mates."

Holy shit.

On the phone, Zander swore under his breath. He'd heard.

"Her only soul mate is herself," Ava said, knowing blunt speech was needed to open Brady's eyes. "We'll find her, but you need to prepare yourself for the worst."

"That she's dead?" He blanched.

"No. That she no longer cares about you."

4

Mason and Ray stepped into the garage of Reuben's home and went silent.

It wasn't shocked silence; it was the silence of awe.

Is this what happens when you work at Home Depot for eight years? And aren't married?

Custom workbenches and cabinets lined the garage along with enough metal tool chests to run a large automotive repair shop. Perfectly lined-up tools hung on the wall. The floor was spotless, painted with that shiny texturized finish that almost transforms a garage into a normal room. Mason wondered if a vehicle had ever been parked inside. Ray nudged him and pointed at the gigantic TV on one wall. "Nice," he said under his breath.

"Rubber mallet could have come from here," Mason suggested.

"Possibly. But could we even tell if it was missing?" Ray asked, studying the hundreds of tools on pegboards.

Mason looked for an empty space on the boards but didn't see one. Everything appeared in complete order. He opened the closest cabinet. Wood glues, stains, and paint. The cans were immaculate, not like his collection with dried paint dripping down the sides. He looked in a tall upright cabinet. Gardening tools. Hoes, rakes, shovels. No crusted dirt.

"Have they even been used?" Ray muttered.

Scratches on the metal indicated they had.

"The house isn't this clean and organized," Mason pointed out.

Ray shrugged. "Priorities."

A uniformed officer appeared in the garage doorway. "We brought the neighbor back. She's ready to talk to you."

"She okay?" Mason asked.

"Pretty rattled. But she can talk. She's on the bench out front."

Mason took one last look around the immaculate garage. His awe was gone. Knowing that the creator would never again enjoy his man cave had soured it.

Outside, Gillian Wood held a cigarette between shaking fingers. She stood and gave the detectives a nauseated smile as she shook hands. Her face was heavily freckled, her eyes an intense green. She wore a T-shirt with PINK emblazoned across the front, and denim shorts. She seemed too thin to Mason. As if she smoked instead of eating.

Ray gestured for her to sit down and took the chair across from her on the wide front porch. Mason stepped back and leaned against a post, trying to blend into the wood. Women warmed to Ray better than Mason, and Ray automatically knew to start the interview.

Gillian shot a nervous glance at Mason and looked to Ray for reassurance.

Every time.

It'd bothered Mason at first. Ava claimed women were careful around him because he rarely smiled. He forced his lips into a wooden smile.

Gillian blinked at him and quickly looked away, taking a long draw on her cigarette.

I tried.

The neighbor said she was thirty-two and had lived next door for nearly a year. She rented the property.

"How well did you know Reuben?" Ray asked.

"Well enough to say hello . . . not much else. He kept to himself." She blew smoke. "He helped me out one time when I had a leak under the kitchen sink. That was nice of him."

"He has a lot of tools in the garage," Ray added.

"I've seen it. Pretty crazy, huh? He works at Home Depot, so I guess the collection is understandable." Her lips quivered on one side. "Probably spends his entire paycheck there. The curse of working retail. I worked at Macy's for a year. I hardly brought home any money . . . always saw something I had to have."

More smoke.

Mason studied her. Gillian was understandably nervous and upset. She'd seen the blood and knew her neighbor was dead. But her discomfiture seemed to mean more than that. He listened as Ray asked about visitors and vehicles that might have been at Reuben's. She'd seen nothing. With every question, her gaze shot past Mason and lingered on the street.

More nerves.

Ray continued to ask about her past interactions with Reuben. She'd only been in his home that one time, when she'd followed him to get a wrench to work on her sink. She didn't know if he had relatives close by. They rarely spoke.

"The officer told me he died," she finally said. "I saw the blood, but he wouldn't tell me if he was murdered." She finally met Mason's gaze. "Did someone kill him?"

"Yes."

Gillian sucked in a deep breath. Her entire arm shook as she raised the now-stubby cigarette to her lips. "I knew it," she mumbled.

Mason waited for her to ask if she was safe living next door to a murder site. She didn't.

"Gillian," Ray started, "you saw the broken glass outside and the blood on the floor."

She nodded.

"To see either one, you had to be in Reuben's backyard. Your fence totally blocks any direct line of sight into his home."

Her face paled beneath the freckles.

She thought no one would notice?

"I'm sure you were just checking on the welfare of your neighbor," Ray prompted. "You must have been concerned."

Mason could drive a semi through the holes in the logic of Ray's suggestion.

Gillian was silent.

"Or maybe you *had* to step into his yard for some reason?" Ray continued.

Her shoulders shook once, and she sucked in a deep breath, meeting Ray's gaze. "I guess I haven't told you everything."

That was easier than I expected.

"I was going to meet Reuben. I always use the back door."

"Always?" Mason asked. "You meet with him frequently?"

She lifted her chin. "Yes. We didn't want other neighbors to see us . . . We had a . . . relationship."

"I see," said Ray. "You must have cared deeply for him."

Mason would have bluntly stated, "You were having sex." Another reason Ray was better in certain situations.

"I did. He was a good man . . . a little obsessed sometimes, but he was kind."

"That's important," Ray said gently. "How long had you been involved?"

"About a month." She frowned, her gaze distant. "Closer to six weeks, I guess."

"What do you mean 'obsessed'?" Mason asked.

Gillian tilted her head to one side as she eyed him. She no longer seemed quite so nervous as she considered her answer. "You ever see that movie *True Lies*?"

"The Schwarzenegger movie," Ray said. "He's a government agent."

"With Jamie Lee Curtis," Mason added.

"That's the one. Remember the idiot who tries to romance Curtis? Tells her he's a spy? He claims people and governments are trying to kill him? How he has to stay off the radar all the time?"

The hair rose on the back of Mason's neck. "Are you saying Reuben talked like that?"

"All the time." Gillian dropped her cigarette butt and ground it out on the porch with her sandal. "He didn't say anything the first few weeks we were together, but recently he needed to get things off his chest. Pillow talk, you know." She gave a short laugh. "I listened but didn't tell him I thought he was full of shit. He worked for Home Depot, for God's sake. Why would he be of importance to anyone?"

"What exactly did he say?" asked Mason.

Gillian patted the pockets of her shorts, and disappointment flashed on her face.

Out of cigarettes.

She settled for twisting the ring on her right hand. "I don't know. I didn't pay that close attention. I thought he was just making it up." Her face fell as she glanced at the front door. "Maybe not," she said softly.

"Did he act differently because of his concerns?" Ray suggested. "Did he worry about going to work? Did he avoid certain people?"

Gillian frowned. "He always went to work. Didn't seemed concerned about that. He would only use a cell phone you buy at a drugstore . . . you know . . . where you buy the minutes instead of having an account. Said he got a new one every few months. He told me I should do that too."

"Why you?"

She shrugged. "Said everyone should. Why give the government more information than they need? Which was a stupid thing to say since he also claimed he worked for the government."

Ray frowned. "He *worked* for the government?"

Mason was lost. They'd found no information that indicated that. "For what part of the government exactly?"

"Whoever would pay him. FBI, CIA, NSA . . . When he talked like that, I knew he was full of it. Claims he sold them information." She gave Mason an incredulous look. "What information would the NSA buy from a Home Depot employee?"

Mason's thoughts raced. Could Reuben have been some sort of informant? The murder appeared to have been done by someone with an ax to grind. Or was he simply a movie fan with grandiose fantasies, trying to impress the woman in his bed?

It happens.

Pulling his little notepad out of his shirt pocket, he reminded himself to look into the possibility of Reuben being a confidential informant. It was a start. A weak start. Reuben's manager and coworkers might know more.

"Was he ever worried about someone specifically?" Ray asked. "Had he angered someone at work? Or maybe had a fight with a friend?"

Gillian shook her head. "I don't know."

"What else did you talk about?" Mason asked, thinking of topics to jog her memory. "Did he talk about trips he'd been on or wanted to go on? Was he planning any big purchases? New vehicles or maybe a new house? What did he like to do during his time off?"

"He liked to have sex," Gillian stated, meeting Mason's gaze dead-on. "I know he had taken trips to Central and Eastern Oregon. He showed me some pictures of Mount Bachelor and the Painted Hills."

"Did anyone go with him?" asked Ray.

"Like another woman?" Gillian's eyes narrowed slightly.

"Anyone," clarified Mason.

"Dunno. I didn't ask. Didn't see people in any of his photos. I'm sorry I'm not more help. If he was moving or buying anything, he didn't tell me about it." She blinked, her eyes growing wet. "He really was a nice guy. I freaked out when I saw the blood. I banged on the back door and shouted his name for a good thirty seconds while I called 911. I beat on some other windows in back before I ran around front and rang the bell." The woman shuddered.

"That sight would disturb anyone," said Ray.

"How did he die?" she asked bluntly.

Both men went silent as Gillian looked from one to the other.

She stiffened as their silence sank in. "Don't tell me—I mean, I know you can't tell me. I understand—I don't want to know." She frantically patted her shorts pockets again, her chest rapidly rising and falling with fast breaths.

"Detectives." A young officer had opened the front door. "The tech has something she'd like you to look at. She says it's extremely important." The officer glanced at the teary witness and looked at Ray with concern.

"Could you take Ms. Wood back home?" Ray asked.

The detectives said their goodbyes, telling her they'd be in touch. Gillian stepped off the porch and then spun around. "Find that asshole," she snapped, her voice cracking.

"We will," Ray promised.

Mason stayed silent. He didn't make promises he didn't know he could keep. Especially to simply make someone feel better.

"What do you think?" Ray murmured as they watched the woman leave with the officer.

"I think she had a thing for our victim."

"What do you think about her *story*?"

"I think Reuben was trying to impress her. Just like any other jerk trying to get laid."

"We don't know that he was a jerk," Ray said.

"He made her use his back door to hide their relationship from the neighbors. Sounds like a selfish asshole to me."

"Could be a private person. Maybe wanted to protect her reputation from the neighborhood grapevine."

"Mmphf." Speculating on their victim's motives was pointless.

"Think she scared off the killer with her noise? It appeared he wasn't finished."

"Possibly."

The house was a one-story ranch. The men passed two bedrooms and the bloody bathroom as they went down a narrow hall. Dr. Trask was hunched over the tub in the bathroom, examining their victim. Mason followed Ray to where a crime scene tech impatiently waited at the end of the hall. "In here," she said. "You've got to see this." The tech led them into a third bedroom that held a large folding table and wooden chair. A clunky-looking laptop and printer sat on the table along with a dozen plastic stacking shelves full of papers.

It looked like anyone's messy workroom except for the heavy blood smears on the laptop, folders, and papers scattered on the table. Mason scanned the room for more blood.

Maps of Oregon, Washington, and Idaho covered the walls. A short, cheap bookshelf held several titles that indicated Reuben liked to hike and camp in the Pacific Northwest. Two large backpacks with aluminum frames were piled in a corner alongside a few clear tubs of various supplies for outdoor living. Small pots, tarps, collapsible containers.

The cluttered room felt at odds with the perfectly organized garage.

Mason didn't see any more blood. It seemed contained to items on the table.

I'll let the crime scene team decide that.

"It's this. I just found it," the tech said, pointing at blood-spotted pages in a manila folder next to the laptop. Her hand was shaking.

"Was the folder laying open like this?" Mason asked.

"No. I'd already documented the entire room, and then I opened the folder. The coffee-cup warmer was on top of it."

Three coffee cups were on the desk. Each had about a half inch of coffee left.

"I assume the blood is our victim's," Ray said.

"Most likely," said Mason. "But I'm wondering if the victim left behind the blood—he could have gotten away from his attacker at some point and come in here—or was it left behind by his killer's dirty hands." He shrugged. "Also could be the killer's blood. Maybe our guy got in some blows too."

"I doubt our victim came in here to read something while he had a killer after him," said Ray.

"Don't assume," said Mason. Until he had proof, he never ruled out anything.

"Please stop talking and read it," begged the tech, frustration in her voice.

Mason looked closely at the top page. He scanned it and then rapidly flipped through the next two, his stomach churning. Three pages of handwritten rants against law enforcement. "What the fuck," he muttered.

Beside him, Ray had gone silent, the blood forgotten.

Mason turned to the last page. It was a blueprint with a single handwritten line below it. "This is a map of the Clackamas County Courthouse." Mason forced out the words.

"It says this afternoon. A bomb is to go off in the courthouse." Ray choked. *"This afternoon."*

Mason was already on his phone.

"What the hell . . . I thought I saw this." Ray had returned to the second page and pointed at a line.

Mason's heart pounded as his phone rang in his ear and he looked. Ava's name jumped out at him.

"This says he wanted to tell Ava about a bomb during one of their meetings," said Ray.

"He was an FBI informant? Ava's informant?" Mason's head spun.

"Looks like he didn't lie to Gillian."

5

Finally making it to her office at the FBI building near the Portland airport, Ava stowed her bag in her desk drawer and turned on her computer. Brady's revelation about Jayne had knocked her world off-kilter, but Ava had a demanding job and work to do. Too much work. She didn't have time during work hours to hunt for her twin.

A missing adult woman who'd left on her own wasn't a high priority for law enforcement. Especially one who'd vanished a dozen times before.

I know she's fine.

She sat silently and closed her eyes, mentally searching—feeling for anything out of sync as a sign that tragedy had struck her sister. Like a sudden physical pain in her heart. An overwhelming sense of emptiness and loss.

Nothing.

How many thousands of times have I done this over the years?

She didn't fully believe she would feel anything, but the ritual settled her mind. A little.

Zander would continue to search for Jayne and do it ten times more efficiently than Ava. Computers and databases were his passion. With his speed and knowledge, he could do his regular work and search for a digital footprint left by Jayne at the same time. Ava didn't even have to ask. He knew what she needed, and their friendship was important to both of them. Zander had watched as Ava's relationship with Mason developed, and now she enjoyed watching Zander and Emily fall in love. Emily had recently moved in with him, and Ava was certain a wedding was in their future, but she wondered if the two of them knew it.

She hadn't seen Zander this happy since . . . ever.

No one deserved happiness more than Zander. Eight years ago, his wife had died of cancer, their unborn daughter too young to survive outside the womb. Ava hadn't known him then, and he'd told no one the story when he transferred to the Portland FBI office. She'd long suspected he had dark pain in his past—sorrow would flash in his eyes at times, but she'd never asked, not wanting to intrude on his privacy. In a bleak moment last fall, when Zander was at his lowest, she'd learned the heart-wrenching story.

Emily had eliminated most of the sorrow in his eyes.

Focused on her computer screen, Ava took a few moments to register that something had happened on her office floor. Brisk footsteps, anxious voices, people leaving. She moved to the doorway of her office and felt a nervous energy flow through the halls.

"What's going on?" she asked an agent as he jogged by.

"Ask Ben," the agent tossed over his shoulder.

"Thanks a lot," she muttered, planning to do exactly that. She strode in the opposite direction, toward Ben's office.

Her supervisor was on the phone, and the same uneasy energy hovered around him. Ben hung up as she entered, and his gaze met hers but then jumped away as he shuffled through some papers on his desk.

Uh-oh.

"What happened?" she asked.

Ben cleared his throat. "We've got a credible bomb threat at the Clackamas County Courthouse. It's being evacuated at the moment and a perimeter established a few blocks out. I'm sending all the bodies I can."

Ava's breath caught as images of the bombed Oklahoma City federal building flooded her mind. Timothy McVeigh had killed well over a hundred people. It had happened more than twenty-five years ago, but she'd studied the bombing at the FBI Academy.

What's today's date?

"It's June," she blurted. The Oklahoma bombing had happened in April, and domestic terrorists sometimes used the date to launch their own illegal acts.

"My first thought too," Ben said. A grim expression covered his face. "But it's June eleventh. McVeigh was executed on this date."

"Shit." *A martyr.* Ava turned to go back to her office. "I'll grab my bag."

"No. Wait."

She froze, one hand on the doorjamb of his office. *Something else is wrong.*

"Reuben Braswell," Ben stated.

The man's face appeared in her mind. A pain in the ass. Braswell was fascinated with law enforcement and saw himself as some sort of necessary source of information for the FBI. Ava placated him, even though his phone calls and visits seemed more about using up her time than providing information. "What about him?"

"When's the last time you spoke with him?"

Ava touched a consistently numb spot on her shoulder. "Before the coast." *Before I was shot this spring at the coast.*

"What did you talk about?"

She shrugged, still fingering her shoulder. "I'll have to check the report. I don't recall anything of use. Sometimes I think he simply likes to feel important."

"He didn't mention a bombing?"

"Hell no." She straightened. "You can't think Braswell knew something about today's bomb threat. Wouldn't he have told us?"

"He's dead. He was murdered in his home at some point overnight."

She blinked, unable to speak.

"They uncovered the plans for today's bombing in his home. Intricate plans. I haven't seen them yet, but there's something in the plans that suggests he wanted to tell you about the bombing. Did he ever allude to something like that?"

Ava fought for breath as she strained to recall her last meeting with the man.

Did he hint at something?

She was positive Reuben hadn't discussed anything of the sort. "He never said anything about a bomb or any other type of violent episode. He provided more of the 'I heard a rumor that so-and-so isn't paying his taxes because he's a sovereign citizen'–type information."

"I want you to stay here. Find all your notes on every meeting with Braswell."

"I can go—"

"Stay *here*. Every law enforcement agency is lending help. They'll have more than they need."

She nodded dumbly, frustrated but knowing he was right. "Got it." She turned to leave again.

"And Ava," Ben said, "you'll find out eventually, but Mason caught Braswell's murder investigation this morning." His gaze held hers as he waited for a reaction.

Her heart jumped, but she maintained her composure. "I see."

Did Mason discover my name connected to the bombing?

She wanted to check her phone even though she knew he hadn't called. Mason wouldn't. He had a protocol to follow, and notifying his fiancée that her name had turned up at a murder scene wasn't part of it.

What is going through his head?

Ava was certain she'd never mentioned Braswell's name to Mason. At the most, she might have mentioned she had a meeting with an informant. The names and topics were confidential.

"I'll get my notes." She walked away, her mind racing.

He didn't mention a bombing. I wouldn't have missed that.

She sat in her chair and tapped her keys. According to her files, she'd met with Reuben Braswell four times and taken three phone calls over the last eighteen months. She had last spoken with him in January at the strip mall Starbucks down the street from her office.

He had originally contacted their office, stating he had information about an unsolved bank robbery. He'd been randomly assigned to Ava for a meeting, and his tip had panned out. One of the robbers had been a friend who'd bragged when he had too much to drink one night.

At least that was Reuben's story. After a few meetings, she wondered if Reuben had known about the robbery all along. He didn't like the FBI; he'd been clear about that. He had a big chip on his shoulder about all law enforcement, but she didn't know why. He didn't have a record.

She suspected he'd had a falling-out with his friend and turned him in as revenge even though it meant talking with law enforcement.

The first time she'd met him he'd been suspicious to the point of amusing her. He'd been stiff, reluctant to speak even though he'd been the one who'd contacted the FBI. The next meeting he'd been slightly more relaxed and even asked for a suggestion on how to get law enforcement help for a friend in a domestic violence situation.

She suspected it had been hard for him to bring up. Sympathy had flashed in his eyes as he talked about a female friend. He said the police had come after her husband had hit her, but nothing had happened. Ava told him who in her local police department his friend should contact and emphasized that the woman needed to be ready to do whatever it took to keep herself safe. Ava looked up some domestic violence help websites and gave the addresses to Reuben.

But at their January meeting in the coffee shop, Reuben had been full of suspicion again.

She'd been waiting ten minutes and was moments from walking out when Reuben finally stepped into the crowded shop and scanned the room for her. They made eye contact, and he nodded but continued his perusal of the other patrons. Reuben was tall and lean but emitted a powerful energy that told her he believed he could hold his own in any fistfight. He walked and moved like a brawler. A type of person she rarely saw in this Starbucks. Due to its location, most of the patrons were white-collar professionals and soccer moms who'd come to shop at the mall.

He didn't order and took the seat to her left so he could view the rest of the place. Just as she had.

"Morning, Reuben." Ava sipped her coffee, wondering what was in store for her today. Reuben was unpredictable. Would it be the guy who wanted to help a friend, or the one who thought law enforcement was always watching him?

"How many agents are in this shop, Agent McLane?" His dark gaze darted from coffee drinker to coffee drinker, lingering on a businessman with a laptop twenty feet away.

"None."

"He filming us?" Reuben jerked his head at the man with the laptop.

She sighed. It was to be a paranoid visit. "No. Do you think the FBI would be that obvious?"

"Maybe they're trying the opposite." His eyes were sharp and assessing.

"I think I should go." Ava started to stand.

"Wait!" He grabbed her forearm, his gaze fierce. "Forget it. You know how I am."

She glared daggers at him. "Do. Not. Touch. Me."

He immediately let go. "I'm sorry."

Ava made a show of rubbing her forearm, fury bubbling in her chest. "Do that again and we're done. Permanently."

"I told you where to find that guy who was violating his parole."

"And I notified the proper law enforcement agency. You didn't need to bring that to the FBI."

"You listen to me. No one else does."

"If you need someone to listen to you, get a dog." She still fumed about him grabbing her arm, but she sat back down. "I have a lot of work to do."

"Wait." He stared at her left hand. *"What's that? You're not married."*

"That's none of your business." She slipped the hand with the engagement ring under the table. She was not sharing personal information with this man.

"You're not married," he repeated, as if saying it again would make it true. Shock registered in his voice.

"Soon," she reluctantly admitted. *"Now. Tell me why we're here."*

Concern crossed his face. *"Who are you marrying? How well do you know him? You know a lot of marriages can turn violent. I've seen it."* His eyes softened. *"I would never hurt you."*

Ava stood. *"Don't contact me again, Reuben. We're done."*

"But I need to tell—"

"Tell it to a dog. Or a cat." She strode out of the shop, her coffee cup gripped tightly, wondering why she'd agreed to the meeting.

Ava reread her notes. She had written that the meeting was a waste of time, that he'd grabbed her arm and made inappropriate comments. Her recommendation had been for no other agent to meet Reuben Braswell in person.

Scanning notes from earlier meetings, she confirmed he'd offered no more information that was pertinent to the FBI. He could have just as easily given any of his leads to the Portland Police Bureau. She'd suspected he was attracted to her. It was in his eyes and his body language, and his concern about her ending up in a violent situation, but she'd ignored it since he'd broken a big case, and she had hoped he'd offer useful tips again. He'd insinuated that he associated with people in antigovernment factions, but that he personally avoided anything illegal. It'd been enough for Ava to continue to meet with him.

She frowned as she looked at all the meeting notes as a whole. At two of the meetings he'd probed her about FBI activity, and he had done the same on all three of the phone calls. In her reports she'd briefly mentioned his questions about the FBI.

Was his overall goal to get information out of me?

She knew he'd gotten nothing of value, but she wished she had noted specifically what he had said.

Note-taking 101. Write it all. No matter how unimportant it seems. *Did he want to tell me something at the last meeting, but I walked out?* Like a plan for a bombing in June.

"Shit." She was getting ahead of herself. What she needed to know was exactly how her name was connected to today's bomb threat. She forwarded all her Reuben Braswell notes to Ben and wondered if it was possible that the early stages of bombing plans had started in January.

She fought the urge to call Mason, certain he must know that she had been informed her name was connected. Instead, she ran a search on her computer for police activity at the courthouse and found a news channel's live helicopter footage of the evacuation. Squad cars lined the blocks near the courthouse.

The courthouse was a big brick historical building separated from the Willamette River by a four-lane highway in a tiny, slightly isolated sector of Oregon City. The small area was only two blocks deep and five blocks wide along the base of a steep cliff that divided it from the rest of the city. A strip of wine bars, little independent shops, and small restaurants filled the narrow space between the Willamette River and the cliffs.

An intermittent stream of people filed out of the building and the surrounding businesses. Uniformed officers guided them out of the area. From the helicopter's feed, Ava picked up the worry and stress of the civilians. The perimeter strengthened as more officers and vehicles joined. The highway traffic was stopped in both directions. In a few more minutes, no one would be within blocks of the courthouse.

Is Mason down there?

He had a murder investigation to handle, but it wouldn't surprise her if he'd sped to the heart of the action after finding the bomb plans. Again, she stopped herself from calling him. Now was not the time for an interruption.

The reporter in the news helicopter talked over the drone of the chopper. Ava tuned him out as he described what she was already seeing. The helicopter flew in circles around the scene, and it seemed close because of the powerful cameras. No doubt it was much farther away, but she couldn't help but worry for the chopper if a powerful bomb went off.

Most bomb threats are fake. No doubt this one will be too.

She scanned the law enforcement on the ground, searching for an indication that a bomb squad had arrived. The courthouse was huge. It'd take forever to search.

There would be no answers soon. She turned away from the screen, knowing it was time to focus on the stack of cases on her desk. She didn't have time for procrastination.

Quiet cracks sounded from the live video, and the reporter gasped. "Were those gunshots?" he shouted in a high voice. "Get us back! Get further out!"

Ava spun back to her screen, her heart in her throat.

The courthouse disappeared from her screen as the helicopter took a sharp turn, leaving her with a dizzying sweep of the Willamette River.

Dammit, Mason, where are you?

6

Mason parked a block and a half away from the courthouse and took a deep breath.

"What a mess," said Ray.

He was right. People streamed past Mason's vehicle, heading away from the building. Officers were directing the masses and tightening their perimeter. He didn't see a mobile command unit yet, but judging by the large group of law enforcement at the far end of the lot, that was the location of the current core of command.

Tension gripped him. He'd been on edge ever since finding the bomb threat, but now the reality was right in front of him. The police had an entire building to search. The plans didn't say where the bomb had been planted, but the killer had a copy of the courthouse's layout.

It could be anywhere.

They got out of the vehicle and headed around to its rear to get ballistic vests.

"A bomb scare *again*?" said one woman to another as they passed by, looks of annoyance on their faces. "How are we to get any work done for the courts?"

Seriously? That's the attitude?

Mason glanced around. Most of the exiting employees looked bored. Nervous shoppers with their bags and kids in tow hustled out of the area much faster than the office workers. Pieces of conversations reached his ears.

"Anyone seen Diane? She was on a break somewhere."

". . . the child murder case going on. Someone must have got nervous."

"My car is parked all the way at the other end."

". . . right in the middle of a transcript."

"Pain in the ass."

Ray caught his eye and shook his head. He grabbed two vests out of the vehicle and handed one to Mason.

A mother with a toddler on her hip stopped next to Ray. "Where are we supposed to go?" she asked him in a frazzled voice. Ray pointed the way as he spoke to her.

Mason strapped on his vest and eyed the large three-story building down the street. No one had come out in the last few seconds. Maybe everyone was out by—

Ray grunted and two shots cracked through the air.

Mason ducked and spun around to see Ray collapse against the woman with the toddler, knocking her aside, his vest on the ground beside him.

He's been shot.

"Ray!" Mason lunged at his partner and shouted at the woman with the toddler. *"Get down!"*

She dived to the ground near the side of the SUV, clutching the child to her chest.

Someone punched Mason in the back, and he fell hard to his hands and knees, unable to breathe, the wind knocked out of his lungs. Pain radiated from his spine, and he closed his eyes against the agony, straining to draw in a breath.

Not punched.

I'm shot.

He dry heaved, feeling the contents of his stomach shift, and he finally caught his breath.

My vest.

His brain came back online, and he knew his vest had stopped the bullet. Sucking in deep breaths and shoving the pain out of his mind, he looked to Ray, sprawled on the ground. Deathly still.

No. Not Ray.

Screams and running feet sounded around him, but Mason ignored them, every ounce of his focus on his partner, who was bleeding from his side and thigh. Ray's eyes were open, looking at nothing, making Mason lose his breath again.

Two more shots. More screams.

Get to cover.

Ignoring the radiating pain in his back, he grabbed Ray's shoulders and dragged him to the side where the woman huddled against his vehicle with her child. She held the toddler's face against her shoulder, hiding the sight of Mason's bleeding partner. "Is he dead?" she choked out.

"No!" *I won't let him be.*

On his knees in the gravel, Mason pressed his shaking fingers against Ray's neck. An eternity passed before he found a pulse, making him weak with relief. "Hang in there," he ordered. Ray continued to stare blankly into the distance.

Mason ripped open Ray's blood-soaked shirt where the bullet had entered. Blood oozed from a hole near his armpit. Not spurting. He rolled Ray onto his side to look at his back, and a low moan came from his partner. A good sound to Mason's ears.

No exit wound in Ray's back. *Shit.* The bullet was still inside.

Must have hit a rib and changed direction.

"You will *not* die on me, asshole."

Ray coughed, and his eyes locked with Mason's.

He's laughing.

Relief and panic simultaneously swamped him.

"Jesus Christ, Ray."

Three rapid shots sounded. Mason ducked lower and scanned his surroundings, knowing they needed to get out.

Where is the shooter?

The open area had immediately cleared of people after the first shots. Most had darted inside nearby stores or were crouched by the other vehicles in the lot.

"I need a medic!" Mason shouted. "Officer down! Officer down!" His shout was taken up by other officers. Calling 911 would be redundant.

They'll get here ASAP.

Mason turned his attention to Ray's thigh. Unable to rip the pants, he pulled out his Leatherman tool, and his hands shook as he fumbled to pry open a blade.

"Here." The woman with the toddler pressed a cloth diaper against Ray's bleeding chest.

Ray's moan of pain reverberated in Mason's every bone, and he dropped the tool. "Dammit."

He finally levered out the blade and slit open Ray's khakis.

Most bullet entry holes in flesh were surprisingly simple in appearance, not the gaping mass of destruction one expected. The exit wound was often a different story.

"What the—" The wound on Ray's thigh was nearly two inches in diameter and flowed freely with blood but didn't pulsate. *It missed the artery.* Slightly relieved, Mason rolled him again to look at the back of his leg and saw a small opening.

"How in the hell did you get shot in the front and the back?"

Two shooters.

"He spun toward me after the first shot, trying to protect us," the woman said. The diaper she held against Ray's chest was fully soaked with blood. "He was shot in the front first." Tears streamed down her face, but her voice and hands were steady. Her son sat on the ground, his back against a wheel, a blank look on his face. He was silent as his wide blue eyes met Mason's.

He's scared speechless.

"Got another diaper?" Mason asked.

She jerked her head toward the open diaper bag. "Yes. And there's a blanket too."

More shots sounded.

Mason dug both out of the bag as more shouts of "Officer down!" came from different directions. *It's not just Ray.*

They were in the middle of a massacre. And his best friend might not make it out.

He handed another diaper to the woman, and she tossed the first aside. It made an audible splat. Mason tucked a fuzzy blue blanket around Ray's torso. It was way too small, but he had to do something. Ray's teeth chattered.

Keep him from going into shock.

A clock started to tick in his head. Time was running out.

Mason shoved another diaper against Ray's leg and shouted for help.

Ice encased his lungs as a thought hit him.

There's no bomb.

His heartbeat pounded in his head.

It was a ploy to draw out cops.

7

Mason couldn't take the mass of people filling the hospital waiting room. Feeling claustrophobic and overwhelmed, he slipped out of the room and escaped down the hall to an alcove with a window. He leaned his forehead against the glass, barely registering the manicured grounds several stories below.

He has to live.

Ray had been unconscious by the time they flew him to Oregon Health & Science University Hospital. He was currently in surgery, and Mason had no updates.

Ray was lucky. Three officers had died, and four others were in critical condition.

No one had found the shooter. *Shooters?*

Yet.

Mason wouldn't rest until the shooter had been found. He'd sworn to Ray as he bled in the parking lot that he'd get the person responsible. Ray hadn't answered but had tightened his grip on Mason's hand.

I've never been so scared in my life.

The shooting had stopped as abruptly as it started. Sirens had wailed for the next twenty minutes as officers combed the area for the shooter. Mason—and nearly everyone else—believed that the shots had come from the top of the cliff. A thick group of trees lined the cliff for almost three blocks. Perfect cover.

Nearly every officer from the local precincts had been down below, helping with the evacuation and perimeter for the bomb threat. Sitting ducks. Waiting to be picked off.

The theory had raced through the media, but the police's public information officers wouldn't speculate—not on camera.

Mason had seen his thoughts reflected in every officer's eyes.

They wanted to kill us.

Rapid footsteps echoed down the hall.

Ava.

He knew her sound. Spinning around, he saw her reach for the door handle of the waiting room.

"Ava," he choked out, unable to say anything but her name.

She locked eyes with him. Even from fifty feet away he felt her concern and fear. She darted toward him and was in his arms. He pressed his lips against her forehead and inhaled, her familiar scent as calming as the smell of the ocean. He closed his eyes and felt his tension fade.

"Is he okay? Will he be okay?" she asked, her voice cracking. "What have you heard?"

"He's in surgery. I've heard nothing."

"How can this be happening?" Ava pressed against him, her hands sliding up his back.

His entire body flinched as he gasped.

She jerked back, her eyes wide. "What happened?"

"Sore back," he forced out. "Strained it somehow."

"Bullshit." She stepped behind him and lifted his shirt. "What the hell . . ." She spun him around to face her, her eyes searching his face. "My God. Your vest stopped a bullet," she whispered. "Your back looks like someone hit it with a sledgehammer."

"I'd worn the vest for ten seconds. That damn bastard Ray was helping someone instead of putting his on." He sniffed, his eyes watering again.

Ava ran quivering hands up and down his arms and then across his chest. "You're all right?" Her voice shook. "No one told me you'd been . . ."

"I haven't mentioned it."

"Mason! You might have broken ribs."

"Others needed help first. Ribs can wait. They really don't do anything for them anyway."

"Internal bleeding—"

"I feel fine."

She stared him down, a smoldering fire in her eyes. "You will tell me if you feel dizzy or sick or if *anything* is wrong. *Anything*. And a doctor is going to look you over before we leave here today."

He felt both dizzy and sick. But he knew it wasn't from the gunshot.

"Is Jill here yet?" she asked.

Mason winced. He'd called Ray's wife on the way to the hospital. "She's in Boise. I suspect she's already on a plane." He took a deep breath. "Calling her was one of the hardest things I've ever done, Ava. Every spouse fears that call."

"I know all too well."

When Jill had answered, Mason had heard the fear in her voice. It wasn't a good thing when your husband's partner called out of the blue. "Ray's okay." Mason had opened with a small lie. "But he's been shot and is on his way to OHSU."

"What happened?" she'd calmly asked, but he knew she was petrified.

He'd told her about the bomb threat and Ray's wounds. And the ballistic vest in his hand.

"Who does that? Who targets cops?" she'd whispered. "Don't answer that . . . I know exactly the type. They've haunted my dreams for years." Her breathing grew uneven.

"Where are Kirstin and Ben?" he'd asked. Ray's two teens were like his own children.

"They're at my sister's. I'll call her right now. I don't want the kids to find out until I can be there with them."

"Instant information," Mason had said. "They'll know something happened, whether it's from social media or a friend texting them about the shooting. At least no names will be released until later."

"I've got to try. I'll be on the first flight back." She'd paused. "Mason?"

"Yeah?"

"Stay with him, okay? I know your initial instinct is to go hunting for the shooter, but someone needs to be there when he comes out of surgery. I can't think of anyone better than you. As long as one of us is with him, he'll make it." Her voice had risen.

But we aren't with him right now.

"I understand," he'd told her and floored the gas pedal, determined not to let down her or Ray.

As he stood in the hall with Ava, déjà vu hit him, and he took hold of her hands. They were like ice. "We were in a hospital like this a few months ago."

Ava gave a stiff nod.

He touched her cheek, unable to speak. *She doesn't want to think about it either.*

Ava had been the one in surgery for a bullet wound, with Mason stuck waiting. He'd driven like a maniac to get from Portland to the coast, where she'd been shot while on a case. He'd been out of his head because he'd been powerless to help her. His sympathy for Jill increased tenfold.

"Still here," Ava whispered, raising her hand to cover his against her face, her smile warm.

She's so important to me. I don't know what I'd do if . . .

"Not going anywhere," she said. "And I won't let you either."

45

A cold shudder racked his shoulders, sending pain down his bruised back. He was hyperaware of how close he'd come to being on the surgeon's table today. Or dead.

None of them could control fate.

Ava opened the door between the garage and their home as Mason parked his car beside hers. Exhaustion made her feet heavy, her limbs slow.

The two of them had stayed at the hospital for five hours. Ray's wife, Jill, had finally arrived, along with their two teenagers. Her daughter's face was pale and her eyes red and swollen. Her son looked the same. Ava's heart broke for the three of them.

And for Mason. He vacillated between looking lost and looking furious.

Ava wondered what he'd do when the shooter was found.

Her brain had wandered, as she thought of movies and books where the cop killer ends up dead in his cell. She had no doubt Mason would strangle the man with his bare hands if given the chance.

Ray has to live.

Grim surgeons had pronounced Ray's surgery a success but were guarded on his prognosis. They'd insisted on talking to Jill alone, but she'd pulled both Mason and Ava along with her.

"The next twenty-four hours are crucial. We're keeping him sedated, so all his energy goes toward his healing."

Jill had looked stricken. "Sedated for how long? I can't talk to him?"

Ava's throat had tightened. *She's afraid he'll die before she can speak with him.*

Mason had scowled at the doctors but hadn't spoken. One of them had glanced his way and done a double take at his stern expression.

"You can talk to him," the doctor had told Jill. "Someone will take you back in a few minutes. I'm sure he can hear you."

"But he can't answer me," she'd whispered, her knuckles white as she clenched her hands together.

"No, ma'am. Not yet. I'm sorry."

The doctors had also allowed Ava and Mason a minute with Ray. Seeing the unconscious big man with tubes and equipment surrounding him had rocked her to the core. Ray Lusco was one of the kindest men she knew, and that kindness had placed him in harm's way.

This isn't fair.

Mason had gripped Ray's hand and leaned close, speaking rapidly next to his ear. Ava couldn't make out the words, but judging by Mason's fierce expression, they were *Dammit, get well* and *I will find the motherfucker.*

The look on Mason's face had haunted her the whole drive home. All the faces had. Jill's, her children's, and Ray's.

Ava set her bag on a chair in the kitchen and reveled in the silence of her home after the nonstop voices and equipment in the hospital.

Too silent.

"Bingo?" she called. Usually the dog was right at the door to the garage when one of them arrived. Even if he'd been in the backyard, he'd dart through his doggy door the moment he heard a familiar car engine. "Bingo?" she said louder, listening for the clack of his nails on the wood floors.

A bark led her to the backyard door. He sat patiently on the deck, his dark eyes pleading.

His doggy door was locked.

"Crap!" Ava unlocked it and he darted through. "I'm so sorry, boy. I can't believe I did that to you." Bingo stopped at his food bowl and gobbled two big bites before bounding to the garage door to greet Mason.

"What's wrong?" he asked Ava as he crouched to scratch the dog's head and rub his ears.

"I locked him out somehow. He must be starving."

"It won't hurt him to be late to a meal."

"I know, but still. I feel horrible." The lock on the doggy door was a necessity. The first month they'd been in the home, they'd left it unlocked at night, allowing the dog access to the backyard if needed. It'd worked well until a raccoon decided to enter in the middle of the night.

Bingo's barking had brought Mason pounding down the stairs to find a raccoon in the kitchen sink, calmly watching their dog flip out over the furry intruder.

Ava had shut Bingo in a bathroom, opened the back door, and then laughed uncontrollably as they tried to herd the raccoon out the door, chasing it from room to room. From then on, the door had been locked at night.

She pulled a bottle of rosé out of the wine fridge. Usually a red was her go-to, but during the hot summer she craved white or rosé. As she removed the cork, she kept an eye on Mason; he looked exhausted as he rubbed and petted the dog. Bingo soon had enough love from Mason and went back to his food bowl, attacking it with gusto.

Poor dog.

She didn't like missing meals either. Grabbing two glasses, she started to pour.

"Beer for me," Mason said, opening the fridge and removing an IPA.

Ava blinked. Usually Mason preferred a milder beer. Either he was too tired to notice what he had grabbed, or he needed the bitterness of the ale to cut through the pain of the day. She didn't say anything, curious to see his reaction at the first sip. They kept the IPAs on hand for Ray.

Her heart contracted as she imagined the brown bottle in the big man's hand.

Bingo lifted his head from his bowl and stared at Mason. Surprising Ava, the dog walked away from a half-filled bowl to sit at Mason's feet. Not begging. Simply sitting.

Mason patted his head and then trailed Ava into the warm air outside, Bingo on his heels.

Mason and his son, Jake, had built an elegant roof over most of their large deck. It had a ceiling fan, electric heaters, and a gorgeous stone fireplace with a TV mounted above the gas unit. With comfy outdoor furniture, it had become their favorite room in the house—or not in the house. Ava couldn't wait to use it when it snowed.

Mason sat on the sofa, gingerly leaned back against the cushion, and tapped the place beside him.

As if I'd sit anywhere else.

She sat and leaned into his side, her body touching him from shoulder to knee. He took her hand and held it in his lap. They should have changed out of work clothes into something cooler, but neither had the energy.

Bingo sat as close to Mason's left foot as he could and rested his chin on Mason's knee, his dark eyes fixed on his master.

Bingo knows he's hurting.

Ava blinked hard.

Mason's phone pinged with a text. "Jake," he said, opening the message.

Ava knew what his son wanted. Jake sent Mason the same question every time there were local law enforcement deaths or violence. She watched the screen.

I heard the news are you ok

I'm fine

That was all his teenage son needed to put his mind at ease. No further questions. No explanations needed. Mason put the phone on the end table with a sigh. "I should have thought to text Jake."

"You had other things on your mind."

"A shitty day," Mason muttered, calmly drinking his beer and staring at the blank television. She watched him swallow, slightly disappointed in his lack of reaction to the bitter beer.

"Definitely. But could have turned out much, much worse."

I won't think about that possibility anymore.

She'd dragged him to the emergency room before they left the hospital and made a doctor check his back. The doctor had flinched when he saw the blossoming bruise. An X-ray had shown no concerns, and he'd offered a prescription for painkillers, which Mason turned down. "Let me know if you change your mind. You're going to be in pain for a few days."

Ava swore she saw Mason silently mouth, "Good."

Stubborn cowboy.

But he was *her* stubborn cowboy.

"Tell me what you found this morning," she said after a few peaceful moments of silence. Neither had mentioned the fact that her name had been in the same document as the bomb threat. She'd felt the question float between them a few times at the hospital, but all their energy had been centered on Ray. Neither wanted to delve into the oddity.

He sighed and took a long draw on his bottle. "Reuben Braswell, age fifty-two. Found dead in his bathtub by a patrol officer after a neighbor reported seeing blood on his kitchen floor."

"Wait. How—"

"I'll come back to that. It's not that relevant." He frowned, his forehead wrinkling. "I think."

Ava mentally shelved her question.

"Braswell had been bludgeoned in the head in the kitchen and then dragged to the bathroom, where he was hit again in the face and mouth." He lifted the beer to his mouth and brought it back down without drinking. "Someone removed eight fingers while he was in the tub."

Ava sipped her wine, no longer tasting it, picturing the tall man. The abuse was bad, but she'd seen worse. Much worse.

"One finger might be missing. I'll ask Dr. Trask in the morning if she found the eighth."

"Gianna was there?" Ava liked the petite forensic pathologist.

"Yes. I didn't get a chance to talk to her much because one of the crime technicians found the bomb plans."

"With my name in the same document."

He nodded and squeezed her hand. "Did Braswell ever mention a bomb threat?"

"No."

Mason nodded again. "I didn't think so."

"I did walk out on our last meeting. He had given me nothing and was being inappropriate."

"Inappropriate how?" he asked, turning to look at her, his dark gaze sharp.

"Your knuckles are dragging." She raised a brow at him. "He made comments about me getting married. It was none of his business." Mason didn't need to know he'd grabbed her arm; she'd handled it.

"Hope you made that clear to him."

"Of course I did, and then I left. That's the only time I can think of when he might have wanted to tell me something but didn't get the chance."

"We thought the threat was real." A shudder ran through him, vibrating into her skin. "Did we jump to conclusions too fast?"

Ava slid to the edge of her seat and turned to face him. "Don't you *dare* take any blame for what happened today. Not a single percentage of it. The only person to blame is the one who pulled the trigger."

"Might have been more than one shooter."

"Not important at the moment." She waved away his concern with the hand holding her wineglass. "What exactly did you find in Reuben's home?"

He scratched his chin. "Detailed layout of the courthouse. Then there was the handwritten diatribe." He took a sip of beer. "I've seen and heard a lot of shit directed at law enforcement, but this was brutal." He slowly shook his head. "You could feel the anger coming off the page. This guy hated cops and anyone to do with them."

Ava tilted her head. "He was paranoid and a conspiracy-theory believer. He always thought he was being watched—believed I had other agents planted in the room when we met." She frowned, thinking hard. "He might have told me he thought he was being watched at home? I'm not sure." She blew out a frustrated breath, wishing she remembered more. "He had weird ideas, but for the most part he seemed harmless to me."

"Those are the ones that surprise you."

"That's been true several times."

"Anyway, your name was in the lengthy diatribe. For as angry as he was with law enforcement, he said you were different. That you were one of the good guys."

Ava didn't know what to say.

"Said you were a one-of-a-kind cop. You looked out for the common man and your fellow law enforcement members."

"I have no idea what I did to deserve his praise. All I did was meet with him a few times and try to stay patient." She thought for a moment. "I gave him some resources for a friend of his who was in a domestic violence situation. That wasn't a big deal. He could have found them on the internet."

"He went on to describe in minute detail his plans to plant a bomb at the courthouse. It would be right after lunch when everyone had returned. He wanted the courthouse full."

"Wow. Are you sure this was Reuben's handwriting?" She couldn't see a killer in the man she'd met at Starbucks.

"It matched the cramped style on the Post-it notes stuck to the maps on the walls and the checkbook carbons found in a desk drawer."

"Okay." Her mind spun, searching for different possibilities that could explain how the angry ranter and her informant were the same person. "Either he has some sort of mental illness or he's an excellent actor."

"He indicated he wasn't alone in his thinking. A like-minded group was mentioned. His tone changed when he wrote about them . . . it felt respectful and admiring."

"He told me he was friends with people in antigovernment factions. It was one of the reasons I continued to meet with him. Many groups stir up hate toward law enforcement. Too many."

"But if Reuben was killed before he could carry out his plans, then who else knew about them? And did they decide to shoot when they saw us rally to the courthouse?" He met Ava's gaze. "Or did they plan it before?"

"You're saying the plans were left for you to find."

"It's possible."

"Discovering Reuben's murdered body was to bring law enforcement into his home, where the bombing plans would be found?" Ava felt the theory was a stretch. A big stretch. "That means someone had to report the death in time for police to respond, the plans to be found, and the courthouse to be evacuated—all before the stated time of the bomb detonation. That's a lot of wobbly domino pieces to line up."

"Reuben had a thing going on with a female neighbor," said Mason.

"A relationship?"

"Sounded like it was purely physical. She was the one who called the police about the blood in the house."

"Was she expecting to meet Reuben at a certain time today?"

Mason winced. "I didn't ask."

"To make the dominoes in your theory fall in line, someone had to know when she was coming."

He held the cool beer bottle against his forehead. "This is making my brain ache."

"Mine too. I heard no bomb was found in the courthouse. They used explosives dogs to search the building and surrounding area."

"I think we both knew they wouldn't find anything."

Silence settled between them. The deadly massacre had struck too close to home. To consider that it'd been carefully orchestrated to take innocent lives hurt her heart.

Why is there so much anger?

"Who will head up the shooting investigation?" she asked.

"Well, the Clackamas County sheriff was running the evacuation and bomb scare, but he has to expect the FBI will assist him in the investigation at some point."

"For a bomb at a county courthouse, you bet."

"But now with the primary focus turning to the shooting, I see the FBI taking the lead in the investigation and the sheriff's department supporting. And OSP will want in since Ray was . . . involved."

He pressed his lips together, his eyes fierce. She knew he wanted to be involved with Ray's case, but he was too close to the victim. OSP would assign it to a different detective.

And Mason would look over their shoulder the entire time.

"The Braswell murder is mine. *No one's* taking that away from me," he stated.

"Of course not." He looked exhausted, barely able to hold his head up. She wasn't about to point out that there was a strong chance his murder investigation would fall under the umbrella of the shooting investigation, and then Mason would be removed from the Braswell case.

He had to know but was stubbornly ignoring the logic.

"We're both worn out," she said. "This is a discussion for alert and peppy people who've had a good night's sleep."

"Peppy? No one would ever call me peppy," he grumbled.

He had a point.

"I think it's bedtime, Peppy," she said, struggling to keep a straight face at the disgusted look he gave her.

"Don't," he ordered.

"Not a good nickname?"

"Hell no. But I agree on bed," he added softly. He dropped his gaze, and she felt his thoughts turn to Ray. He was hurting, and it was more than his back.

She took the beer bottle from his hand and set it with her wineglass on the end table. Moving to his lap, she took his face in her hands and lightly pressed her lips against his cheek. She moved her kiss to his forehead and then his other cheek. All soft touches, offering comfort and understanding. He closed his eyes and leaned his face against hers, tightening his arms around her.

"I'm tired." The weight in his voice broke her heart.

"That makes two of us." She stood and pulled him to his feet. "Tomorrow will be better."

"Will it?" he whispered, gathering her against him.

She leaned into him and said nothing, knowing the question was rhetorical.

Tomorrow could be worse than today.

What if Ray doesn't make it through the night?

8

Mason didn't know how long he'd slept, but it couldn't have been longer than three hours. He'd woken a dozen different times. Sometimes from the pain in his back, sometimes from thinking about Ray.

He'd checked his phone each time, expecting a text about changes in Ray's condition.

There had been none. He'd lie back down, relieved. No news was good news. But then he'd wonder if Jill had forgotten her promise to notify him. He refused to text her during the night to ask, hoping she was getting some sleep at the hospital.

Jill's text had arrived as he drove to the medical examiner's office.

No change overnight

Ray's condition wasn't headed in the wrong direction. Mason took that as a positive.

Inside the building he was directed to one of the autopsy suites. Two autopsies were going on, but Mason immediately knew which was his. Dr. Gianna Trask stood on a small stool near her stainless-steel table as she leaned over Reuben Braswell. Her assistant made notes as Dr. Trask spoke quietly, the doctor's words recorded by a dangling overhead microphone.

Mason slipped on a gown, booties, and a face shield from the shelves near the door. If his eyes were shut, he'd know where he was by the smell alone. The constantly running air-filtering system did the best it could, but the autopsy suites always smelled like iron from blood, strong detergents, and refrigerated meat that was starting to go bad. Depending on the case, sometimes the odors were worse. Advanced decomposition and burned flesh were the two that Mason hated the most.

The room was chilly, and a popular song from the nineties played in the background. Mason couldn't remember the band's name, but he could picture them clearly in his head. A group of English guys with morose faces.

Working on the other autopsy, at the far end of the room, were Dr. Seth Rutledge and two gowned assistants. The doctor raised a hand to acknowledge Mason, who did the same as he went to join Dr. Trask.

Reuben's body was stark white under the bright lights. Mason dragged his gaze away from the stubby, brutalized hands, remembering the fingers scattered on the bathroom floor. The head was worse.

"Good morning, Mason." Lines appeared at the corners of Gianna's eyes as she smiled. He couldn't see the rest of her face behind her mask and face shield. The small woman was swamped in her personal protective equipment, and she had an organ in her hands that Mason couldn't identify. She set it on a scale, and the assistant made a notation on his clipboard.

Mason hated being late, but his restless night's sleep had caused him to accidentally turn off his alarm instead of hitting SNOOZE. Ava had had to shake him awake.

"Sorry about being late."

"Don't worry about it. I can catch you up to speed." She straightened and arched her back. A pained look crossed her face. "Ouch. I've been in one position for too long."

Mason's gaze locked on the small bulge under her gown. "You're pregnant," he blurted. "Ah . . . I mean—Um." His face heated. *What if she's not pregnant?*

Dr. Trask met his stare but didn't say anything.

Shit. She's going to tell Ava I fucked up.

"Gianna," her tall male assistant muttered, shaking his head. "Be nice."

Her eyes crinkled, and she gave a muffled laugh behind her mask. "Yes, I'm pregnant. But jeez, Mason, you should be more careful."

"Surprised me, is all." He tried to calm his pounding heart.

How did I not notice her pregnancy at the crime scene yesterday?

Some detective he was—his job was to notice things that other people didn't. The one bright spot was that Ray hadn't noticed either.

"Congratulations to you and Chris," Mason said. "What does Violet think?" he asked about Gianna's teen daughter.

"She's ecstatic."

"That's great." He wondered if Ava knew about the pregnancy and hadn't told him. His jaw tightened. They'd discussed having kids. It was still up in the air. Both hesitant to talk about it.

Mason had already done the family path. Jake was in college, and he couldn't imagine becoming a father again at fifty. Or even later. But being twelve years younger than he, Ava felt different. Sometimes. She hadn't said anything in months.

Focus on the case.

"What do you have on Mr. Braswell?" he asked.

"I never had a chance to tell you yesterday that I had estimated his death to be between midnight and four a.m."

He'd forgotten to ask about the time of death.

Dr. Trask tipped her head, studying him. "You were very busy and preoccupied yesterday. And I assume most of the night. Don't be so hard on yourself."

She has a point.

"Keep going."

"Manner of death is blunt force trauma to the skull. I can't tell you specifically which blow . . . there are too many."

He stole a glance at the head. One side of Reuben's skull was sunk in, and his right cheekbone and eye socket were indistinguishable. The blood coating his face had been washed off, exposing ripped and split skin and what was left of his teeth and lower jaw.

Reuben Braswell looked like a horror-movie extra.

"External exam revealed numerous abrasions and bruising all over his body. Eight fingers had been removed. But I only have seven." She gestured at a shallow silver bowl.

A bowl of horror-movie props.

"Where in the hell is the eighth finger?" Mason muttered.

"A keepsake?" suggested Dr. Trask.

"Probably." *What will he do with it?* "What else have you found?"

The doctor gently prodded a spot on the sunken skull. It sank farther, and Mason looked away, bile burning his esophagus. "I don't think I'll be able to reassemble this skull. I'll give it my best shot."

Mason studied the destroyed face. Reuben's would not be an open-casket funeral. "I don't think you need to attempt to make it look better."

"He's somebody's son."

"His parents are dead. He never married . . . I haven't checked to see if there might be some kids. He has a brother and sister, but they live in Nevada. I'll try to contact them today."

"Mason?" He turned and found a tall woman covered in protective gear. She'd been at the other autopsy table. He recognized her eyes.

Detective Hawes.

"Nora . . . why are—" Mason cut off his words. The OSP detective could only be here for one reason. He looked past her to the male body on the other table. "Is that one of the . . ." He couldn't finish.

"Deputy Tims. From the courthouse yesterday."

One of the murdered officers.

A subtle dizziness came over him, and the other body blurred in his vision.

That could have been Ray on that table. Still might be.

"I hadn't heard you were assigned to the shooting," Mason said lamely.

"Last night. I'll be working with the task force that the Clackamas County sheriff put together."

He took a deep breath and his vision cleared. He and Detective Hawes both worked out of the Portland office. She hadn't been there long, but she'd impressed Mason with her thoroughness and work ethic. She would have been his choice to find Ray's shooter.

Concern shone in her eyes as she studied him. "Ray's going to be fine. And we'll get the guy—or guys—who did this."

"I have no doubt you'll find the shooter."

"You heard there are four deaths now?" Nora asked, sadness in her eyes.

Shock rocked Mason, and he shook his head, unable to speak.

It's a never-ending nightmare.

"The injured Oregon City officer didn't make it," she said.

His face flashed in Mason's mind. "Young."

How many more police will die?

"Twenty-five. Married with a two-month-old son."

Anger swept through him, and Mason bit his tongue. There was nothing that could be said to fix what had happened.

"Mason?" Dr. Trask asked. "I'd like you to look at this."

"I'll let you go," Nora said. "We both have a lot to do."

He watched the detective return to Dr. Rutledge's autopsy and sent up a fervent prayer that there'd be no more deaths.

Especially Ray's.

9

Ava rubbed the smeared mascara below her right eye. She'd glanced in the mirror by her front door as she was leaving for work and had done a double take. "How on earth did I do that?" She'd put on her makeup a half hour ago, before Mason left for the medical examiner's office. "He would've told me if he'd seen it," she mumbled. "I think."

Sometimes men didn't notice that type of thing.

Her phone rang, and she smiled as the name of the winery they'd reserved for the wedding showed on her screen. She was in love with the place. It was a Tuscan-style building that sat on top of a hill out in Yamhill County. The views were spectacular, but it wasn't pretentious. It was small and homey and welcoming. Their wedding wouldn't be large, maybe forty people.

"This is Ava."

"It's Erin. I'm so glad I reached you."

Ava would have recognized the young woman's British accent anywhere. She'd spent many hours chatting with the winery's manager. Discussions about wedding plans had led to discussions about wine and then discussions about Italy. Erin had spent two years there and had advised Ava on her honeymoon plans.

"Hi, Erin, what's up?"

"Is everything okay? When my assistant told me you canceled your date, I had to call you. I was really worried."

Ava's hands turned to ice. "What?"

"You canceled your reservation. Monica said you called ten minutes ago."

Panic shot up her spine. "No! I didn't call! Oh my God, Erin. You didn't give my date away, did you?"

"No, of course not! I wanted to hear it from you personally." She lowered her voice. "I did wonder if something went wrong between you and Mason. It does happen."

"Who—who would . . . ?" Ava's shoulders fell. *Jayne.*

Her sister was back in the States, and it appeared she was up to her old games.

"I'm so sorry to scare you like that. Who on earth would do such a thing? Do you or Mason have an angry ex who would call?"

"No exes." Ava pressed two fingers above her right eyebrow, a headache blossoming. "I think someone was playing a joke."

"Well, it's a shitty joke." Erin's accent thickened. "I'll leave it to you to dole out the tongue-lashing. What a horrible thing to do. What if Monica had gone ahead and filled the date?"

"Then you would have kicked them out because you know that is *my* date—our date," she corrected.

"You bet your arse I would."

Ava ended the call a minute later.

Do I tell Mason?

She wouldn't do it now. He had enough on his plate. And she still hadn't told him about Brady Shurr's visit and Jayne's disappearance. It felt as if she had learned about Jayne much longer ago than yesterday. But yesterday had turned into a lengthy nightmare.

No wonder she'd forgotten to bring up Jayne.

She sent a text to Cheryl, her next-door neighbor and wedding planner, asking if she was home.

Yep. What do you need?

Can I come over for a minute?

The door is open

Her anger starting to boil, Ava gave Bingo a head rub and then marched over to Cheryl's house. The door was literally open, and Ava walked right in.

"Cheryl?"

"Kitchen."

Cheryl's home always gave Ava the feeling that she'd walked into an eclectic art studio. Bright colors popped everywhere, and it worked perfectly, creating a lush and opulent atmosphere. If Ava had tried to decorate with colors like that, the result would resemble a toddler's playroom.

Ava never dreamed she'd use a wedding planner. How hard could it be to make some reservations and choices? Now she was thankful she'd allowed her neighbor to talk her into using her services. Ava didn't have time to think about details; she was too busy with work. Hiring someone to think for her had been one of her best decisions ever.

She found Cheryl in the kitchen, pouring something over a glass of ice. The odor of fresh espresso hit Ava and she sighed.

"This one is yours." Cheryl shoved the drink into Ava's hand.

"I can't. I have to drive to work."

The tall blonde rolled her eyes. "There's no alcohol in it."

"That's a first." Ava took a sip. A perfect iced vanilla latte. "This is fantastic. Thank you."

Popping a pod into an espresso machine, Cheryl met her gaze. "That's better. You looked like you wanted to kill someone when you first walked in." She hit a button, and the tiny machine made a huge noise and espresso immediately streamed into a cup.

Ava waited until it quieted. "I did want to kill someone. My twin." She gave Cheryl a rundown of her phone call from the winery and Brady's report on Jayne.

Cheryl's jaw hung open as she mixed her own iced latte. "Holy cow, girl. Are you sure you're related to her?"

"Positive," Ava said dryly.

"Good thing Erin thought to give you a call."

"That's just it. What if other vendors haven't called to confirm something was canceled?"

Cheryl's eyes widened. "Shit."

"Exactly."

"But how would she know the details? I assume you mentioned the venue to her at one point, but would you have told her who is doing the flowers or photos?"

"No, but it doesn't matter. She's very resourceful. If she put half the energy into bettering herself that she put into causing trouble, she'd be a CEO of a Fortune 500 company by now."

Setting down her latte, Cheryl grabbed the iPad on the counter and started typing. "I'll call and confirm everyone, no matter how small their involvement is. Thank God you already picked up your dress. It took months for that order." Cheryl shuddered. "You'd have to pick something off the rack."

Ava was positive that wouldn't have been the end of the world. "Everything is replaceable except that winery view. I know there are other locations, but anything as fabulous will have been reserved months ago."

"Tell me about it." Cheryl glanced up. "Did I tell you about the young bride who wanted me to arrange a reception at the Portland Art Museum in three weeks?" She snorted. "I'm not a miracle worker."

"I've found you to be a miracle worker a few times. My dress, for example."

"You're my first bride who custom-dyed a wedding dress in teal. If the designer found out what you did, she would have a heart attack."

"It's not teal."

"Whatever you call it, it's definitely a unique color." She gave Ava a side-eye. "And your choice of dress completely surprised me. It wasn't what I expected."

"I loved it." She'd stored the dress at Cheryl's house, not wanting Mason to accidentally find it.

"I did too." Cheryl sighed. "Okay. I have a dozen calls to make. I'll request they contact us about any cancellations made over the phone."

Ava grimaced. "They should call you to confirm even if I show up in person to make a change."

"Noooo! She wouldn't impersonate you!"

"She would."

Cheryl swore. "I'm sorry you have to put up with that."

"It's my reality. Nothing new. I'm relieved her long silence is over. I've been walking on eggshells waiting to see what would happen next and constantly looking over my shoulder."

"You can't win. Either she's acting out or you're waiting for her to act out."

The perfect description of Ava's life.

"Did you talk to Jill about being your attendant?" Cheryl asked, still tapping on her tablet.

"Not yet." *Will Ray make it to be Mason's best man?* "I don't think I should ask her after what happened to Ray."

Ava's stomach churned, and her wedding plans suddenly seemed petty and frivolous.

"Who were your other choices? That FBI agent in Bend, right? Or the hunky reporter's wife? You need to line up someone quickly. They should know since it's only a few weeks away."

"I know."

Cheryl set down her iPad, her gaze scrutinizing Ava.

She sees too much. Ava took a drink of her latte, pretending she hadn't noticed.

"It's your twin, isn't it?" Cheryl said softly, placing a hand on Ava's arm. "Some part of you is hoping she'll be in your wedding."

Ava's eyes burned. "It's ridiculous. She's made my entire life hell."

"She's still your sister."

"It's the worst idea ever. She'd do her best to destroy the day . . . She'd try to seduce Mason in a coat closet or offer the minister a blow job or *accidentally* knock over the cake." Ava coughed out a rough laugh. It wasn't funny; it was true.

"I'm sorry. I'll watch out for you," Cheryl said in a fierce voice. "I won't let anyone sabotage your special day."

"It's just another day. Nothing changes after we get married except legal stuff." All the wedding details she'd chosen felt insignificant. Thinking of Jayne had enveloped Ava in a dark mist.

What is the point of all the planning and decisions?

"Don't you *dare* try to downplay your wedding day. It's important. You're announcing your commitment to the world, and I *know* your relationship will feel different afterward."

"Impossible. We can't love each other more than we already do." Ava knew their love went deep, to a fathomless depth that she'd never dreamed existed.

"Oh, honey." Cheryl squeezed her arm. "I should make you put money behind those words, because you are in for a dreamy surprise. Now don't give me that exasperated look. I'm the expert here. Love is my business." She checked the time. "Shouldn't you be on your way to work? Get going and let me handle these details."

Cheryl was right; Ava was going to be late. She appreciated Cheryl's little pep talk, but Ava was practical. Love was love, and she and Mason were already deep in it.

It can't get better.

Can it?

◆ ◆ ◆

An hour later Ava looked up as Zander stopped outside her office.

"I've been assigned to the courthouse-shooting task force," he told her. "It's made up of the Clackamas County Sheriff's Office, OSP, Oregon City police, ATF, and us. I told Ben you should be on it too, but he argued that since one of the victims is a close friend, you shouldn't be involved. I told him it didn't matter. You're the best for this job."

Ava was touched. "I appreciate that, but I understand Ben's reasons. You'll be an asset to the group." *I'd give big money to be on that task force.*

Ray's prognosis was still guarded. Ava had texted briefly with Jill after leaving Cheryl's house. Even through Jill's texts, Ray's wife sounded tired.

Zander grinned at her. "I convinced Ben to send you."

Surprise froze her. "You did? Are you serious? He gave in?"

Ben appeared behind Zander. "I don't give in." He poked Zander's upper arm. "I made my own decision based on the information, not someone's personal argument." He turned a serious gaze on Ava. "You are to respect the boundaries of the investigation."

In other words, Mason is not to be my shadow.

"Of course. But I do have a full caseload at the moment."

"This is the priority. The shooting was all over the national news and internet last night, and the public is angry."

"Some of the public," added Zander. "The usual anticop commenters are out in full force on the internet. They seem to think it's some sort of holiday."

"That's horrible," said Ava. "But I'm not surprised one bit."

"Me neither," said Ben. "The sheriff's department is holding a task force briefing at noon in Oregon City. I told them you'd both be there." He nodded at them and strode down the hall.

Ava exhaled. "This is big." The enormity of the crime swirled around her. Being forced to sit on the sidelines of an active investigation was tense, but having the case abruptly land in her lap carried heavy stress and intense pressure to solve it. Her stress level had risen immediately at Ben's words, but she embraced it. The pressure would push her and help focus her mind.

Her stakes were personal and professional. Someone had ambushed a close friend, her fiancé, and fellow law enforcement members, making her angry and upset.

"You're right. It is big," said Zander. "And you already have a lot on your plate."

His tone caught her attention. "You found something on Jayne?"

"Not yet."

"You won't believe what she did." She told Zander about the winery cancellation.

"You can't be positive it was her," he pointed out.

"Who else would do that to me? It's a personal attack."

"It doesn't involve just you," Zander said. "Losing the venue would affect Mason too."

She stared at him. *He's right.* "I hate it when you act all logical."

"For that matter, it could be aimed at your wedding planner. Maybe someone is trying to affect her business by making her look bad. It would be a major screwup on her part."

Ava thought it through. "I don't think that's it . . . but you're right that it could be aimed at Mason too." She slumped back in her chair. "Now I'm doubting that it's Jayne."

"Just expanding the possibilities. I find it telling that I can't find a credit transaction or car rental in her name—or yours. She must be using someone else's identity."

"Brady said she had access to a lot of cash."

"Still needs a credit card to rent a car or hotel room."

"Maybe she stole identification from someone at the rehabilitation center in Costa Rica."

"I'll call to ask if they've had any thefts."

"You don't have time for this. Neither of us does . . . especially now."

"I can make a quick call while you drive us to the briefing in Oregon City. Before Ben assigned me to the task force, I did some scouring in San Diego but didn't find a trace of her—or you—anywhere. But I did learn your father is at the Oregon coast at the moment. Did you know that?"

"I did," Ava said reluctantly. "It's a family trip. He has his kids and grandkids with him. David invited me." She couldn't call him Dad—or Father—yet. He was David. Using his first name felt safe, like keeping a small wall between the two of them. Jayne was able to fully embrace the father she'd never known existed, but Ava wasn't there yet.

Baby steps.

"Could Jayne be with him? Was she invited?"

"I don't know." Ava imagined her sister playing on the beach with David's grandkids. It was the type of opportunity Jayne wouldn't pass up. The chance to pretend she had a real family.

It is her real family.

"Can you call him?" Zander asked patiently.

"I'll text." Ava picked up her phone. *No small talk needed.*

"No one makes phone calls anymore," Zander complained. "It's becoming a lost skill."

She sent David a text asking if Jayne was with them.

"Why didn't you join them at the beach?" Zander asked. "You could have popped in for a day visit."

"Do I seem like a pop-in kind of person?"

"No, you seem like a person who is terrified of being a part of something unfamiliar . . . or terrified that it could become something very good."

"Not terrified. Cautious."

"You've known this family for almost nine months and you're still hesitant? They could have been a bunch of jerks, but instead each one has reached out to you."

"I like Kacey. We talk sometimes." David's daughter was the type of person Ava wanted to be friends with, but the blood connection made her hesitate.

She waited a few moments, staring at her screen. "I don't think David is the type of person that always has their phone in hand. I might not hear back for a while."

"I envy those people."

"I do too. But I've accidentally left home without my phone and felt as if I was missing a limb."

"Let's head out to the meeting," Zander suggested.

Ava nodded and stole another look at her phone. No text. She slipped it into her pocket, grabbed her bag, and followed Zander.

Why do I feel this day will get worse?

10

Mason welcomed the heat of the sun as he stepped out of the medical examiner's office. Even the waiting room had been cold. He turned his face to the sky, appreciating the warmth and realizing how drained he was. It was barely noon and he wanted to go home, take a nap, and not wake up until someone could tell him Ray was out of the woods.

Instead, he had to go back to Reuben Braswell's home and pick up where he and Ray had left off yesterday. At least the crime scene team should be gone. No one to distract him.

Why am I not rushing over there?

The need to nap swamped him again. As important as the Braswell murder case was to him, he desperately wanted his finger on the pulse of the shooter investigation. The image of the dead officer in the medical examiner's office haunted him.

It could have been Ray.

He and Ray went back more than a decade. Mason had been an experienced detective when Ray was assigned to the Major Crimes division as a rookie, fresh off being a state trooper for years. His easy talkativeness and snappy way of dressing had annoyed Mason at first, but he'd soon learned the former college football player had a big heart and a brain as sharp as a knife. They had become friends, and Ray and Jill had pulled him into their lives when his own was cold and empty after his divorce from Jake's mom. He'd dragged his heels, not wanting to bring down the upbeat family with his taciturn ways.

With strong encouragement from Jill, Ray had prevailed.

Mason was a better man for having known both of them.

"Callahan."

Mason stiffened at the familiar voice. Michael Brody leaned against an SUV parked twenty feet away at the yellow curb.

Not now.

He didn't like to admit it, but Mason grudgingly admired the investigative reporter. As a whole, reporters drove him nuts. And it'd only gotten worse with the hundreds of online "news" sites cropping up. Facts and truth weren't high on their list of priorities when it came to sniffing out a story.

But Brody was one of the good ones. The two of them had butted heads a few times but eventually recognized they shared a dedication to finding answers. Ava adored the reporter for some reason. Probably because he usually rubbed Mason the wrong way. Brody had no filter and no respect for authority. Mason suspected Ava pushed him and Brody together as much as possible so she'd have a sociology experiment to analyze.

The younger man was cocky and laid back and always looked as if he'd just returned from the beach. Currently he wore loose shorts—with two ragged holes—and a faded T-shirt. He didn't look like a man with two master's degrees. The Range Rover and expensive watch were the only indications that the reporter had money to burn. Family money. His mother had been a skilled surgeon, his father a state senator, and his uncle the governor of Oregon.

Mason shielded his eyes from the sun as he squinted at the vehicle. It was navy. Last time he saw the reporter, it had been black. "New Rover?"

"Yes."

"What do you want, Brody?" Mason asked. The casual displays of wealth never failed to trigger Mason's annoyance.

"What's the connection between the death of Reuben Braswell and the shooting yesterday?"

How did he find that out?

It was another thing that irked Mason. Brody had sources that he shouldn't have and refused to reveal. The reporter had friends in both high and low places.

"Why do you think there is one?" Mason inserted annoyance into his tone. He wasn't about to acknowledge anything. "If you have questions, we have public information officers to help you."

Brody grinned, his teeth white against his tan face. "I like you better. You don't mince words."

"No shit. Go away."

"See?"

Mason put on his cowboy hat as he headed for his vehicle. "I'm exhausted. Fuck off."

"Hey, Mason . . . I'm sorry about Ray."

He halted and looked back. Brody's tone was sincere and so was his expression.

He knows when to stop with the crap.

On some twisted level, Mason enjoyed their arguments. "Thanks."

"If something at the Braswell murder scene led you to that bomb scare at the courthouse, I might know some avenues you can pursue to find the shooter."

"Are you being serious right now?"

"Deadly serious."

"I'm not on the shooting investigation. My job is to find who murdered Reuben Braswell."

"I think this might open up some leads for that murder too."

"You use the word *might* a lot. That doesn't instill confidence."

Brody shrugged. "You know I have resources."

Do I want to open this can of worms?

"I could use some coffee," Mason finally said. He could spare twenty minutes to hear Brody out if it might help with either investigation.

"I'll even buy," said Brody.

"That was a given."

Ten minutes later the two of them were at a shaded table outside a coffee shop. Mason had ordered an iced black coffee. Brody had a gigantic frozen drink with four shots of espresso, whipped cream, and extra caramel drizzle.

"That's not coffee," said Mason as he realized he wanted a taste of the froufrou drink.

"It's caffeine. That's what's important."

Mason leaned forward. "What do you have for me?"

Brody drew a happy face in the condensation on his plastic cup. "A couple of months ago I was working on a story about conspiracy theories. Where they originate, what draws people to them, how they perpetuate, and so on."

"Ava said Braswell was a conspiracy theorist."

"Let me finish," Brody said, raising a brow. "I found several online-message-board sites dedicated to discussing these theories. It was pretty entertaining. Especially when people would present proof. Blurry pictures, links to unreliable web pages, testimony from relatives. Great stuff. It was one of my most fascinating research projects."

"Your research is reading what crazy people write." Mason wished his job were as laid back.

"Some of the writers are as normal as you and me, but they seem to have a weakness for the bizarre."

"You mean a weakness in their heads."

Michael ignored his remark. "After a while one commenter frequently caught my attention. He had all sorts of theories about our government—and several other governments around the world. Believed there was a one-world government forming behind our backs. He would trumpet that law enforcement was a weapon of the government to keep us down, created to make a permanent working class that simply supports the rich. No chance to build something of themselves. Arrest the middle-class working guy who's barely supporting his family and throw big fines at him that he can't afford, or lock him up long enough to lose his job and rely on government handouts. Said law enforcement only pretended to help the public. That they would ignore regular people in real trouble."

"Sounds like it was personal to the commenter."

"That's what caught my attention too. But then his rants turned to killing cops. He proposed to take away the government's human weapons, so the government would be powerless to keep us down."

Mason's hand tightened on his coffee cup. "Seriously?"

"Yep. He caught a lot of flak from other commenters, which didn't seem to bother him. He could argue with the best of them, but he also had plenty of supporters. I got the impression he frequented other message boards where this law enforcement conspiracy to keep the average man down was commonplace. I looked but couldn't find another one that he participated in. He probably had a different username."

"Who was this guy?"

"After some deep digging, I found the email for this poster belonged to Reuben Braswell."

Mason's coffee turned to acid in his stomach.

"Think one of his like-minded associates could be involved in his murder?" asked Brody.

"That doesn't make sense. If they had the same ideologies, why kill him?"

"Maybe he had a change of heart . . . Maybe the shooting was part of a big plan and he wanted to back out. That could have made one of his associates very angry." Brody looked evenly at Mason. "What at the Braswell scene alerted you to the bombing threat at the courthouse?"

I can't go there.

"Considering your number of sources, I'm surprised you haven't figured that out."

"I've heard rumors. Nothing substantiated. I know an alarm was raised while you and Ray were inside the home, and then you were out of the house within minutes."

"Everybody responded to the threat. City, county, state, federal . . ."

"But no one else was investigating the murder of a cop-hating conspirator and then rushed into a massacre."

I hate it when he does that.

Brody had a knack for solving puzzles when he didn't have all the pieces. Mason took a long drink of his coffee, searching for how to respond.

The reporter leaned back in his chair and nodded. "Thought so. You're really bad at hiding your thoughts. What was it? Something on his computer? A diary?" Brody crossed his arms as he considered. "His computer wouldn't be searched until it went to a lab—unless something was immediately visible on the screen. Braswell didn't strike me as a diary-keeping type of guy." He looked expectantly at Mason.

"You know I can't tell you anything."

"How is Ava involved in this?"

Holy shit.

Brody snorted. "You should see the shock on your face." He grew sober, his eyes concerned. "She's not in any danger, right?"

Mason hadn't even considered that since her name was in Braswell's diatribe, Ava might be a target. "Christ."

If Braswell singled out Ava as a good cop, does that make her a target for Braswell's killer?

"What on earth did you find in that house?" Brody leaned forward, his stare probing.

"Give me the websites and username you linked to Reuben Braswell."

"I emailed them to you before we sat down."

Cocky bastard.

"Someone was furious with Braswell," Brody continued. "Who and why?"

"When I learn that, I'll know who killed him."

And possibly shot Ray.

11

"She shouldn't be here," the Clackamas County detective said to Zander. The young county detective had marched over the minute he learned Ava was in the task force room for the briefing.

"I'm right in front of you," Ava said in a calm voice to the detective. "Vent your complaints in my direction." She saw a muscle twitch in Zander's cheek.

He's trying not to laugh.

She didn't find the situation funny. Due to her name being in the Braswell notes, she had been prepared for pushback against her presence on the case. "If you don't want to discuss it with me, then you can call the Portland FBI ASAC. He assigned me to this case in spite of my name showing up *for no good reason* in that man's house because he knows I'm the best for the job." She knew her boss would back her up.

"There's got to be a hundred agents in that office," the detective said. "Your ASAC can send someone else."

"Then you call him. But we've already had this discussion, and he won't care about your concerns. He cares about finding out who murdered four police officers." Ava held the detective's gaze.

She sent up her hundredth silent prayer for Ray.

After a long moment, the detective turned away. "Find a seat," he tossed over his shoulder.

Ava let out a breath she hadn't realized she'd been holding. "Ass," she muttered.

"He's doing his job," Zander pointed out as they took two seats in the front row. "If he hadn't protested, it wouldn't have looked right. He had no intention to send you packing."

"You don't think so?" Ava studied the detective with a skeptical eye and a new sense of respect as he huddled with two men in deputy uniforms.

"Nope. And he only addressed me to see how you'd react. I think you passed his test."

He did back down rather easily.

"He's so young." She was miffed she'd misread the detective's tactics. She glanced around the room, recognizing police uniforms from a half dozen agencies, big and small. Several people were also in plain clothes. More detectives, she assumed. She was one of six women of about twenty-five people. A tall blonde in a pantsuit caught her eye, and Ava waved her over. She liked Nora Hawes, who was in Mason's department. Ava had considered recruiting the detective for the FBI a number of times, but Nora seemed to relish the assortment of cases in OSP's Major Crimes division.

Nora sat in the row behind her, and her lips turned up on one side. "I saw you put that detective in his place."

"He was just doing what was necessary," Ava replied, ignoring the twitch in Zander's cheek again.

"I ran into Mason this morning at the medical examiner's office. He looked exhausted. You two holding up okay?"

"As well as can be expected," said Ava. "This case is very personal."

"It is for a lot of us," answered Nora. "Ray is one of the good ones." She sat back in her chair as the Clackamas County sheriff stepped behind the table at the front of the room. Everyone else immediately found a seat.

Ava watched the sheriff shuffle through some papers and wished Mason were also on the inside of this investigation. He had left an odd message on her phone earlier, essentially telling her to watch her back. It made no sense.

Is he worried there will be another shooting?

Ava briefly closed her eyes. So many unanswered questions.

There were five rows of chairs facing the front, and computer stations filled one side of the room. A few techs moved from computer to computer, checking wires and moving plugs. Four uniformed officers sat at a table answering phones, taking tips from the public. She'd heard the tips were coming in as fast as the officers could answer the phones. More were arriving via email and on social media. Sorting through the information would take most of their hours. Task forces weren't glamorous; they meant long, dull hours spent wading through minutiae.

The walls of the room had a dozen whiteboards and bulletin boards. Currently only one bulletin board was in use, but Ava knew they would all be full in days. Photos were pinned to the first bulletin board, showing shots of the streets around the courthouse. Two of them had uniformed bodies lying in the street.

She looked away, her stomach tight. If Ray hadn't been holding a ballistic vest, would he still have been targeted? The other victims had been in uniform. The crack of the shots she'd heard while watching the news video had echoed in her mind all night. Mason said Ray had been one of the first people shot. Had she heard one of the shots that hit him?

"Okay, folks, let's get started." The sheriff addressed the room and proceeded to introduce himself and a few other commanders from various agencies. As she listened, Ava appreciated his leadership skills. The sheriff didn't waste words and made everyone feel like they were a part of a team. Not every commander could do that.

He tapped on a laptop, and a PowerPoint display popped up on the screen behind him. "Here's what we've got so far. Twenty-two .300 AAC

Blackout casings were found in this area at the top of the cliffs." He used a red laser pointer to indicate an area under the trees in the huge photo.

"Heavy rounds," Zander muttered under his breath.

"No other locations?" asked someone in the audience.

"Not that we've found." The sheriff cleared his throat. "Based on interviews from people at the scene, it's looking like one shooter, but we haven't ruled out the possibility of two or more. We're still reviewing all the camera footage we recovered in the surrounding area. A 7-Eleven turned over quite a bit of footage, and three churches in the area did the same. Data from traffic cameras has been pulled, and interviews with people at the scene are still in process."

Ava sighed. It was easy to miss important details when they were buried under so much information.

"Channel 8 turned over the helicopter coverage. There were a couple video sweeps of the cliff area that are being analyzed second by second." He paused. "Some bystanders filmed the shootings."

A low mumble of disgust filled the room.

"Don't complain. They might give us some answers."

"They turn up on social media yet?" asked Nora in a sour tone.

"Yep. And we've got people hunting them down for removal. I haven't heard of anything graphic being posted. Most of the social media platforms have algorithms in place to prevent that from happening now."

"Most," whispered Ava. The thought that Ray's kids could find footage of his shooting enraged her.

"I'm hearing that police are nervous to respond to calls or gather in public," said a man to Ava's left. More mumbles rippled through the group.

Can you blame them?

"I've heard the same," the sheriff said. "We'll do what needs to be done. This threat isn't new. It's been a part of our lives from the moment we took the badge. Public safety is our priority. No one will ignore that."

"Have they tracked the source of the bomb threat?" asked the same man.

Ava pressed her lips together and noticed the sheriff did the same as he pondered the question. *Are they not sharing where the threat was discovered?* Zander shifted in his chair as they waited for the sheriff's answer.

The sheriff made eye contact with Ava and held it. She gave him a small nod. There was no point in hiding that her name was linked.

"You will all have access to copies of information that turned up at a murder investigation yesterday. Handwritten pages were found in the home of a fifty-two-year-old male victim, Reuben Braswell. These documents warned us of the bomb threat."

"But there was no bomb," a woman said from the back.

"Nope."

"So the rumor that the threat was created to pull dozens of law enforcement officers to one location could be true," she said faintly.

"We haven't disproven that," said the sheriff. "We're not crossing off any possibilities this early in the investigation, and I trust all of you know better than to talk to the media. If I find out you have, you'll be off my task force immediately, and I won't listen to excuses. Now, I've made assignments, and you'll find them on the table at the back. We're going to work nonstop on this until we catch our killer. Our family in blue deserves the best."

He picked up his stack of papers, signaling that the briefing was over.

"Thought he was going to out you there for a moment," Zander said in a low voice as they stood.

"It's not a secret," said Ava. "Everyone here will see my name in his notes sooner or later."

Behind them Nora cleared her throat, and they turned around. "I've been assigned to dig into Braswell's past," she told them, eyeing Ava. "We'll need to talk."

"Definitely," said Ava. "But honestly, I've racked my brain over my interactions with him and can't come up with anything that helps."

"Maybe I can prod your memory or see something you don't."

"True." Ava knew it was important to use a fresh set of eyes and ears. "You know you'll be working parallel to Mason's murder investigation."

"I do. I think the sheriff gave me this assignment since we're both with OSP." She shouldered her bag to leave. "I'll see you two later."

"Logical to give that to another OSP detective," said Zander to Ava. "I checked our assignments before that detective got on your case. We're to start with a 7-Eleven clerk who wasn't around for interviews yesterday. He'd gone home before the shooting started but told his manager today that he has something to share. We're also to hit the businesses in the area that were missed and review the canvassing notes."

"A full day or two," said Ava. She turned and nearly bumped into the sheriff.

"I've questioned whether you should be here, Agent McLane," the sheriff said in a voice only she and Zander could hear.

"You and everyone else."

"I don't like politics when it comes to police work," the sheriff said.

"No one does."

"I believe having a bit of a personal stake in an investigation makes someone work harder."

"I wish others thought like you do," Ava said fervently.

"I know your record."

Ava said nothing and simply held his gaze.

"You've successfully hunted a cop killer before," he stated.

"I have," she said stiffly. That case had also been personal. Mason's supervisor and several other law enforcement members had been murdered last fall.

"Can you get 'em again this time?"

"Absolutely."

Ava had no doubts.

"Then get to work." The sheriff gestured toward the door and walked away.

"Ready?" she asked Zander. She knew she'd just received a compliment and added not letting down the sheriff to her list of motivations for finding Ray's shooter.

A good leader inspires.

Outside the room her phone rang.

It was David's number. She had forgotten she'd texted to ask if Jayne was with him at the coast. "Dammit. Why didn't he just text a yes or no?"

"Because he wants to talk with you."

Ava gave Zander a side-eye. "I'm not in the mood for a family chat at the moment. We have work to do." She answered her phone.

"Ava?" A low female voice like her own.

"Kacey?" Ava frowned as her half sister gasped for breath. "What's wrong?"

"It's Dad." More wet gasps for air came through the phone. "He went for a run on the beach this morning and someone attacked him."

Ava stopped in the parking lot, her throat tightening, an image of the kind man in her mind. "Is he okay?"

Kacey sobbed. "He's dead."

12

At noon Mason sat in his SUV in front of the Braswell home, trying to decide what to do. He'd left a message on Ava's voice mail, saying he was worried that her name in Braswell's document could mean trouble for her. Since Braswell was dead, would someone target her too?

He didn't know why it would happen, but he had to say *something* to feel he'd addressed it. And get it off his mind. Distractions were pulling him in a dozen directions.

Ray was number one, and Jill had been silent since that morning.

No news is good news.

He took a deep breath, fighting the urge to text Jill, and focused on the house.

Solving this could lead to Ray's shooter.

Mason would go through the home more thoroughly, but he also needed to follow up on the notes from officers who'd canvassed the neighborhood. One neighbor hadn't been home when they knocked on the door, but now there was a vehicle in that driveway. Mason knew he should go ask the usual "Did you see anything?" questions.

He didn't feel like talking to people.

He'd already met with Brody. That was enough for anyone in one day.

According to the officers' canvass, no homes on the street used a doorbell camera, and only one had an outdoor security camera, but an officer had checked the video and said it only picked up the outer edge of the street.

Maybe the house he needed to visit would have a security camera.

He would walk the Braswell home first and then talk to the neighbors. Decision made, he got out of his car and was slapped in the face by the heat. The high temperatures were very unusual. Typically June was quite wet. No doubt the local media would start worrying about a drought any day.

He let himself into the house, took off his hat, and stood just inside the door. He hadn't paid much attention to the living room on his right yesterday. He'd gone straight to the body and then checked the kitchen and the "map room." The living room was nondescript. Brown furniture. Oak coffee table and end tables. A framed poster of Mount Bachelor and another of the Columbia River Gorge. Couch cushions were slightly askew—they'd been searched. Black fingerprint powder on the tables. The crime scene techs had been thorough even though there didn't appear to have been any violence in the room.

The kitchen was next. More black powder. Mason pulled up the photos he'd shot of the kitchen on his work phone yesterday and compared them to the scene in front of him. Except for the powder, nothing had changed. The pools of blood had dried and were now darker.

A vision of Ray's blood in the gravel popped into his mind. His lungs suddenly tightened, and he wiped sweat off his forehead. The air in the home abruptly felt stagnant and thin.

I need to get out.

Mason strode back out front. Breathing deeply, he leaned against the same pole on the porch that he'd stood at for the Gillian Wood interview. His gaze fell on the neighbor's car across the street, and he immediately moved in that direction. Now, talking to people sounded much better. The house could wait.

The home was a ranch nearly identical in shape and size to Braswell's, and the vehicle was a little red Toyota pickup that had seen better days—probably over a decade ago. Mason rang the doorbell and stepped back a few feet, his business card in his hand and his badge visible on his belt.

The door was opened by a lanky teenage boy in long athletic shorts and a tank top. His hair poked out in all directions, and he clutched a game controller in one hand.

Mason introduced himself. "Your parents around?"

"I live with my dad, and he's out of town." The teen studied the business card Mason had given him. "This about Reuben?"

"Is school out already?" Mason's son, Jake, had always been in school halfway through June.

"I'm at PCC. No class today. What happened to Reuben? I mean, I know he's dead, but how did it happen?"

"How old are you?" Just because he attended the community college didn't mean he was over eighteen. Mason wasn't about to talk to a minor without his parent present.

The teen scowled. "Twenty-two."

Mason didn't believe him. "You got ID?"

"Am I under arrest? You can't just come here and ask me to show ID for no reason."

"You want to talk about Reuben? I want to know you're over eighteen."

He instantly vanished and was back moments later with a driver's license. Kaden Schroeder was twenty-two. "I heard it was pretty nasty," Kaden said as Mason studied the license, at first wondering if it was a fake so Kaden could buy alcohol, but it looked legit.

Mason handed back the license. "Who told you that?"

Kaden shrugged. "Dunno."

The shrug and answer reminded Mason of Jake. So did the game controller and messy hair.

When I was twenty-two, I had my own apartment and a full-time job.

"What are you studying?"

"Why does it matter?"

"It doesn't. Just curious what you're working toward in your life."

The young man squinted at him. "Uh-huh. I think we're done." He started to close the door.

"You got any security cameras that cover the street?"

The door swung back open, interest bright in Kaden's eyes. "Nah. You got a suspect?"

"How well did you know Reuben Braswell?" Mason ignored Kaden's question.

Another shrug. "Not that well. He helped my dad repair our fence. Seemed cool. Big *Twilight Zone* fan. Found out we liked a lot of the same episodes."

"The original series?"

"Of course. All the reboots suck."

"The two of you talked about a TV show. What else?"

"Dunno."

"Did you help your dad repair the fence?"

"What does that matter?"

That means no. "Have you seen anyone over there or on your street recently?"

"You mean like someone new? There was a Mustang in his driveway a couple times over the last week or so. Didn't see it before that."

Mason made a note on his pad. "Color?"

"Silver. Sweet car."

"You don't think it was Reuben's?"

"Nah, seen him driving his truck the other day. The Mustang wasn't around."

Mason froze, his pen hovering over his pad.

Where is Reuben's truck?

He scribbled a note to get the make and the plates of the truck to put out a BOLO. The killer could have driven off with the truck . . . but then how had the killer arrived at the home?

Two people?

It wasn't confirmed that a single shooter had done the courthouse shooting.

He needed the Braswell report from the crime scene team to see if their findings indicated more than one person had committed the murder.

"Who'd you see driving the Mustang?"

"Didn't see no one. Just saw it in the driveway."

"Overnight? Just during the day? Short or long periods?"

The young man wiped his nose with the back of his hand as he thought. "Not sure. I know it was there when I got home around two a.m. last Saturday. Don't know if it stayed all night. It was never there consistently. Figured it might be a new girlfriend."

Mason mulled that over. "You know Gillian who lives next door to him?"

"Yeah." Kaden looked away. "Know her a little. She's okay."

The expression on his face reminded Mason of Gillian's expression when she'd first lied about her relationship with Reuben. Mason lowered his notepad and took a hard look at Kaden. "You got something going on with her?"

Shock flashed in Kaden's eyes. "Hell no. I mean . . . I wouldn't mind . . . but hell no." He twisted the game controller with both hands.

Mason believed him. "Did you ever see her at Reuben's?"

The shock flared again. "Are you saying she's a suspect? That she killed him? *Holy shit.*"

Mason held up both hands. "Slow down! I'm not saying that at all."

"Then why the fuck are you asking about her? She's really nice. She wouldn't do something like that." Concern filled his tone, but doubt flickered in his gaze.

"Let me ask again. You ever see them talking to one another? And I'm not asking because I think she killed him." *But she's not off my list.*

Gillian was thin. She'd have to have caught Reuben by surprise with a powerful swing of the mallet to overpower him.

Could happen.

I need to interview her again.

Mason recalled Ray's easy manner with the woman and clamped his teeth together.

Don't think of Ray now.

"I can't think of a time when I saw them," Kaden was saying. "They're next-door neighbors, so I'm sure they talked."

Mason's phone vibrated with a text, and he checked the screen. It was from Jill.

Call me asap

Dread swamped him. "I gotta make a call. Thanks for your help." The words tripped out of his mouth. "Call-me-if-you-think-of-something-else." He pointed at the business card in Kaden's hand, turned away, and speed-walked across the street to his SUV.

I need to sit down. It could be bad. Shit, Ray.

He sat in his vehicle, and his fingers shook as he hit the screen to call.

"Mason?" Jill answered.

"What happened?" Every muscle in his body tensed.

"Ray was struggling to breathe. It set off alarms." Her voice quivered. "They're taking him back to surgery."

Shit.

"Oh, Mason. He was still sedated. I haven't even spoken with him yet, and now . . ."

Mason closed his eyes. "I'm sure they'll take care of it."

"No one's telling me anything. The kids . . . Can you . . ." Soft sobs came across the phone.

"I'm on my way."

13

Ava had moved to the passenger's seat of Zander's SUV, her half sister Kacey still on the phone sobbing and babbling about her father's death.

This isn't happening.

"Slow down," Ava repeated as a gush of garbled words spilled from Kacey's mouth again. "Take a few deep breaths. Is anyone with you?"

"Yes." Kacey noisily sucked in air. "Kevin and his wife. My husband flew back to San Diego yesterday for work."

"Kids there too?"

"Yes. They don't know yet." Kacey's voice cracked. "How do I tell them their grandfather is dead? Kevin's kids are way too young to understand."

Ava thought that was a blessing but didn't say it out loud. Her half brother's toddlers were adorable, and Kacey's two kids were eight and ten. They were going to take the news hard.

"What did the police tell you?" Ava asked. "How did they know where to find you?"

"We've been here for two weeks," Kacey said. "We've met everyone, and you know how Dad is. He's everyone's friend within seconds of meeting. The couple that found him recognized him immediately." She took a shuddering breath.

"How did he die, Kacey?" Ava asked gently.

"H-h-he was shot . . . in the head," she whispered.

Ava sagged into her seat.

Why this man? Why this kind man?

"I'm so sorry, Kacey."

"I don't know what to do."

"Just keep your family close. You don't need to do anything. The police will guide you. Was it the Seaside police?"

"Yes. But the detective was from Clatsop County."

Ava had known the small city's police department would ask county or state for assistance in the murder. Seaside police were more accustomed to handling drunk tourists and speeding teenagers.

"I know the Clatsop County sheriff," Ava said. "I worked with him on a case over there a few months ago. I'll call him and get an update." She paused. "Do you need me there?" she asked tentatively. Ava knew it wasn't practical; she had just been assigned to one of the most important task forces in recent history.

But it was her family.

Sort of.

"No," said Kacey. "You'll just sit around with the rest of us waiting for information. You must have a ton of work."

Guilt swamped Ava. She'd only known Kacey for nine months, but the woman had already learned that Ava's work would always come first. Ava had used the excuse several times when David or Kacey had invited her to San Diego.

Is my work more important than this?

She met Zander's gaze. He was in the driver's seat, watching her intently, sympathy in his eyes.

"What do I do?" she mouthed silently at him. Confusion warred with responsibility in her brain.

"What do you want to do?"

That's no help. She covered her phone's microphone. "I don't know. I feel like I should be there for them, but we have a huge case on our hands." Ray's face flashed in her mind. She wanted to track down his shooter. "I wouldn't be able to help the case in Seaside. I'd simply be standing around with the rest of them."

"You've told me a dozen times you don't feel a connection to this family."

She had said that. And it was true. Sort of.

What is wrong with me?

"I want to find Ray's shooter at the moment," she admitted.

"Since he's injured and his prognosis is up in the air, that makes sense. You've had a tight connection with him for a few years." Zander gestured at her engagement ring. "Mason is tightly intertwined with the case here too."

The mention of Mason was the deciding factor. Ava immediately knew she had to stay but didn't know how to explain it to her grieving half sister.

"Kacey? I'll get back to you after I call the sheriff and see what information he has so far. That will help me decide if I should be there or not."

Her excuse was lame, and she cringed as she said it. It focused on the murder, not the family.

"Okay."

"I'll call you as soon as I can," Ava promised. "Oh, Kacey . . . have you heard from Jayne? I thought she might have accepted your invitation to the coast."

I nearly forgot to ask.

"No. I haven't heard from her in weeks. She never answered my invitation to join us here."

"I'm sorry about that, Kacey. She's . . . Well, you know."

"I'm learning. You're two very different people," Kacey said softly. "Dad really did love you two, you know. He was so happy when he found both of you. He'd always felt a piece of himself was missing." Quiet crying came through the phone. "Call me when you can." Kacey ended the call.

Ava slowly lowered her phone. "I don't know if I'm doing the right thing. I feel horrible." She was numb, drained.

I wouldn't be any help to that family.

My family.

"I'm really sorry, Ava," said Zander. "I know how confused you are about David and his family, but I also know you hoped for the fairy tale."

Her fairy tale.

One big happy family. With both a mother and a father.

She turned wet eyes his way. Zander always saw everything. "I did," she admitted. "It was stupid."

"No, it wasn't. It's absolutely normal for children who never knew their parents to hope they'll appear in their lives one day and they'll live happily ever after."

"I should have tried harder," Ava said. "I should have accepted all their invitations and sent them Christmas presents. Did you know David sent us a case of expensive Italian red wine and the most beautiful wineglasses I've ever seen?" The present had compounded her guilt about holding the family at arm's length. But not enough to push her into action. "I'm a horrible person."

"Considering your upbringing and your twin, I'd say you turned out to be an amazing person. You're driven and caring. You've done a lot of good for a lot of people . . . including Jayne."

"I'm not looking for a pep talk."

"I know. But I needed to say it."

Jayne, where the fuck are you? Ava rubbed her temples, feeling overloaded and anxious. Everything was happening at once. A perfect storm.

Ray, David, Jayne.

"Did I ever tell you about the time Jayne told my junior high school crush that I had herpes?" she blurted. The memory had leaped out from behind a door in her mind that Ava kept tightly shut and locked.

Zander shot her an incredulous look. "No, you told me about her sleeping with boys and telling them she was you, and how she stole your driver's license since she flunked her driving test, and how she threatened to cut herself if you didn't take a history test for her, and—"

"Got it." Ava cut him off. Her list of grievances with Jayne was long and painful and didn't need to be rehashed at the moment.

"What happened with your crush?"

"He went out with Jayne, of course." She wrinkled her nose. "They had sex. I've always hoped he used a condom, because if anyone had herpes, it was Jayne."

"In junior high?"

"You wouldn't believe the number of teens—and men—she slept with."

"Men with a girl in junior high? That's fucked up. And illegal." He paused. "She needed mental health care."

"I know. I mean, *now* I know. Back then I just thought she was mean."

Would Jayne's life have been different if she had received the proper help?

"I'm sorry, Ava."

Ava didn't answer. She usually hated when people felt sorry for her, but Zander was an exception because his sympathy was aimed at the past, not the present.

"Let's go talk to that 7-Eleven clerk," Ava said. "I'll call the Clatsop County sheriff about David's case on the way."

Zander started his vehicle and put it in gear. "On it."

Ava had been on hold in the car for five minutes before Clatsop County sheriff Greer picked up the line.

"Special Agent McLane!" The sheriff sounded genuinely pleased to hear from her. "I've been wondering about you. I hope you're fully recovered?"

"I am. Thank you." The truth was her shoulder and collarbone still ached, except for the areas that were numb. And she occasionally shuddered as she drove past men watching traffic as they stood on the side of the road. She'd been a vehicle passenger in the sheriff's county when a killer shot at the car. If the shot had been a few inches higher, she'd be dead.

"And Agent Wells? How's he doing since he persuaded Emily Mills to leave the coast? Their romance is still the talk of the county."

Ava glanced at Zander behind the steering wheel. "Zander is fine. I don't think anyone persuaded Emily. She does exactly what she wants."

Zander nodded emphatically, his eyes on the road.

"I'm calling about the shooting in Seaside this morning." Ava struggled to keep her tone even.

"Sad business," said the sheriff. "The victim had a big family, and I'm hearing over and over how kind he was."

Ava winced and struggled to align her words. "I know. He was my . . . father. But I didn't know he existed until last fall. My mother never told us about him."

The sheriff was silent for a long moment. "Well, now, that's just horrible. I'm very sorry for your loss, Agent McLane. I had no idea he was your father."

"My mother thought she was doing the right thing at the time." Ava cleared her thickened throat. "What can you tell me about . . . the incident?" She couldn't say murder. Not yet.

"I just got an update from the detective who caught the case. David Dressler left for a run around eight this morning. His family wasn't sure of his route but believed he was headed south down the beach from the promenade."

Ava knew the promenade was a central spot in Seaside, where the touristy Broadway Street met the beach.

"He was found by a couple of tourists in some taller vegetation."

"Was he still in sight of the city homes along the beach? Or past the golf course?"

"The vegetation blocked him from any home's view. And the golf course was further south."

"Weapon?"

"Found a nine-millimeter casing. We'll know more details after the lab looks at it."

"His injury?" Her voice was hoarse.

"One shot to the temple. No stippling. No exit wound."

Hopefully death was instantaneous.

"Witnesses?"

"None so far. Only the folks that found him. Medical examiner said he hadn't been dead more than a few hours. We've been canvassing the area but haven't found anyone who heard a shot."

Did they use a suppressor? The roar of the ocean was loud, but not enough to muffle a gunshot.

"Anything else?"

"A report of an assault on a woman early that morning near a bakery shop not far from where he was found. We've requested the bakery's video."

Hope rose in Ava's chest. "Did she give a description of who assaulted her?"

The sheriff sighed. "She hasn't come forward. The bakery clerk reported it during our canvass. He saw them in front of his shop around eight a.m. He said the man slugged her in the face, making her drop to her knees."

"Why didn't the clerk report this earlier?"

"He claimed he had his phone in hand, ready to call it in, when the man helped the woman up and they walked away together, his arm around her shoulders. He said the woman didn't appear to be coerced or fighting him off, so he let it go."

"She was probably petrified that he'd hit her again if she fought back."

"Could be," agreed the sheriff. "My intuition says it's not related, but it's all we've got so far. Two violent acts that close together warrant some speculation in a small town of that size."

"Agreed," said Ava, trying to make the pieces fit together. They didn't.

"We also had an early-morning home break-in about two blocks away from where your father was found."

"Cameras?"

"Nothing caught on camera. The rental house was empty, and the alarm system went off after a window was broken. When the local police got there, it was all quiet. It appeared the alarm scared them off. This one feels like teenagers to me . . . or possibly someone homeless looking for a place to sleep."

Ava didn't know what to make of the break-in. It was another incident that didn't seem to be related to her father's death. "Um . . . where is the shooting victim being examined?"

"We sent him to the medical examiner's office in Portland." His voice took on a tender tone. "I'm very sorry again, Agent McLane. Even if you didn't know him that well, it's a shock."

"Thank you. It is."

"I'll call you immediately when I get updates. Say a word to Agent Wells for me."

Ava promised and then ended the call. She sat in silence for a few minutes as Zander drove. "Sheriff Greer says hello," she finally said.

"He's a good man. What was that about someone being assaulted?"

She shared the sheriff's stories about both incidents.

"The clerk didn't see a gun on the man? Or the woman?" Zander asked.

"Not that he reported."

"I agree the crimes being so close together is odd. It's a sleepy little city."

"Not this time of year," Ava pointed out. "I'm sure Seaside is crawling with summer tourists."

"But no one heard a gunshot."

"No one that they've found yet."

The two of them were quiet for a long minute. "Do you need to go to the coast?" Zander asked. "Have your thoughts changed?"

Ava inhaled deeply through her nose. "No. I'll stay here. The sheriff will keep me informed." She pictured Kacey's friendly face and her two children. "I'll keep in touch with Kacey several times each day."

"And after our investigation is over?" Zander asked. "What will you do?"

"I'm sure they'll be back in San Diego by then."

"Won't they be at the wedding?"

"Shit. You're right. I totally forgot they were coming." She rubbed her forehead. "Do I need to push off the wedding? It feels wrong—"

"No!" Zander said firmly. "You've waited long enough, and a wedding might be just what that family needs. Something joyful after this hell." He turned into a 7-Eleven lot, parked, and looked sternly at Ava. "If you delay your wedding, I'll shoot you. And that's after Mason and Cheryl shoot you first."

"Don't know if *shoot* is the right word to use today," she said softly.

"Dammit." He tipped his head back against his headrest. "You're right. I'm sorry."

"It's okay. I'm feeling rather numb after everything that's happened over the last two days."

"I hear you."

"A wedding is the furthest thing from my mind."

"I understand that too." He tilted his head and met her gaze. "Ready?"

Ava looked at the 7-Eleven. Three teenagers with skateboards loitered near the front, cans of caffeinated drinks in hand. The usual colorful promotional posters plastered to the glass blocked her view of most of the interior, but she could see a tall older man behind a cash register.

"Yep."

Moments later they had brought the tall clerk outside for a chat, leaving his coworker to cover the registers. He leaned against Zander's vehicle and sized up the two of them.

"Mind if I smoke?" The clerk, whose name was Todd, had already shaken out a cigarette from a battered pack. It was in his mouth and being lit before Zander or Ava agreed. He had the longest fingers Ava had ever seen. They matched the thin legs sticking out of his shorts and his bony arms. She estimated he was in his late fifties.

He inhaled deeply and turned to glare at the three skateboarders. "Hey!" he yelled at them. "How many times do I have to tell you to beat it? Can't you read?" He pointed to a No LOITERING sign directly behind the teenagers.

The teens sneered. "Why is the carpet all wet, *Todd*?" said the dark-haired teen as his friends burst into laughter.

"I don't know, *Margo*," answered the one with a shaved head, setting the three of them into peals of laughter. They dropped their boards in the parking lot and pushed off. Two of them flipped off Todd with both hands as they sped away.

"As if I haven't heard those lines a million times since the eighties," muttered Todd as he inhaled more smoke.

"What?" Zander looked confused.

"It's from *Christmas Vacation*," said Ava. "The Chevy Chase movie."

"Ahhh." Light dawned in Zander's eyes. "Never watched any of his vacation movies."

"Seriously?" asked Todd, skepticism in the tilt of his head. "You grow up in a foreign country?"

"Don't watch a lot of TV. Or movies."

"Huh." Todd examined Zander as if he were a new species of bug.

"You told your supervisor you saw something yesterday before the shootings that the police should know about." Ava changed the topic. "What time did you get off work?"

"I was off at noon."

"An hour or so before the shooting happened."

"Yeah, I was home taking a nap when it happened. I went to work at three a.m. yesterday. Needed some sleep."

"When did you find out about what happened at the courthouse?"

"Not until around dinnertime. Saw it on Twitter."

"What did you do then?"

"Called Paula because I knew she had been working at that time, and everyone online had said the shooter took his shots not far from here."

"Paula had spoken to the police?"

"She told me they'd just left when I called. Said they took copies of the day's video coverage and questioned her, but she hadn't seen anything. She heard sirens at one point, and some customers had come in all jacked up about the police activity, but no one knew what had happened for a good half hour."

Ava nodded. So far Todd's story matched the officer notes from Paula's short interview.

"You don't know who did it yet?" Todd asked, looking from Zander to Ava.

Realizing she could smell his body odor, Ava studied the older man. He didn't seem nervous, just interested. The smell was understandable for the hot day, but he worked in an air-conditioned store.

Maybe he just didn't wear deodorant.

"We're following leads," said Zander smoothly. "Lots of information pouring in."

Todd nodded. "So you've got nothin'. That's why you're talking to me."

"We're talking to you because your supervisor said you had something to share."

"Yeah. Another asshole. Comes with the job." He didn't sound annoyed, just resigned. "I bet you deal with them a lot too."

"Absolutely," answered Zander. "What happened?" he asked to steer the man back on track.

"It was when I got off. I left through the back door 'cause that's where we park, and some dick had just parked in one of the employee spaces. It happens sometimes. The street parking here can get tight around lunchtime."

"What did you do?" Ava asked.

"Told him to move his car." He laughed. "Dude had already walked to the sidewalk, so I went after him, telling him I'd have his car towed if he didn't move it."

"Can you show us where this happened?" Zander asked.

Todd nodded and gave a jerk of his head for them to follow as he walked around the side of the store toward the back. At the rear of the store were four parking spots. The yellow lines separating the spots were nearly worn away, and Ava didn't see a sign stating they were for employees only.

The clerk pointed at the spot closest to the side street. "Right there. Since I kept bitching at him to move, he finally turned around and came back." Todd raised his eyebrows. "Dude was pissed. He didn't say a single word, but the look he gave me had me backing up a few steps. He wore sunglasses, but I could tell how angry he was. Was in the way he held himself, you know?" He ran a hand through his hair. "After I heard about the shooting, I thought of this guy. He definitely had enough bottled-up anger to shoot someone."

Ava silently sighed. An angry man wasn't a great lead. Were they wasting their time?

"Cameras?" Zander was scanning the back of the building.

"Used to be one right there way above the door," Todd said. "Got stolen last week. Probably to sell it for a quick buck. They must have had a ladder to get all the way up there and unscrew the bolts. Took the whole thing."

Last week? Removed in planning for yesterday?

"No video of it being stolen?"

"Nah. We checked it out. You can't see anyone. They stuck close to the building out of view. The camera shakes and jerks for a few minutes; then it goes black." He dropped his cigarette and ground it out with his shoe. "Can't really be worth much."

"What happened with the angry guy?" Zander asked. "You must have got a good look at him."

"He backed out of the spot, spun his tires, and left. Of course I got a good look at him. I said I talked to him." He gave Zander a suspicious side-eye, as if worried the agent was missing a few marbles.

"What did he look like?" Ava asked, amused at the clerk's misunderstanding. "Was he carrying anything? What was he wearing?"

"Oh . . . black baseball cap, sunglasses. Dark pants. Long-sleeved black T-shirt. Pretty good-sized dude—"

"Taller than you?" asked Zander.

"Nah."

"How old?"

Todd thought for a moment. "Hard to say. Moved like a young guy and had the attitude of a young guy, but his face was weathered—that might be from working outside. Anywhere between thirty and fifty, I'd guess. If I'd seen his eyes, I'd have a better idea."

"Shoes?"

"Ah . . . tennis shoes?" Todd looked uncertain. "Wasn't looking at his feet."

"Hair?"

"Sort of a dirty blond. Had it pulled back in a ponytail that stuck out under the cap." Todd wrinkled his nose. "Had a backpack on one shoulder."

Ava perked up. Black shirt and pants on one of the hottest days of the year and a backpack that could carry a weapon.

A possibility.

"What was the vehicle?"

"Dunno." Todd shrugged. "White. Four-door little boring sedan that looks like every other car. I guess not very old because the paint was shiny. I only remember that much because I thought it was funny that he burned rubber on a lame car like that."

"Which way did he go?"

"Turned left."

The opposite direction of the shooter's location.

They asked a few more questions, trying to prod Todd's memory, but he had no other useful details. Ava gave him her card. She and Zander silently walked around the store to the front parking lot. "What do you think?" she finally asked as they reached his vehicle.

"We've got a description. We'll see if it matches up with any other possible leads. Maybe he's on camera somewhere else. We can check in the direction he went."

He didn't sound very confident.

"Why park behind a 7-Eleven? That's a good way to get towed."

"I don't know how a tow truck could get into that tight space," Zander said quietly. "It'd be nearly impossible, so not too bad of a choice if he knew there was no working camera." He lifted both hands. "It could happen. The guy shot into a crowd of cops. He's a risk taker."

Ava couldn't argue with that.

Just as she was about to get into Zander's vehicle, she checked her phone. It'd vibrated three times while they talked with the 7-Eleven clerk, but she'd ignored it.

The three texts from Mason made her gasp.

Call me

Call me

Ray's in surgery. Took a bad turn. Headed there.

"What happened?" Zander asked sharply.

She'd frozen with her hand on the door handle, staring at her phone. "It's Ray. Something happened and they took him to surgery." Her heartbeat pounded in her ears.

"Do we need to head that way?"

Indecision flittered around her head. *What do I do?*

"I don't know." She fired off a text to Mason asking what happened.

For the second time that day she was pulled in two different directions. Stricken, she looked at Zander, unable to make a decision. *Work or family?*

He read her face. "Get in. I'll run you back to the office, and you can drive from there. I'll handle our assignment for now."

Relief flooded her. "Are you sure?"

"I can tell you wouldn't be an effective investigator at the moment."

"That's true. My focus is completely shattered."

They both climbed in the vehicle, and Ava gripped her phone, willing Mason to text her back.

Her phone was agonizingly silent.

Hold on, Ray.

This will destroy Mason.

"This isn't happening today," she whispered. "I can't have two people taken away in one day." With a sharp pang in her heart, she suddenly felt David's death very keenly; she'd lost the what-could-be. While he lived, there had always been a chance that she'd lower her walls and they'd get to know each other in a deeper way. Now she could lower them all she wanted and it no longer mattered.

"I'll never know," she mumbled, staring straight ahead.

"You're right," Zander said. "You'll never know what might have happened with David in your life."

Zander is too perceptive.

"But do you know what?"

"What?" she asked flatly.

"You've got two half siblings with nice families waiting to get to know you. The potential for something great between all of you still exists." He turned and caught her gaze. "Don't turn your back on it."

She hated it when he was right.

What do I have to lose?

14

Mason called back as Ava was getting into her car at the FBI office to drive to the hospital. Her heart jumped at his name on her screen.

"What happened?" she asked.

"Ray's all right. There were some really bad moments for a while, but he's breathing normally now."

Ava exhaled and leaned back in her seat, drained. "How's Jill?"

"A wreck. Just like the rest of us. But relieved."

"Do you need me up there?" she asked.

"No, I'm going to leave in a few minutes now that he's out of danger again." Mason sounded as if he hadn't slept in two days.

The shooting was barely twenty-four hours ago.

"Ava . . ."

She waited.

"We lost another one. A deputy," he whispered.

Her eyes smarted. "That's five deaths now."

"I know. Could've been six."

Silence stretched between them.

Ray will be fine. He's going to make it.

Ava kept the thoughts to herself. Mason was never comforted by the usual words of encouragement. They were empty to him, meaningless. She felt the same.

"There's a service tomorrow," he finally said.

"We'll be there, of course." The police funeral they'd attended last fall suddenly felt as if it had occurred yesterday.

Mason didn't reply. His supervisor had been murdered in October, and Ava knew he was suffering through unpleasant memories. She wished she were standing beside him.

"What are you doing?" he asked, his voice flat.

He wants a distraction. "Zander and I were assigned to follow up on some interviews in Oregon City." She wished she had nonshooting news to share. She still hadn't told him about David's death on the coast—there'd been no time.

"Mason, I hate to bring this up now, but you should know." With hesitant words she shared what she knew about David's shooting.

"Ava . . . I'm so sorry." Concern flooded his tone. "Are you going over there?"

"No. I'm needed here. The sheriff seems to have it under control."

"That's not what I meant."

He was asking about her joining her . . . family. "I know," she said quietly. Like Zander, Mason knew all her insecurities about the Dresslers. "I'm staying here. For now."

"What a fucked-up couple of days," he muttered.

"There's something else. I forgot to tell you last night because . . . well, because," Ava said awkwardly. She told him the story of how Brady Shurr had shown up, and Zander's discovery that Jayne had used a fake passport in Ava's name to get into the country.

"Are you okay?" he asked sharply.

He'd been the buffer between Jayne's rehab journey and Ava for quite some time. "Is it wrong that I'm almost relieved to hear she's up to her old tricks?"

"Makes sense. We've both been waiting for her relationship with Shurr to blow up somehow. This is the Jayne we understand."

"I don't think *understand* is the right word. *Expect* is more accurate." She grimaced. "There's one more thing."

Mason cursed long and loud at her story about the wedding-venue cancellation.

"Zander has a point that we can't assume it was Jayne. It could have been someone getting back at you or at Cheryl's business."

"We both know that's not true. Jayne enters the country and that happens? It's not a coincidence."

Ava caught a movement out of the corner of her eye. Zander was waiting at his SUV two rows over, watching her talk on the phone. *Good. He didn't leave after dropping me off.*

"I'm going back to work. Zander is waiting," she told Mason as she held up one finger to Zander. "I think I've covered everything."

"That was a lot to catch up on. David . . . Jayne . . . the wedding."

"I know. Too much has happened in a short period of time. We both need a breather. Hopefully there will be good news about Ray soon."

"I'm ready for some good news," Mason admitted. "It's all been shit."

"I love you."

"I love you too. Keep an eye out for Jayne. And anything else odd."

She straightened, remembering the message he'd left on her voice mail. "What was with that message earlier? You essentially told me to watch my back. Why?"

"Brody told me he thinks Reuben Braswell wasn't alone in his anger against law enforcement. Even though Braswell said you were one of the good ones, someone else might not feel that way."

"Michael is involved now? Is he writing a story?" Ava grew very still. Michael Brody had excellent instincts. She'd learned to pay attention when the reporter had something to say.

"He was working on something else when he stumbled across Braswell. He sent me some links I haven't looked at yet, but Braswell may have been active in organizations that want us gone."

"By 'us,' you mean law enforcement. Not you and me specifically."

"Right."

Mason's answer was a split second too slow for her comfort. "You heard something about me," she said flatly.

"I didn't, honestly. I just want you to be aware."

"I will. I always am."

"I know," he said reluctantly. "But I had to say something."

"And I love you for it." She'd dated men who'd tried to micromanage her work life. Mason didn't, and she knew he battled protective urges about her and her job. She did the same with him. But with jobs like theirs, all they could do was trust.

And they both did.

Mason sat at his desk, keenly aware of Ray's empty space across from him. The entire room was quiet, most of the detectives out of the office. The silence was eerie.

He made himself focus; he had work to do.

Brody had forwarded his user ID and password so Mason could snoop and observe on the websites the reporter had mentioned. A few minutes later Mason knew that everything Brody had said was supported by what he saw on the message boards.

The hate was overwhelming.

"Fucking pricks," he muttered. He'd wanted a shower within the first minute of visiting one site.

Every profession had its bad apples, but the law enforcement ones were thrust into the media spotlight. The website Mason was currently viewing appeared to be encouraging attacks against these bad apples. But there were cops with good reputations listed too. He was alarmed to find law enforcement officers' home addresses and phone numbers, and even pictures of their kids. The comments were brutal.

put them in prison

funded by the deep state

take away their families

Ice formed at the base of his spine. The comments were designed to incite violence. No doubt most of the commenters rarely left the chairs in front of their computer screens, but it just took one to absorb the hate as fuel and act upon it. He scrolled rapidly, searching and skimming for names or pictures of people he knew.

Or himself. And Ava.

The website was an amateur mess. No search function. Just a long, long list of discussion topics.

There was no way he could scroll through every discussion; it would take hours.

He took several deep breaths. There was nothing he could do even if he did find a familiar name. He and Ava already lived their lives with the utmost caution. They had to for their own peace of mind and safety. Getting worked up over this site was pointless.

In the email, Michael had listed the topics where he'd discovered Reuben's comments. Mason cringed at the one titled "FBI: the well-dressed weapon of the deep state."

Do they believe there are real men in black?

He snorted. Ava was always struggling to find clothing she liked that was acceptable according to the dress code. She would be the first to say it was difficult for female agents to be well dressed. She was especially grumpy when it came to shoes.

To Mason, shoes were simply something that covered feet. He preferred his cowboy boots, which brought him a fair bit of harassment from the other detectives, but he couldn't care less. He was comfortable.

Ray was a sharp dresser. Even when he wore a simple golf shirt, Ray looked as if he'd stepped out of a sports magazine.

Not now.

Refocusing on the website, he clicked on the FBI topic and scanned for Reuben's user ID: LOCKEMUP.

Classy.

Brody's was BUGLEFAN. Mason pondered the name, assuming Brody would use satire to go over the heads of the other posters. His best guess was that it was a reference to the *Daily Bugle*, the newspaper from *Spider-Man*. Made sense for a reporter.

Or maybe he really liked the processed crunchy corn snack.

Mason found Reuben's comments. Unlike some of the other commenters', they were spelled correctly and had punctuation. Mason didn't understand why punctuation and grammar were frowned upon these days. Remembering that Reuben had been of the same generation as he, Mason figured he'd felt the same . . . or simply hadn't noticed the change.

The comments supported what Brody had told him. Reuben believed the purpose of law enforcement—especially federal law enforcement—was to keep the working man down and under control.

Mason pushed back from his desk, fury rushing through him. Ray had put his life on the line to help get people out of the courthouse area. Ray loved people—all people. "Everyone has a story to tell," he'd said to Mason once. "If you ask the right questions, it will open your eyes to the struggles and joys of lives outside your own. It's fascinating."

The big man had a helper's heart. Giving and empathetic.

Why did it have to be Ray?

Mason logged out of the website. He'd seen enough. His stomach couldn't take any more.

But who'd carried out Reuben's plans after he'd been murdered? Who was his accomplice? Or accomplices? Had the person who killed him also shot law enforcement at the courthouse?

Or were the murders unrelated?

Mason doubted that but couldn't rule it out.

Flipping through his notes, he turned his attention to Reuben's family. Ray had written that supposedly they were estranged, but perhaps they'd have some insight into who would murder the man.

He verified that Reuben's parents were both deceased, and that Reuben hadn't ever married. Remembering that he'd wondered about children, Mason checked the state's records for child-support orders but didn't find any.

Doesn't mean no kids.

At fifty-two, Reuben could easily have a child in his or her early thirties. As far as Mason could tell, Reuben had only lived in Oregon. But there could be a child in another state.

Something to keep in mind.

Reuben's brother was two years older than he: Shawn Braswell of Reno, Nevada. Mason started digging. He found a current Nevada driver's license and pulled up the photo. Shawn wore a tight beard and glared at the camera. Mason eyed his height and weight, relieved to see he wasn't huge. Simply from his stare, Shawn Braswell wasn't someone Mason would want to have angry with him. The photo resembled an irate mug shot.

Is he really like that, or was he just an ass for the camera?

He recalled the photo of the two happy boys and the pony on the wall in Reuben's home.

What happened to estrange the brothers?

Mason's brother lived in Eastern Oregon. They talked once or twice a year, which was normal for them but maybe not for other families. He had no doubt that if he needed help and called, his brother would drop everything to respond.

He searched for Shawn's employment records but found nothing recent. Shawn had worked for several construction companies over a ten-year span. He had to be working somewhere, and Mason wondered if he was being paid under the table. His criminal history was clean; Mason couldn't even find a speeding ticket.

No phone number was associated with his name, and Shawn's last known address appeared to be in an apartment complex. Mason studied the building on Google Maps. Looked decent. He made a quick phone call to the Reno police, asking them to do a door knock to let Shawn know about his brother's death and to pass on Mason's contact information.

He felt bad about using outsiders to inform family of deaths, but he didn't have the time or budget to go to Reno. He turned his attention to Reuben's sister.

Veronica Lloyd was six years younger, married, and lived in Mosier, Oregon. A tiny town along the Columbia River, an hour east of Portland.

Well. What do you know?

Ray's initial notes had said she was in Nevada.

Her Oregon driver's-license picture showed a dark-haired woman with a timid smile and kind eyes, but he could see a faint resemblance to Shawn and Reuben.

A little research revealed she and her husband had bought a home in Mosier less than a year ago. They'd lived in Reno before that.

A Google search told him Mosier had fewer than five hundred residents. Mason didn't think he could live in a town that small. No anonymity. Everyone would know everything about their neighbors, and he was fond of his privacy.

Veronica didn't have an employment history, but her husband worked for the Hood River County School District. Previously he'd worked for the Washoe County School District in Reno.

Did they want a change of scenery?

If Veronica had moved to Oregon, surely she had been in touch with her brother. Mason wondered how deep the estrangement went.

Or maybe there was no estrangement . . . The information about her location had been wrong. This could be too.

He tapped a freshly sharpened pencil on his keyboard, mentally figuring the length of time it would take him to drive to Mosier. If traffic was decent, he'd be there by 6:00 p.m. He could send the local police to notify her of her brother's death, but Mason had a strong urge to talk with the sister. She was relatively close by, and Mason liked to do as many interviews as possible face-to-face.

"Hey." Nora Hawes approached his desk, her heels rapping on the cheap tile flooring. "The task force assigned me to dig into Reuben Braswell."

"Thank God." Mason meant it. He'd assumed someone from the task force would be working parallel to his investigation, and luck had shone on him. Working with Nora was a breeze. She was sharp and funny and worked her butt off.

"Can you catch me up?"

He tossed her a fat three-ring binder. The murder book he'd started on Reuben Braswell. So far it didn't have many pages, but he knew it would fill up fast. "You can read that on the way to Mosier."

"Who?"

"Mosier the town. Just past Hood River."

"What's in Mosier?"

"Braswell's sister."

Nora hefted the light binder in her hands. "These aren't supposed to leave the building."

Mason said nothing.

She gave him a side-eye. "Feels like we have a lot of work to do." She tucked the notebook under her arm, clearly planning to take it with her. "I saw Ava at the task force meeting."

"Then you've seen more of her today than I have."

"She's catching some crap for being a part of it. Her name turning up in Braswell's documents isn't doing her any favors."

Mason's gaze sharpened on Nora.

"Don't worry. She handled it like the professional she is."

"Asses."

Nora shrugged. "A lot of driven people were in that room today. The energy and anger were palpable. We'll get the job done."

"Good."

"Reuben is at the core of that shooting." Nora said. "He may be dead, but from what I've seen so far, it originates with him. Have you dug back further?"

"A bit. He didn't hang out with the nicest people." Mason stood and grabbed his hat. "I can tell you about it on the way. Ready to go?"

She rapped her knuckles against the binder. "Yep. Good thing reading doesn't make me carsick."

"Reading what? I don't see a binder under your arm."

"I'm blaming you if someone reports me walking out with it."

"No one is going to protest. Not today." He swallowed hard. *Five dead officers.*

Nora caught her breath. "True. Let's go."

15

"There's the camera," Ava stated as she pointed through the windshield of Zander's vehicle. He took a sharp left into a church parking lot. They'd been canvassing the area near the 7-Eleven in the direction in which the clerk had seen the white car turn. Zander had tried to get Ava to take the afternoon off even though Ray was out of danger, but she'd assured him she needed the distraction.

Past the 7-Eleven, the streets were lined with small homes. The roads were narrow, just wide enough for two cars to pass. There was no street parking. Most of the homes sat far back from the street and had skinny, long driveways that led to garages behind the homes.

Two blocks away from the 7-Eleven, Ava had spotted a white camera perched high on the corner of a small stone church. Its parking lot had several dozen spaces, but none were currently occupied.

"Looks like no one is here. The lot is empty," said Zander. He parked as Ava checked the church address against the log of canvassed properties.

"An officer came by yesterday evening, but his knock went unanswered. He walked the building and noted two cameras."

"That one doesn't cover the street. Don't know if it will help us," Zander said, nodding toward the one that had caught Ava's eye. "Let's find the other one."

"You check. I'll see if anyone is here." She headed toward the wide steps that led to the building's front entrance. Zander nodded and went in the opposite direction. "This building is lovely," she said under her breath, wondering how old it was.

It was made of rough square stones and had steep peaks that gave it a European feel. The windows were arched, as was the wide entrance to the covered area in front of the door. She stepped through the big arch and felt the temperature drop ten degrees inside the roomy alcove. She hesitated at the tall double doors. *Do I knock? Do I go right in?* She knocked.

After waiting a moment, she tried the large brass handle and was surprised when the door pulled open.

A church smell wafted out. Old carpet, wood polish, and history. And some guilt. Ava had been raised Catholic, but it hadn't stuck after she left home. Although some of the clichéd Catholic guilt occasionally cropped up. Like now. It wasn't a Catholic church, but the shame flared anyway.

Zander's quick stride sounded on the stone steps behind her. "I found the camera in back. It only covers a back entrance and more of the parking lot." He stopped beside her. "We going in?" he asked after a long pause.

"Of course," Ava said quickly. "I was waiting to see if someone was coming first." She stepped inside the vestibule and he followed.

"Gorgeous," Zander stated. They'd stopped outside the sanctuary. It had high ceilings with wide beams, and the walls were filled with the lovely arched windows Ava had noticed outside. Ava eyed the front of the sanctuary, where three carpeted steps led up to a pulpit. A wedding scene flashed in her mind. She and Mason standing side by side in front of those steps. They had agreed not to have their wedding in a church.

Guilt hovered again. *Sorry, Mom.*

Zander's phone rang, startling her. He frowned at the screen. "It's a foreign number—oh!" He immediately answered. "Wells."

Foreign number? Ava didn't answer those.

"Thanks for getting back to me," Zander said, holding Ava's gaze. "What did you find out?"

"Who?" she mouthed at him.

He covered the microphone. "Costa Rica."

She'd completely forgotten he'd called to see if anyone at the rehab clinic had lost their license or had their identity stolen.

"Uh-huh. Can you spell the name?" Zander said into the phone. His eyes darted from side to side, and Ava knew he was storing the information. He had amazing recall and could memorize pages in a short time.

She'd asked him once how he did it, hoping for some tips. But he'd shrugged and told her he saw the page in his head and simply read it back. That didn't help her at all.

He ended the call. "One of their patients, Camila Guerrero from Los Angeles, had her wallet stolen a while back. It hasn't turned up. Nothing was charged on her credit cards, but she immediately canceled them."

"Jayne would want the ID, not the cards. Surprisingly," Ava noted wryly. Jayne had done her share of stealing credit cards and going on shopping sprees, telling Ava that it wasn't hurting anyone because the bank would cover the fraudulent charges. But now, with Brady Shurr in her pocket, Jayne apparently had access to plenty of cash and credit.

"I'll email and have someone search to see if 'Camila Guerrero' has turned up in the area. Maybe at a hotel or car rental place."

"She'd still need a credit card," Ava pointed out.

"Depends on the place." He raised a brow.

He was right. Some might accept a large cash deposit. Or bribe. Depending on the quality of the business.

"True." Ava sighed. "Jayne is the least of my concerns at the moment." Footsteps sounded, and she turned to see a man walking their way.

"Can I help you?" he asked as he approached. His jeans had several holes and he wore battered flip-flops. Ava guessed he was in his midthirties. His faded T-shirt had an image of actors from the TV show *Portlandia*, and his curly brown hair nearly covered one eye. She wanted to brush it out of his face.

Ava introduced herself and Zander while trying not to stare at the man's broken front tooth. His name was Pat Arthur.

"Is this about the shooting yesterday?" he asked, tucking his thumbs in the front pockets of his jeans.

"Yes. We'd like to review your camera footage from yesterday. It's possible it picked up something."

"Like what?" Simple curiosity filled Pat's dark eyes.

"Are you a church employee?" Zander countered with a question of his own.

Pat pushed his hair out of his face, to Ava's great satisfaction. "Yeah. I'm sort of the do-it-all guy. A little maintenance, set up for meetings, basically I keep an eye on the place. I have a small room at the back. They wanted someone on the premises at night after a break-in several months ago. They also had a pipe burst last winter. A lot of damage could have been avoided if someone had been around." He lifted one shoulder. "My parents attended here for years. When they told me what the church needed, I figured it was a good fit since I'm in school."

"You get a free place to stay in exchange for being sort of a watchman?" Ava asked.

"They pay me too. Not a lot. Doesn't really matter. I'm saving a ton on rent."

"Where do you go to school?" Zander asked.

"Reed. I'm off for the summer, but I work at a deli over on Division." He gave a satisfied nod. "I get free food there."

Ava was familiar with Reed College in Portland. It was a very small liberal arts school.

"You've got it worked out, don't you?" Zander asked. "Free rent, free food, and you get paid by two jobs."

Pat grinned. "Yep."

"You know how to access the camera footage?" Ava asked.

"I'm the one who told them they needed it and then did the installation." He turned and gestured for them to follow. "They needed to catch up with the twenty-first century."

"Have the cameras been helpful?" Ava asked.

"Eh. I guess. There haven't been any other break-ins, but I had put up signs saying we had surveillance in place. The only time I've had to review some footage was when Joe Pender backed into Samuel Owens's new truck. I thought they were going to start hitting each other. Both claimed it was the other person's fault, but once they saw the footage, Joe admitted he hadn't checked before backing up," Pat said with satisfaction.

"Handy," said Zander.

"Yeah, but now they don't speak to each other anymore. It's pretty awkward to watch them avoid each other on Sunday mornings."

Ava and Zander followed Pat down a long hallway. He stopped at a door and pulled a thick ring of keys out of his pocket, easily picking the right one for the lock. He flipped a light switch and led them into a small office. Ava blinked as she spotted a dusty typewriter on top of a small filing cabinet and hoped the dust meant it'd been retired. Pat dropped into a chair and accessed a desktop computer. He hummed as he clicked the mouse and tapped the keys.

"What time do you want to check?" he asked.

"Let's start at ten a.m.," Zander suggested, picking a time two hours before Todd had seen the man and white sedan behind the 7-Eleven. Pat nodded and continued to hum. The screen was split into quadrants, showing four camera views in color.

"You've got four cameras?" Ava said, slightly embarrassed that they'd missed two—not that they'd looked very hard.

"Yep. Takes four to cover everything."

Ava noted in disappointment that none of them showed the street. They covered a large part of the parking lot, all sides of the church, and all the doors.

Pat found the requested time and started the videos simultaneously, quickly speeding them up. Ava stepped closer and watched as an older couple holding hands jerkily speed-walked through the parking lot, rapidly moving from one camera's feed to another. Two people on bicycles whipped through at high speeds. A truck used the parking lot to turn around.

"Hello," Zander said under his breath as a white sedan seemed to recklessly veer into the parking lot. "Slow it down. Super slow if possible," he told Pat.

The time stamp read 12:10. Right after Todd said the white car had left his store.

"His plate is legible," she said, watching the sedan slowly drive through the lot. There were two parking lot entrances. One on the street Ava and Zander had come from and another on the cross street of the church's corner lot. The sedan had entered from the same location as Zander. The car showed up on three cameras as it slowly drove through the L-shaped lot and then went out of sight. Ava held her breath, hoping it would come back. After a few seconds, she asked Pat to return to the view of the license plate.

"Let it keep going a little longer first," Zander said, glancing at her. "But speed it up again."

"Got it," said Pat. "That what you wanted to find? That white car?"

"Possibly," Ava said, unwilling to share much.

Moments later the car was back, and Pat immediately slowed it down. "He's looking for cameras. I'm sure that's what he was doing the first time he drove through too," Pat stated, and he tapped one of the views. "This camera is completely hidden. He's going to think nothing is there."

"I didn't see it," said Zander. "I only saw the one near the rear door."

"Yep. I deliberately placed that one and the front camera in plain view. Hid the other two. Wanted anyone scoping it out to think our coverage wasn't as good as it appeared."

Sure enough, the white sedan parked in view of the hidden camera.

"Nice!" Pat held up a hand and then gave himself a high five.

"Can you zoom in?" Ava asked.

The other views disappeared, and the white sedan filled the screen. It had backed into a spot under trees near a dumpster. Ava spotted the Chevrolet logo on the front of the four-door vehicle but couldn't make out the figure behind the wheel.

Come on. Get out.

Her wish was granted seconds later as the driver's door opened. Dark pants. Long-sleeve shirt. Hat. Backpack. Excitement rose in her chest. "That's him," she whispered to Zander.

Pat froze the video. "That's your shooter?" he asked. "He parked at *my church?*"

"We don't know that," Ava said quickly. "This guy caused a disturbance at the 7-Eleven before the shooting, and we wanted to see where he went next."

"The dumpster blocks him from the other street," Pat pointed out. "There're no windows facing him from the back of the church, so he thinks no one will notice him there. People park in the lot sometimes, but I ignore them unless it looks like they're sleeping in their car or doing something illegal. I don't mind if someone parks here for a few hours."

"An officer said no one was here when he came by yesterday evening," Zander said.

"I was at the deli. Heard about the shooting while I was working."

"There aren't any other cars in the lot," Ava mentioned.

"I bike." He put the video in motion at normal speed. The driver walked a few feet from his car and studied the back of the church building and then glanced back at the car near the dumpster.

Ava watched, her entire focus on the man. Todd was right. He moved like a younger person, and through his shirt, she could see the definition in his arms and chest. *He takes care of himself.*

But was this their man?

He turned and she leaned closer, studying the backpack, hoping to see something that indicated he had a weapon inside.

As if he'd be that sloppy.

"He's still uncertain about his decision to park there," Zander said.

"Got the license?" Ava asked without looking away from the screen.

"Already sent it off."

The dark figure hefted his backpack into a better position on his back and took off at a jog toward the parking lot entrance. The entrance closest to the 7-Eleven.

"He's going in the right direction," Ava whispered. Her heart pounded in her chest.

Don't jump to conclusions.

They all watched the man leave the view of the cameras. "Speed it up again," Zander requested.

No one else entered the parking lot. Ava held her breath as she watched the time on the video get closer to 1:00 p.m. At 1:20 he entered the view of one of the cameras, and Pat slowed it down.

"He changed," Ava said. He was now wearing a white short-sleeve shirt and dark shorts. The hat was still in place over the blond hair.

"The shirt was probably under the other one. Same with the shorts," Zander said.

"Nah, I think those are those rip-off pants things," said Pat. "You know . . . you unzip them around your thighs. Good for hiking when it warms up."

"Either way, he deliberately changed." Her voice was high. *This has to be him.* "There's no other reason for him to change."

"Sure there is," Pat argued. "He was jogging, remember? Maybe he was trying to work up a sweat and then stripped down a bit when it got too hot. Maybe there are weights in the backpack. He could be training for something intense."

The man in the video wiped sweat off his forehead as he stopped at his car. He lifted one foot onto the bumper and leaned in, stretching out his back leg.

As an athlete would.

Shit.

They continued to watch as he did the same with the other leg. The energy in the office dissipated. "He's just a cranky athlete? Is that why he got pissed at the 7-Eleven?" Zander asked, straightening his back. He'd been bending closer and closer to the screen.

"I'd be cranky if I had to run in this heat," offered Pat.

"Keep the video going," said Ava. She pressed her lips together.

The man on-screen took off his backpack and set it on the hood of his car and did a few bouncing jumps in place as if working kinks out of his calves.

He's not in any hurry to get away. Disappointment filled her.

"We'll keep looking," Zander said. "This is only our first stop."

The man opened his car door and grabbed his backpack off the hood. He took three steps to the dumpster, lifted the lid, and hurled the backpack inside.

"Holy shit!" Pat said as Ava's jaw fell open.

The man dropped the lid, got in his car, and drove away.

16

Mason drove in silence as Nora studied the file.

He'd offered to turn on music, but Nora said she couldn't read and process while listening at the same time. He respected that. It was a beautiful day for a drive through the Columbia River Gorge. Blue skies, blue water, green trees, tall cliffs, and the occasional waterfall.

"What's the deal with the parents' deaths?" she asked as he took the Mosier exit off the highway.

"What do you mean?"

"You saw they died one day apart, right?"

He started. "No, I didn't. I saw they died about five years ago, but I guess I didn't notice the dates."

"Maybe a car wreck where one survived a day longer than the other," Nora speculated. "Where did they live?"

"Redmond . . . or was it Madras?" The Central Oregon towns weren't that far apart, but Mason was annoyed that he wasn't positive about the answer.

"Go easy on yourself," Nora said.

He glanced over. She was watching him closely.

"You've been through a lot in the last two days."

"We all have," he stated.

She said nothing else but gave him the same silent look that Ava did when she thought he was being unreasonable. "No evidence reports from the crime scene team yet?"

"I saw some in my email. I need to print them out and add them to the book. Haven't had time to read them yet."

"What's Veronica's husband's name?" Nora asked. "If he works for the school district, he might be home since it's summer."

"Alan."

Mason took a right turn and parked in front of a two-story older home in a quiet neighborhood.

"Cute," Nora commented. "Looks straight out of a Hallmark TV movie."

Mason agreed. The white home actually had a white picket fence around the spacious yard and a huge tree with a swing. *Kids?* He spotted two bikes propped up against a post in the carport. They were pink.

He hadn't come across anything that indicated the Lloyds had kids, but it made sense for the midforties couple. He hoped the children would be out of hearing distance during their talk.

Mason stepped out of the car, and Nora tucked the binder into her large bag. He was about to tell her to leave it in the vehicle—several graphic murder scene photos were inside—when he realized they'd both be in hot water if it was stolen. Best to not take chances.

He scanned for a dog, opened the low gate, and followed her up the brick-lined walkway. The lawn was pristine. Green and freshly trimmed. Rosebushes full of blooms. The attention to detail continued on the home. Crisp paint and cheerful pots of flowers next to the front door. Mason knocked. "Might be best if you started the interview," he told Nora.

She raised a brow at him and nodded.

Footsteps sounded, and Veronica opened the door. He recognized her immediately from her driver's-license picture. Her eyes were just as kind as in her photo but now had a question in them.

Mason and Nora held out their identification. "Good afternoon," Nora said. "I'm Detective Nora Hawes and this is Detective Mason Callahan. We're from the Oregon State Police."

Veronica tensed. "What happened?"

"Can we come in?" Nora asked. "Or if you prefer, we could sit over there." She gestured at a wicker love seat and two chairs on the wide porch.

"Is it Reuben?" Veronica whispered, her eyes wide.

Nora paused. "It is. Your brother died yesterday."

Veronica placed a hand on the doorjamb, her gaze moving between Nora and Mason. "Please come in," she said in a steady voice.

"Are your children home?" Mason asked.

"No. They're at a friend's."

"Good."

Veronica shot him an alarmed look.

I didn't mean to scare her.

"We can speak more freely that way," Nora said, smoothly covering Mason's gaffe.

They followed Veronica into her home and directly to a formal living room on the right. Veronica sat on one end of a sofa and Nora joined her. Mason chose an uncomfortable-looking chair across from them and sat. The wooden back was nearly perpendicular to the seat.

Yep. Uncomfortable.

He felt as if he were sitting in school.

A gray tabby wandered in and studied Nora and Mason with interested blue eyes. Then it chose Nora's shoes to investigate and rubbed its head against them.

"What happened to Reuben? You're detectives who have driven all the way out here to inform me in person, so I assume it's bad," Veronica said. She grabbed a box of tissues from an end table and held it on her lap after pressing one tissue against her eyes.

"I'm really sorry to tell you, but your brother was murdered," Nora said in the gentlest voice possible.

Veronica's head shot up, and she clenched the tissue in her hand. "Who? Who did it?"

"We're trying to find that out. Our investigation is just getting started."

"Was anyone else hurt?" Veronica asked.

Mason found the question odd. "No," he said. "Why do you ask?"

Veronica peeled a strip off her tissue, her eyes downcast. "That's good. I just didn't want anyone else . . ." She trailed off.

"Veronica," Nora began, "should we be worried about someone else?"

"How did it happen?" Veronica asked, tearing another strip, ignoring Nora's question.

"Someone assaulted him," said Nora.

Veronica blew out an audible breath, and her hands shook. "My parents died a few years ago," she said. "Police also came to my front door that day. I'm having a bit of déjà vu."

"You lived in Reno at the time of your parents' deaths?" Mason asked, knowing the answer.

Speculative eyes turned on him. "I did. We moved here a year ago . . . but I assume you already knew that."

"We did," he admitted, holding her gaze. "We need as much information as possible to figure out who harmed your brother."

"He died yesterday?" Veronica's brows came together. "Wasn't there an attack on the police in Portland yesterday?"

"Yes," Mason said as his curiosity rose. "Why would you bring up that shooting?"

"Was his death part of it?" she asked faintly, her gaze going from Mason to Nora.

"He wasn't killed near the courthouse," Nora said. "The attack was in his home earlier yesterday morning."

Veronica relaxed a degree and slowly nodded. "I see."

Mason wasn't satisfied. "Ms. Lloyd, why did you immediately mention the shooting? What would a police incident have to do with your brother's death?"

Her eyes widened. "I don't know . . . I just watched it again on the news a half hour ago. When you said my brother was murdered, my brain sort of went there."

She's lying. Mason decided to back off for the moment.

"Ms. Lloyd," said Nora, "do you know of anyone who would want to harm your brother?"

"I don't really keep in touch with Reuben."

That wasn't an answer.

"You haven't talked since you moved to Oregon?" Nora asked.

"A bit. We text here and there. He's not someone I invite for Thanksgiving."

Nora frowned. "Why is that?"

Veronica returned to shredding her tissue. "Differences. He's older than me. We've never been close."

"What about Shawn?" Mason asked. "You closer to him?"

A guarded gaze turned his way. "Not really. None of us really talk to each other. Well . . . both of my brothers talk a bit to me, but not to each other. They don't get along. Haven't in a long time."

You don't say . . .

"It's hard when family members don't get along," Nora said. "What about when your parents died? Did that bring you all together?"

"No. I was the only one who went to their funerals."

Caution emanated from Veronica. She sat stiffly, rarely holding their eye contact as she had at the beginning of the interview.

"Can you tell me what happened to your parents?" Mason asked.

"What does that have to do with Reuben's death?"

Defensive. "Probably nothing. We're trying to get a complete picture of his background."

The tabby jumped on the couch beside Veronica and pushed against her arm. She scratched its head. "I'm sure you can find the police report on my parents' deaths," she said quietly.

Mason's ears pricked up. "Police report?"

Veronica's chin came up. "My father shot my mother and then himself," she said bluntly.

Nora leaned closer to Veronica. "How awful for you."

Veronica's gaze was flat as she met Nora's. "My father was a horrible man. All the way to the end. I swear he did that to my mother to guarantee his children's lives would always be miserable."

Mason held very still, studying Veronica, hearing truth in her tone. She was bitter—understandably—and her words implied a dreadful childhood. Had her brothers suffered the same? "I'm sorry," he said, knowing how inadequate the words were for the tragedy in her life.

"Thank you."

"What city did this happen in?" Nora asked, beating Mason to the question. He was greatly interested in the police report.

"Coeur d'Alene."

"They died a day apart?" Mason asked.

"Yes. He held on for a day at the hospital." Hate flashed in her eyes, and Mason felt scorched.

The anger clashed with the kind gaze he'd seen when they first met. *She was raised around hate. She's bound to have some deep inside. It's inevitable.*

His phone buzzed and he glanced at the screen. The call was from a Nevada area code. *Shawn Braswell?*

"I need to take this. Excuse me for a minute." He moved outside and down the stairs of the porch before answering.

"Callahan."

"Detective Callahan. Sergeant Davies. I took your request for a knock on Shawn Braswell."

Disappointment filled him that the call wasn't from Shawn. "Yep. Not home?"

"No. My officer questioned a few neighbors, and according to them, Braswell hasn't been around for at least a week. His parking spot has been empty."

Curiosity flared. "What's he drive?"

"Hang on."

Mason heard computer keys. "Silver Ford Mustang. Two years old."

Bingo.

"I believe he's been up here in Portland," Mason said. "That car was recently seen at his brother's house."

"The deceased brother?"

"Yes."

"Well, shit. Don't know if that's good news or bad for you." The sergeant cleared his throat. "We all heard about the ambush yesterday. Didn't realize that was in your area when I spoke to you before."

Mason didn't say anything.

"We'll be sending officers for the funerals."

"Thank you." Mason meant it. It was what police did when tragedy struck. It was impossible to describe what the show of outside support meant to stricken departments.

"Found the asshole yet?"

"Working on it."

"Let me know if you need anything else."

Mason ended the call and stood silently in the perfect front yard. Reuben Braswell was dead, and according to his neighbor across the street, Shawn Braswell's car had been seen in his driveway.

Unless it was someone else's silver Mustang.

Mason doubted it. He didn't believe in coincidences.

He'd just learned from Veronica that the brothers did not get along.

But was there enough bad blood for murder?

Did that mean that Shawn had also been the shooter yesterday?

It was a large leap in logic. A personal death by bludgeoning and a mass murder by rifle. Two very different scenarios.

It didn't sit right with his gut. Something was wrong. Too many pieces of the puzzle were missing.

A muscular man in a tank top and shorts stepped out of Veronica's front door. He approached Mason and held out his hand. "Alan Lloyd. I just heard about Reuben."

Mason shook his hand, taking his measure. Alan's gaze was direct and open, and he didn't sound surprised.

Veronica had immediately asked if we were there about Reuben.

They'd expected Reuben to come to a bad end.

"What were your first thoughts when you found out, Mr. Lloyd?" Mason skipped the small talk.

"Not too surprised. Reuben was a reckless, angry hothead, and Veronica knew this. She loved her brother, but we all knew he walked an edge."

"An edge?"

Alan thrust his hands in his shorts pockets. "I understand you know about Veronica's father."

"I know he murdered his wife," Mason stated.

"Never saw such an angry man," Alan admitted. "And the sons have the same anger. They believe the world is against them. Veronica told me that their father beat on the boys regularly—she claims he never touched her." Alan shook his head. "Don't know if I fully believe that, but I'm just happy that Veronica turned out normal since she grew up with a father like that."

"That's good. Do you know anything about his death?"

"Her father was about to lose his property when he died," Alan continued in a low voice. "It was a heavy blow for the proud man."

"What happened?"

"Didn't pay his taxes." Alan shrugged. "I'd told him it would catch up with him, but he blew me off. Said the land was his and the government had no right to tax it. He'd bought it fair and square."

"That's not how it works."

"You and I know that. Her father was pretty impressionable, you know? He tried to tell me that the government was ripping us off by collecting property taxes. When I asked why he believed this, he just gave me a lot of mixed-up mumbo jumbo that I think he found on the internet. He was easily influenced—especially if someone said what he wanted to hear, like it was illegal for the government to collect taxes."

"Reuben paid his property taxes," Mason said.

"He did. Bitched to high heaven about it but understood he'd lose his home if he didn't."

"What else did Reuben bitch about?" Mason asked evenly.

Alan's lips turned up on one side. "Sounds like you already have an idea." His gaze dropped to the badge on Mason's belt.

"Would it surprise you if I said Reuben was somehow involved in the massacre in Oregon City yesterday?"

Alan's eyes flared and he took a long moment to answer. "Yes. And no." He stared at the ground. "Don't see him as a killer. But . . . I've heard him talk. Talk doesn't mean action," he added quickly. He looked back at Mason. "Should I have said something?"

"Did you know something?" *If this guy knew about the courthouse . . .*

Alan thought for a long moment. "No. Nothing. We haven't heard from him since last February or so—at least I haven't. Reuben was always complaining about something related to the government, but I never saw a hint that he'd take action." He gave Mason a questioning glance. "What did Reuben do? Your partner told me he died yesterday morning. Wasn't the shooting in the afternoon?"

"It was," Mason said. "But it appears he had prior knowledge that it was going to happen."

"I'm really sorry about that. I had no idea." He gave Mason a sharp look. "And I doubt Veronica did either. Her brother barely spoke to her."

"That's what I understand." Mason paused. "Your wife mentioned that Reuben didn't get along with Shawn." He purposefully left the statement wide open for Alan to continue as he wished.

"That's putting it mildly. I haven't seen them in the same room for ten years. And that's a good thing. Those two used to beat the crap out of each other in the past. Veronica said that they've always been like that." He paused. "She told me Reuben was always the instigator. She thinks he funneled his anger at his father toward Shawn."

But Shawn's car was at Reuben's house?

"You heard from Shawn recently?"

The man thought for a moment and then shook his head. "Hear from him less than Reuben. Especially since we left Reno."

"Why did you leave?"

"Job opportunity."

"Would Shawn come up here to visit Reuben?"

Alan snorted. "Hell no."

Mason considered telling him about the silver Mustang in Reuben's driveway, but something made him hold back. "Know anyone who might want to hurt Reuben?"

"Like I said, we barely heard from him. I have no idea who he hangs around with or might piss off."

"Daddy!" Racing footsteps sounded on the sidewalk. Both men turned to see two young dark-haired girls sprinting toward the gate. A woman holding another girl's hand wasn't far behind. She waved at Alan.

"No more talking," Alan said in an aside to Mason as he stepped forward to intercept the girls as they burst through the gate. They flung themselves at him as he crouched down, arms wide open.

Mason watched as the excited girls both talked to their father at once, happiness shining in their faces and voices. Alan dropped kisses on both their heads.

These girls aren't being raised around hate.

The parents were putting an end to the cycle.

His stomach clenched as Reuben's abused corpse flashed in his memory. The chatter of the innocent girls clashed with the violence their uncle had experienced. The bloodshed was barely removed from their everyday lives.

The woman had entered the yard and was now chatting with Alan, casting a few curious glances Mason's way. He stayed back from the happy reunion. He didn't want the death hovering around him near the girls.

He quietly went up the porch stairs, intending to get Nora and leave. They'd brought bad news to the charming white home, and he had an overwhelming desire to get out before the kids entered it.

Hopefully Nora and Veronica are finished, because I certainly am.

17

Ava and Zander jogged out of the church, Pat right on their heels. They stopped at Zander's SUV to grab gloves and evidence bags out of the back.

"Please tell me the garbage hasn't been picked up since the shooting," Ava said to Pat as they dug through the large kit.

"Nope. Tomorrow is garbage day."

"Ready?" Zander said to Ava as she pulled on her second glove. His eyes were bright.

"Absolutely." They strode over to the dumpster, and Zander told Pat not to walk where they'd seen their suspect move between his car and the huge bin. The dumpster was much taller than it had seemed on the video. The top was even with her forehead. Zander threw open one side of the lid and met Ava's gaze as a foul odor filled the air.

"Who's going in?" he asked.

"I'll leave that honor to you." The smell turned her stomach.

He grinned, braced his foot on a small ledge on the dumpster's side, and easily clambered up to the edge. "I see the backpack. There's not much garbage in here."

"Slow week," said Pat. "No meetings or gatherings were scheduled."

Zander awkwardly shot a few one-handed photos of the inside of the dumpster and then dropped inside, out of sight. He cursed.

"What is it?" asked Ava.

"Don't know what I landed on, but it was big and it squished. Luckily it was inside a garbage bag. Hey, Ava, can you take some more photos as I grab this?"

"Sure." She eyed the narrow ledge that Zander had stood on and tentatively tested it with her foot, glad she'd worn flats.

"I'll balance you," offered Pat.

"Thanks." Otherwise she would have had to hang over the edge on her belly to take photos. She hopped up and Pat grabbed her waist, holding her firmly in place. She took a deep breath and snapped some photos as Zander picked up the black backpack.

"Definitely something heavy in here," Zander said. He palpated the pack. "A few hard and narrow items."

"Where do you want to open it?" asked Ava.

"Not in here. Let's get a cloth spread out and open it over that. We'll just look. If it's what we think it is, we'll call a team in to process it."

Ava hopped down and grabbed the pack as Zander held it over the edge. It weighed about ten pounds, and something inside clunked as she handled it, metal on metal. She squeezed it in a few places, feeling long pieces. *A takedown rifle?* Zander nimbly climbed out of the dumpster and landed beside her.

"Let's open it in the back of my vehicle."

Adrenaline rushed through Ava as they returned to the SUV. Zander lifted the rear hatch, pulled a thin cloth out of his evidence kit, and spread it out on the floor of the cargo area. Ava set down the pack and pulled out her phone to snap photos. "Go for it."

Zander unzipped the pack and peered inside. "Hello there, Mr. Ruger." He spread open the main compartment for Ava to see.

She didn't have the weapons knowledge that Zander had, but she knew an AR-15-style rifle when she saw one. Even in pieces. "I'll get an evidence team out here," she said, placing a call to her ASAC. "Need to inform the sheriff too."

"I'll check my email to see if they got back to me about the license plate." Zander continued to peer in the backpack, opening it as wide as he could. "SR-556. It's the Cadillac of takedown rifles."

"Takedown?" Pat asked.

"Means you can break it down. I've handled one of these before and can break it down into three pieces in about ten seconds." He jiggled the pack, trying to see into the bottom. "Three magazines."

Ava's skin went cold, her phone to her ear, waiting for Ben to answer her call. Zander hadn't said how much ammunition each magazine held, but she guessed it to be thirty rounds. The shooter could have done a lot more damage at the courthouse than he had. She met Zander's flat gaze, reading he'd had the same thought.

"Jesus Christ," he muttered. He gently laid the pack back down and checked his email. "Shit. The license plate on our white car leads to a Toyota pickup."

"Stolen plates," Ava said, stating the obvious.

"Now what will you do?" asked Pat, his face full of curiosity.

"Start with the serial number on the rifle and whatever evidence the team can lift from this site." She decided to get Pat out of their hair. "Pat, can you get me a copy of the video we watched? Send it to my email." She handed him a business card.

Ben finally answered her call.

"We found a weapon," she told him, unable to control the glee in her voice. "And we've got him on video, and we have a witness who talked to him face-to-face. I need an evidence team."

Stunned silence greeted her words.

"Well, I'll be damned," Ben finally said. "Nice work."

Finally, one thing had gone right in her shitty day.

Ava leaned into Mason, appreciating the comfort of his arm around her shoulders. It'd been a long day of ups and downs. They sat on a bench in the park at the end of their street, with Bingo at Mason's side, the dog's head on his thigh. It was nearly 11:00 p.m., but neither of them wanted to go to bed, both still running on adrenaline from the last thirty-six hours. Instead, they'd taken a walk.

A few streetlights added a little light to the park, but where they sat it was almost pitch-dark. During the day a perfect view of Mount Hood was visible from the bench. Tonight there was only darkness, the air still warm from the day's high temperatures. The park's grass had been mowed recently, and the fresh scent added to the peace of the evening.

Peace?

The day had been full of turmoil. Right now they were avoiding it, pretending all was right in their lives. Jayne was fine. Ray was fine. No one had died at the courthouse.

Mason exhaled and shifted on the bench.

"Stop thinking," Ava ordered.

"I can't."

"Clear your head."

"I know you can do that mind-clearing meditation crap, but it's never worked for me. Too much going on in my brain. Gotta stay on top of everything."

Ava didn't tell him her thoughts also intruded when she attempted to seek quiet for a few minutes. She'd learned to step back and watch thoughts flow by, letting her mind rest, but it was a constant struggle to keep them at bay when she was supposed to be relaxing and refocusing.

Sometimes the struggle to let go was more tiring than the constant bombardment of the million things she tried to keep track of.

"Then pet Bingo," she said. "That might work better."

"I haven't stopped." He scratched the dog's head with renewed vigor. "How did the evidence collection go at the church?"

Ava had hoped to keep work away for a few hours. But she also wanted to talk about it. Mason was the best sounding board she had.

"One of them chewed out Zander for climbing into the dumpster."

Mason snorted. "Seriously? How else was he to get the backpack?"

"This tech said they should have been called first." Ava saw the point but also knew she'd have felt guilty if the evidence team had come out for a false lead.

"Ridiculous." Mason tugged on one of Bingo's ears. "You watched the suspect lift the lid and drop in the backpack. You knew exactly where to avoid what he'd touched."

"I know."

"Tell me about the weapon."

Ava described the Ruger. One of the techs had removed each piece from the backpack, and Zander had explained how they went together.

"The ammunition in the magazines is the same that was found at the courthouse," she said softly. The courthouse scene had plenty of ammunition evidence. Further tests would check to see if the rounds and shells found at the scene actually came from the Ruger. Ava had no doubts they did.

"The church video went to our team," she continued. "They'll try to get an image of his face." She'd reviewed the video again. The man's hat had shadowed his face the entire time. She didn't know how it was possible to get a good image, but she'd been surprised by their work before.

"Did anyone check with the owner of the vehicle whose plates were stolen?" Mason asked.

"Turns out the plates came from two different vehicles. When we looked at the video again, we realized the fuzzy view of the rear plate didn't match the clear front one. Both plates came from Medford."

Mason was silent, mulling over the information. Ava had been surprised too. The city of Medford was nearly three hundred miles away. Someone had planned well ahead. "How much do you want to bet the car will turn out to be a rental?" he asked.

"I won't take that bet because I suspect you're right. Four-door nondescript sedan. Every rental agency uses them." She thought for a moment. "Any leads on Reuben's truck? Or the silver Mustang?"

"No. I've got BOLOs out for both vehicles. It bothers me that Reuben's truck is missing. How did our killer get to Reuben's house?"

"Maybe he took an Uber," Ava suggested.

"Good point. I'll check with Uber and Lyft. Cab companies too. Maybe someone had a drop-off in the area. Didn't think of that until now."

"Glad I could help."

He tightened his arm around her shoulders and kissed her on the temple. "I swear my head isn't completely in the game. I've got to step it up."

Ava didn't mention his worry about Ray as an excuse again. Mason had already heard it a dozen times. "What did the fingerprint evidence show?" she asked.

"One bloody set on the mallet and bathtub. Same bloody set on Reuben's desk. This adds a point in the column for a single killer."

"Doesn't rule out that another person was there."

"I'm keeping it in mind." He paused. "Jill gave me a good report on Ray earlier," he said. "He appears to be stable. She said a doctor actually smiled. That told her more about Ray's condition than anything he said to her."

"I'm glad to hear it." A small weight lifted from Ava. "Was Nora helpful today?"

"She's always great, and she'll make me stay focused."

Ava elbowed him. "Stop it. Now that Ray's doing better, you'll be less distracted."

"I hope so. Got any other tips? I'll take whatever I can get."

She thought for a moment, considering everything they'd discussed. It helped to talk to another person. They often thought of possibilities the first person hadn't or looked at evidence from a different perspective. "Not that I can think of. There's been no sign of Reuben's brother, Shawn?"

"Nope. It's like he evaporated. I'm sure he'll crawl out from under a rock somewhere."

"He could be our killer. For Reuben *and* the courthouse."

"He's first on my list."

"Always look at family first," Ava said, knowing the statement was unnecessary. "His sister didn't have any ideas where he could be?"

"No. Her husband didn't either."

"Do you believe them?"

Mason was quiet for a long moment. "I do."

"Do they think Shawn killed Reuben?"

"I didn't tell them about the Mustang at Reuben's. As far as they know, Shawn is still in Nevada. And neither of them brought up Shawn as a suspect when I asked who might hurt Reuben."

"Might not have been Shawn's car."

"True. But Shawn's neighbors said he's been gone. Too big of a coincidence."

"It is," Ava agreed. She raised her head to hold her cheek against Mason's warm one. They sat in silence, their breathing the only sound.

"Ready to go back?" he asked.

"Not yet." Going back to the house meant preparing for the next day. For some reason she believed that as long as they sat on the bench, tomorrow would stay away.

At this moment everything was perfect.

Even if it wasn't.

"Any word from Kacey?" Mason asked gruffly. She knew he hated to break the perfection of the long moment too.

"Yes. David's funeral will be in three days. Back in San Diego."

"We'll go."

"Of course." Her father had died. She would leave work for his funeral and show Kacey and the rest of the family that she wasn't a working robot. When Kacey had told her, Ava's first thought had been how tough it would be to get away from the investigation. But she'd promised Kacey she'd be there. "I need to check with Sheriff Greer and get a progress report on David's murder investigation."

Mason turned his head, moving his lips against her cheek. "I'm so sorry."

"I know." *Shouldn't I be experiencing grief?* All she felt was surprised and stunned.

Which led to more guilt.

"We should be talking about a wedding, not our work."

Ava didn't say anything, shocked to realize she hadn't thought about the wedding once that day. *This is insane.*

"It's okay," Mason said. "This is why you hired Cheryl. If there were any issues, you'd have a dozen texts from her. The silence means everything is going smoothly."

She bit her lip. *Smoothly?* Ray was in the hospital, and Ava hadn't chosen an attendant. It might be just her and Mason standing before the minister. The thought left a hollow feeling in her stomach.

Mason moved Bingo's head off his leg and stood, pulling Ava to her feet. He placed his hands on her cheeks, making her look at his eyes in the dim light. "Everything is going to be perfect," he said. "And if something goes wrong, I bet we'll laugh about it in twenty years."

"Like Jake accidentally knocking over the wedding cake?" Mason's son wasn't the most coordinated teenager.

"Exactly like that." He grinned. "That would be pretty funny."

Ava could clearly see it. "I almost want it to happen now."

"He'd be humiliated."

"I'd laugh," she admitted. "I'd probably cry, I'd be laughing so hard."

"It wouldn't matter," Mason said, slipping his arms around her and pulling her tight to his chest. "All that matters is what happens between us that day."

Ava closed her eyes, feeling his heartbeat. *How did I find this man?* He understood every fiber of her. Her needs, her insecurities, and her fears. And easily balanced them with love and patience.

"Ready to go back home?" Longing sounded in his voice.

"Yes."

18

Mason was waiting outside the Home Depot when it opened at 6:00 a.m. He knew Reuben Braswell had worked graveyard, and he wanted to talk to people who worked the same shift. Several customers milled around the front doors. Mostly men in ball caps and Carhartt pants, waiting to pick up their supplies for the day. Mason had noticed the parking lot had a large contingent of pickup trucks. Big diesel rigs and long beds. Some shiny new and others battered with heavy use.

The large glass doors slid open, and the group didn't rush the door. This wasn't the holiday shopping season, when being first might make the difference between getting that big-screen TV or not. The group casually strolled in, leaving space between them. Inside, they dispersed, each headed to a different section of the store. Mason made a beeline for the customer service desk as he inhaled the scent of fresh lumber and made himself not stop to look at the colorful display of wheeled plastic coolers.

He liked Home Depot.

A dark-haired woman in an orange apron cheerily greeted him from behind the tall counter. "What can I do for you this morning?" She quickly scanned him from head to toe; he wasn't their usual 6:00 a.m. shopper.

"I'm looking for Gloria Briggs."

She grinned. "You found her."

Mason's gaze dropped to the handwritten name on her worn apron. In large block letters it read RIA. "Ria," he corrected. "Sorry."

"Not a problem. What do you need?"

Mason showed her his ID. "I'd like to ask you about Reuben Braswell. Is there somewhere quieter we can talk?" The store was actually very quiet, but he felt exposed at the central desk.

Her face fell as she heard Reuben's name. "Let me get someone to cover the desk." Mason nodded and stepped away, eyeing the coolers. They were twice the size of the three he already had.

I don't need another.

But damn, the price is good.

Ria joined him. "Let's head down this way," she said, gesturing to an aisle. He followed, and they stopped under the light fixtures for sale near the back of the store. It was deserted. "No one comes in looking for chandeliers this time of day," she stated. She met his gaze. "I heard about Reuben. Rumors are flying. What happened?"

"I can't say much," Mason said. "The investigation is ongoing." Always a handy phrase that most people respected. "I'd like to know what kind of employee he was."

"Excellent," she immediately said, crossing her arms. "He's worked graveyard for several years and seems to enjoy it. He'd rather work with the merchandise than the customers, so it seemed a good fit for him."

"What do his coworkers think of him? He get along with everyone?"

Something flashed in her brown eyes. "He gets his work done and does his part. Not a slacker."

Not what I asked.

"Who's he hang around with?"

Ria twisted her mouth as she thought. "I see him talking with Joe Cooper a lot."

"He around?"

She checked her watch. "Yes. He should still be here."

"Ria." Mason paused, searching for a tactful way to ask his question. "Did Reuben have any arguments with his coworkers? Or maybe an issue with a customer? Wait . . . you said his job didn't require him to interact with customers."

"He works until seven a.m.," she said. "He dealt with customers during that last hour of his shift."

"Anyone get angry with him?"

She cocked her head to one side. "Are you asking if he got someone mad enough to kill him?"

"I am," Mason said reluctantly.

"You don't have a suspect in his murder?"

"We have a couple of good leads, but I'm looking into every aspect of his life."

The woman searched his eyes, disappointment on her face. "I've never had a customer complain or heard about someone having an issue with Reuben. The guys who work with him will tell you he keeps to himself." She lifted one shoulder. "That's not a bad thing."

"Can you hunt down Joe Cooper for me?"

"Stay here." She passed under the lights and fans, headed to the back of the store.

Mason spent the next few minutes absently studying light fixtures as he waited, wondering if Ria didn't want to say anything bad about a dead employee. Many thought it was respectful of the dead, but it didn't help solve a murder. People needed to be frank.

He remembered how Ava kept grumbling about the light fixture in the dining room, and a shiny rectangular fixture with hundreds of tiny hanging glass balls caught his attention.

No.

A man appeared from the direction in which Ria had vanished. Mason judged him to be in his late twenties. Wide shoulders. Bearded. Huge hands. "You Detective Callahan?" he asked in a deep timbre.

"I am." Mason shook his hand. "Sorry about Reuben. I understand you were friends."

Joe scratched his beard. "Yeah. He was a good one. Pulled his weight, unlike some of the guys."

"You hang out after work?"

Amusement sparked in Joe's eyes. "After work is breakfast time. Yeah, we'd go to that pancake place over off Barbur Boulevard."

"Good pancakes."

"The best."

"What kind of guy was Reuben?" Mason asked.

Joe lifted his chin, his gaze suddenly shuttered. "You know who killed him?"

Mason used his favorite line again. "The investigation is ongoing."

"Cop speak for 'We're not telling you shit.'"

"Pretty much," Mason answered evenly. "I assume you understand why. This is a murder investigation."

The man looked away and ran a hand through his hair. "Reuben had ideas . . ."

"I know he wasn't fond of law enforcement and government."

Joe's gaze flew back to Mason's in surprise. "Yeah. He could get pretty fired up about it. I'd listen to him when he ranted, but it mostly went in one ear and out the other. I don't see the point in complaining about something like that. It's not going to change it."

"He ever tell you someone was angry with him?"

"Nah. He didn't care what people thought about him."

"He pisses off people."

"Not at work. He walked a straight line here."

"But outside work . . . ?"

"Didn't hang with him other than breakfast a few times. But he'd tell stories of how he'd get the cops mad at him."

A small chill touched Mason's neck. "Cops mad at him?"

"He liked to rile them up."

"How?"

Joe shrugged. "Dunno. He'd just come into work all happy and shit. Said he managed to ruin some government worker's day. Wasn't always cops."

"Doesn't sound like a nice guy."

"Never said he was. We got along."

Mason didn't know what to think.

Could be as simple as harassing his mailman.

He gave Joe his card. "Let me know if you think of anything odd that Reuben did or said."

Joe scoffed. "He was always saying odd shit."

"You know what I mean." Mason shook his hand and took his leave, wondering if stopping at Reuben's workplace had been a waste of time.

Near the front of the store he stopped and stared at the cooler display. Swearing under his breath, he grabbed a huge red cooler and headed for the checkout line.

Ava checked the time again. The task force meeting had been scheduled to start at eight, and it was already a quarter after. She sighed impatiently and crossed her legs for the tenth time.

Why is Zander late?

Zander was never late, and he hadn't answered her texts from the last fifteen minutes. She glanced around the room, willing the Clackamas County sheriff to get the meeting rolling so she could get her day started. The sheriff was nowhere in sight, but most of the chairs were full. Impatience flooded the room.

They'd managed to keep the discovery of the weapon in the dumpster out of the media. It had been sent to forensics last night. Ava doubted there were any fingerprints to detect, but it did have a serial number to trace, and there were rounds to analyze that were recovered at the courthouse scene.

She'd checked her email every time she'd woken up the night before, hoping to see a report on the weapon. The plan had been to process the gun overnight. The forensic technicians hadn't complained about the extra hours. In fact, they had been eager to work on the weapon.

Everyone wanted to find the shooter.

Zander appeared and dropped into the chair next to her.

"You're late."

"I know. And yes, I saw all your texts. I was outside on the phone."

His tone caught her attention. "With who?"

"The manager of a small motel down in Merlin."

"Where is Merlin?" She'd never heard of it.

"A little north of Grants Pass. Off I-5 just a bit." He raised a brow at her. "Looks like your sister spent the night there."

"Jayne? When?" Ava glanced around, realizing her voice had been too loud.

"Seven days ago. She used the Camila Guerrero ID, which is how I tracked her. Two days before that she used it in Maxwell. It's a small town south of Red Bluff in California."

"She was working her way north." Ava closed her eyes for a moment, wondering where Jayne had ended up. "I assume she paid cash at these places?"

"She did."

"Must have been convenient to have some of Brady Shurr's money. I wonder where her final destination is."

"Maybe she's coming for the wedding." Zander didn't sound pleased.

"She knows the date," Ava admitted. "I mentioned the wedding twice in an email. She never asked any questions. I assumed she didn't want to hear about it."

Why did Jayne try to cancel my wedding?

Jealousy.

Ava couldn't think of any other reason. Even though Jayne had snared herself a rich boyfriend who was clearly wild about her, she had still gone out of her way to attempt to ruin Ava's wedding.

"There is video of her at the motel's front desk in Merlin. The manager found it while I was talking to him. He's forwarding it to my email."

"Did you get it yet?" Ava leaned close, peering at Zander's phone.

"Not yet."

"Dammit." She sat back in her seat and crossed her arms, itching to get out of the room and hunt down her sister.

That's not my priority right now.

Fine. Ava would get to work on the courthouse shooting. "They didn't need a task force meeting this morning. We've got work to do."

"Everyone has work to do, but the other teams need to be caught up."

"Couldn't they just send an email?" she grumbled. "I want to go check for cameras near the church. See if someone caught a clear image of his face."

"There's the weapon report," said Zander, touching his phone's screen.

Ava whipped out her phone, her heart racing as she opened the email, noting it had also been sent to the Clackamas County sheriff. She rapidly scanned the report.

"Oh, shit," she said.

"I agree," said Zander.

She took a deep breath and continued to read.

"The good news is the rounds match the weapon," Zander said softly.

"But the serial number is a dead end." Ava kept reading, her heart sinking. The report said the weapon was part of a stockpile of weapons that had been stolen from the ATF while in transit outside of Nevada.

The theft had resulted in a big shoot-out, and two ATF agents had died. The weapons had disappeared.

"I remember when this happened a couple of months ago," she said.

"We all do," Zander said solemnly.

"How did our shooter get this gun?"

"Probably bought it off the street somewhere. Which is where the ATF got most of them in the first place."

"Okay, folks. Let's get started." The sheriff strode to the front of the room, a stack of papers in his hands and two men following. The room quieted down, and everyone shifted in their seats, focused expectantly on the sheriff. He set the papers down, and the detective went to the open laptop on a table. The video from the church appeared on the big screen at the front of the room.

The sight made her breath catch. The video hadn't started, but she knew it by heart. It was their biggest lead on the shooter.

The sheriff immediately launched into an explanation of what they were about to see. "And according to the lab report I just received, the weapon found in this church's dumpster is a match to the rounds at the scene. This is our guy—or at least someone working with him." He nodded at a detective, who started the video, and someone lowered the lights.

Even though the group had been told the weapon had been found in the dumpster, an audible gasp went up as the figure on-screen threw his backpack inside. The video ended, and enhanced stills of the man appeared on-screen. Ava automatically leaned forward, trying to get a better look. The images were still fuzzy, but much clearer than what she'd seen yesterday. There were no good views of his face.

Dammit.

"There's a good chance this is Shawn Braswell," the sheriff said. "His height matches what's listed on his driver's license, and the weight appears to be about the same. The hair is the wrong color, but we all know that can be changed."

"Priors?" asked someone.

"No record," said the sheriff. "Neither he or Reuben have ever been in trouble with the law."

The fact bothered Ava. *How did someone go from a law-abiding life to murdering his brother and others?*

The sheriff went on. "It's believed his vehicle was seen at the home of his brother, Reuben Braswell, where we discovered the plans for the courthouse bombing."

"Which were just to get us in place to be murdered," mumbled a voice behind Ava. Murmurs of agreement trickled through the room.

"The relationship between the brothers was volatile," continued the sheriff. "But it looks like they had hatred of law enforcement in common."

"Assuming that's him," Ava stated.

The sheriff nodded at her. "Correct. This is only a theory. Either way, I want this guy found. We'll be pulling some of the teams and moving them to the area around the church. We want more video. He walked down the street. Surely a home security system or doorbell camera caught a better image. We'll be checking traffic cameras in the area too."

"What about the car?" asked a woman from the back.

"Plates are stolen," the sheriff said. "We're still trying to figure out where the car came from. You've all got the information on the missing vehicles belonging to Shawn and Reuben Braswell. Keep an eye out for them as you search. New assignments are at the back of the room."

Everyone started to stand, speaking quietly to the people around them.

"Two more things," the sheriff said loudly. Everyone quieted, their attention back to the sheriff. "The weapon used at the courthouse has been traced to a shipment of weapons stolen from the ATF not long ago."

An angry buzz of voices immediately filled the room.

The sheriff held up his hands in a calming motion. "I know, I know. Two ATF agents were murdered during that Nevada robbery. We don't know whether or not this guy is tied to the theft or their deaths. But either way, those weapons might be back on the street again. We'll find out when we catch him."

Ava had researched the robbery. Hundreds of weapons had been stolen. A drop in the bucket when compared to the nearly four hundred million that were believed to be in the United States. But most of those belonged to responsible gun owners. The odds were good that the stolen weapons would not end up in the hands of that group.

The sheriff continued. "I think you all know there's a memorial service tonight."

The room suddenly went silent. A moment later there were nods and quiet affirmations.

"Good. I'll see you all there."

The families of the fallen officers had asked for private funerals but agreed to a public memorial service. The shooting was still national news, and Ava knew the families had been mobbed by journalists and the nosy public. She didn't blame them for having wanted the funerals kept secret.

"I've got the motel video," Zander said in a low voice.

"Good. Let's go look at it out in the hall."

He nodded and followed her out of the room, the two of them weaving their way among other task force members. Near a windowed alcove, they stopped, and Zander pulled his laptop out of his bag as Ava tried not to dance with impatience.

What are you up to, Jayne?

"Should we contact Brady?" Zander asked as he pulled up his email.

Ava considered. "Not yet."

"Poor guy is probably wondering if she's all right," Zander pointed out.

"Well . . . we know she was all right a week ago," Ava said. "We don't know about right now."

"I think you should say something to him."

Ava remembered how distraught the young man had been. He truly cared about her twin even if Jayne didn't seem to care about him. "I'll tell him," she agreed.

Zander turned his laptop so she could see. The indoor camera view showed a reception counter and the front door of the motel. The desk was crowded with stands of flyers and open snack and candy displays where customers could buy something for a dollar. Ava always wondered how many people helped themselves to a handful without paying. A middle-aged man worked behind the counter, and light glared off his balding head. He sat on a stool, his focus on an old computer, its deep monitor taking up a large portion of the counter.

The door swung open and Jayne walked in, pulling a small roller bag.

Ava caught her breath and leaned closer, her gaze raking over the image of her sister, whom she hadn't seen since last fall. Jayne wore large sunglasses, an oversize sundress, and a perky straw hat with a wide brim. But Ava recognized her immediately.

"That her?" Zander asked uncertainly.

"Yep."

Jayne stopped at the counter and took off her sunglasses, but the hat hid her face from the camera. *Shit.* Ava ached to see her sister's face. The hand motions and shoulder movements were definitely Jayne. The clerk was immediately attentive, running a self-conscious hand over his balding pate. Ava grimaced, wondering what Jayne had said to charm him.

"You move your hands like that when you talk," said Zander.

"No, I don't." Ava scowled.

"Yes, you do. Exactly the same."

Jayne continued an animated conversation with the clerk, and her hands continued to move, pointing to the front door and then holding them up in a "What do I do?" gesture. The clerk shifted on his stool and cocked his head a few times, reluctance in his posture.

Jayne opened her bag. Ava couldn't see what she brought out but assumed it was cash. "She's sweet-talking him."

"She's good at that."

"She can be very persuasive," agreed Ava, waiting to see if Jayne teased the clerk with a view of her cleavage.

It wasn't necessary. The clerk nodded several times and took Jayne's money. She received a key, and he pointed at something behind her, clearly giving directions to her room.

Through the silent video, Ava picked up on Jayne's profuse thanks. Jayne moved out of the camera angle, and the clerk watched her leave as he wiped his forehead. He gave his head a little shake and turned his attention back to his monitor.

Ava straightened and sighed. *At least I know she's not dead.*

But wondering about Jayne's current goals was torture.

"There's more," Zander said, opening another attachment.

This angle was a long view of an outdoor walkway on the second level with a sliver of the parking lot below. Motel-room doors were visible at regular intervals. Jayne appeared at the far end, pulling her bag. She stopped and leaned over the railing, waving at something.

"She's gesturing for someone to join her," said Zander.

Ava was silent. *Oh, Jayne. What have you done?*

Jayne continued to a door closer to the camera and slid her card into the slot. She pushed open the door and waited, looking down the hall in the direction of the camera. Ava finally got a view of her face. She studied her twin, looking for changes.

No facial piercings.

Her hair was its natural dark brown like Ava's and went just past her shoulders.

She looked healthy. No gaunt cheeks or sharp jawline, which had been common during her drug addiction.

Ava relaxed a degree. Maybe the time at the rehab clinic had done Jayne good.

But Ava knew better than to expect the change to last. There was one consistent thing about Jayne: she was predictable in her unpredictability.

The back of a man's head and shoulders appeared in the camera view as he joined Jayne. His hair was dark and short, and he wore shorts and flip-flops.

Of course it's a man.

"Is that Brady Shurr?" Zander asked.

"No."

Jayne stretched up to give him a kiss, and then he stepped back to allow her into the room first.

Ava caught her breath, unable to speak.

No.

"Shit!" Zander gasped.

Jayne's hand had stroked down her stomach to cup below the gentle curve.

She was pregnant.

19

Mason read the Coeur d'Alene police report on Reuben Braswell's parents' deaths, intently focused on every sentence, his temper simmering under his skin.

Reuben's parents had come to a brutal end. Mason had dealt with murder-suicides before, and it made him furious every time. This case was no exception.

Heat built in his chest as he read the neighbor's interview, which stated she had seen Olive Braswell with black eyes and bruises multiple times. Olive had brushed off the neighbor's concerns, admitting that the injuries were from her husband but saying that it was normal.

Normal?

Nothing is normal about a husband who beats his wife. Or his kids—which Mason had learned from Alan Lloyd. He agreed with Alan that it was doubtful Veronica had escaped her father's wrath, but at least she hadn't turned out bitter and angry like her brothers.

Their mother had been seventy-two when she died. Fury bubbled in Mason's chest.

Who beats a woman that age?

Why didn't she report him?

He put the questions behind him. The deaths had happened five years ago, and there was nothing he could do about it now. He concentrated on the details of the report. Olive Braswell had been found in her bed in her nightgown with a single gunshot wound to the head.

Shot in her sleep.

Asshole.

Tim Braswell had still been alive when the first responders found him. He had been on the floor in his living room, shot in the chest. Mason frowned and reread the line. Most suicides chose a head shot. A better chance of death. As Tim had done with Olive. Mason flipped to the autopsy report and read that Tim had nicked a major artery. He'd bled heavily but held on to die in the hospital the next day.

Tim deserved to die on the floor.

But the father didn't die on the floor, because he had called 911, stating he'd shot his wife and was shooting himself next.

Coward. Wanted help for himself but not for his wife.

He flipped to Olive's autopsy, and his brows shot up. Olive had been dead for more than twenty-four hours when the medical examiner arrived at the scene.

Tim had waited a full day after shooting her before he decided to end his own life.

Or it took that long to work up the courage.

That fact that Tim had shot himself in the chest continued to nag at Mason.

Mason read the rest of the report. Tim had had heavy stippling at the bullet's entry; the handgun had been close to his chest, if not up against it. His hand had tested positive for gunshot residue.

But he'd shot his wife the day before.

GSR was hard to get rid of and easily created cross contamination. If a responding officer had previously been at the shooting range and come in contact with Tim's hand, it would test positive. Mason searched for a particle count on the GSR evidence, hoping to see high numbers that would indicate that the weapon had been in Tim's hand. No one had taken a particle count. The GSR test had been deemed sufficient.

But the fact that Tim had shot his wife could have given him high numbers even if the test *had* been done.

Is it possible someone else shot him?

One of his sons? Angry about their mother's death?

Mason grimaced. To the Coeur d'Alene police, it had been a pretty open-and-shut case. They had the 911 call saying that Tim was about to commit suicide. They'd arrived and found he had attempted to. He'd killed his wife, as he'd admitted on the phone . . .

Or did he?

Could someone else have made that 911 call?

Mason blew out a deep breath. Why was he picking apart the Braswell deaths? He tossed the report aside. If they ever caught up with Shawn Braswell, he'd look into it then. Right now the parents' deaths were moot.

He banished the murder-suicide to the back of his brain, but he knew he wouldn't forget.

Sighing, he checked the time. He'd called Gillian Wood, Reuben's neighbor and . . . love interest? They were to meet at eleven, and he'd been burning time in his vehicle in front of her house until the hour arrived. He got out and went to knock on her door.

As he waited on her porch, he glanced at Kaden Schroeder's home, noticing that the red pickup was in the driveway again. Remembering the young man's fluster when Mason had mentioned Gillian Wood, Mason tried to think if he had any more questions for him. Kaden had been the only one who'd stated he'd seen a silver Mustang at Reuben's home.

I wonder if Gillian knows of his interest.

Mason doubted it. He'd thought Kaden was a high schooler and doubted that Gillian saw him as anything more.

Gillian opened the door. She smiled, but her eyes were still haunted. Mason didn't know how it was possible, but she seemed thinner than before. She hesitated after his greeting, and he got the impression she didn't want to invite him into her home.

"Let's sit out here." Mason indicated her front porch. Identical to the porch at Reuben's home. All the houses on the street were cookie cutter. Only the colors and different landscaping differentiated them.

Relief flashed on her face, and they sat. Mason noticed there were no cigarettes in sight.

"Where's the other guy?" Gillian asked.

Ray.

A wave of pain hit Mason, and he was unable to tell the truth. He wasn't ready to discuss it. "He couldn't make it today."

She blinked and shifted in her seat. Nervousness hovered around her, but she didn't seem ready to bolt.

An improvement over last time.

"You said you had more questions for me?" she asked, tentatively making eye contact. "I could've answered them on the phone."

"I needed to come out here anyway," he hedged. He didn't have plans to go in the Braswell home again. Not yet, anyway. "I wondered if Reuben mentioned his brother, Shawn Braswell, in any conversations lately."

"Is that his name? If he told me his brother's name, I don't remember it. He wouldn't talk about his family at all. Reuben didn't like personal questions."

"But the two of you were . . . an item?"

Her lips quirked at the word, and he was keenly aware of how out of touch he was with certain popular terms. "I wouldn't call it that. Yes, we had a physical relationship, but he was an expert at putting up walls. Anytime I asked personal questions, he cut me off, telling me to keep it light." She snorted lightly. "Who doesn't discuss their feelings? I mean, we'd been sleeping together for more than a month, and I simply wanted to know where his head was at. He wouldn't answer. He never wanted to know what I was feeling either."

He's just not that into you.

Mason didn't say it out loud. Gillian wasn't in need of relationship advice—not that Mason was any expert, but if a man was interested in a woman, he talked to her. "Strong, silent type, huh?"

"Definitely." Pain flashed in her eyes.

She liked the guy.

"I learned to hold back any questions about personal stuff. One time I asked what his tattoos meant to him, and he clammed up." She traced a circle on her right bicep and touched her shoulder. "Isn't that one of the points of tattoos? To show off things that are important to you and have meaning? Everyone expects questions about them."

Mason wouldn't know.

She turned and lifted her hair so he could see the small round tattoo on the back of her neck. "It's a yin and yang. I'm fascinated with the idea that opposites can be complementary." She turned back to him, tossing her hair over a shoulder. "I showed it to him, and all he said was, 'It's nice.'"

"He wasn't one to ask questions either?"

"Nope. I honestly think it's simply how he was. It was one of the more frustrating relationships I've ever had. My grocery checker is more interactive."

The natural follow-up question would be why she stayed. But Mason wasn't interested in that can of worms. "He ever show signs of a temper? What would set him off?"

"I never saw him get angry," Gillian said. "Sure, he was annoyed by things. He'd talk about things like store customers and politics. I think I'd told you before, I'd just listen. He needed to rant sometimes."

"Did you ever worry he would hurt you?"

She drew back, distaste on her face. "God, no. Why would you ask that?" Her confusion appeared genuine.

"Heard he could get physical if pushed."

"I never felt that. Even when he told me I asked too many questions." She looked expectantly at him, clearly finished with the topic.

"Did you see a silver Mustang in his driveway recently?"

Her forehead wrinkled. "No. Why?"

"What about any other unfamiliar vehicles?"

"None. Only his truck."

Mason glanced at his notebook. He was out of questions. Frustration filled him.

"I think I saw a silver car across the street last night. There's been so many vehicles coming and going since . . . you know. I assumed it was part of the investigation."

His frustration evaporated. "A Mustang?"

"Not sure."

"Where was it?"

"In front of the Schroeders' house."

"How well do you know them?" he asked.

"Not that well. I say hi to Kaden when we're both outside—he's the teenage son. Not sure of the dad's name."

Mason wasn't the only one who thought the twenty-two-year-old man looked very young. "What time did you see the car?"

Gillian gazed across the street at the home as she thought. "Don't know the time. It was dark, though, so maybe close to ten?" She nodded as if confirming her thoughts. "I was locking up before bed." She met Mason's gaze, uncertainty in her eyes. "I double-check every lock before bed now. Windows too." Her voice lowered. "I've asked to break my lease. I can't live here anymore."

"I don't blame you." He stood and offered his hand. "Good luck, Gillian."

"Thank you."

He strode across the street to the Schroeder home. He was certain no one related to the investigation had been in the neighborhood at

10:00 p.m. The crime scene team had wrapped up, and Nora drove a black SUV.

Probably a friend of Kaden's.

He knocked on the door, waited twenty seconds, and then pushed the doorbell as he wondered if Kaden was gaming with headphones on. Mason's son Jake never heard his phone when his were on and he was deep in a game.

Impatient, he pressed the bell again.

He took two steps to the side to glance in the window just in case Kaden was gaming within sight, and he found himself peeking into a casual living room. No screen or gamer was visible. Mason looked back at the red truck, noticing the PCC parking pass hanging from the rearview mirror. The vehicle was definitely Kaden's.

Mason pulled out a business card and wrote a note on the back for Kaden to call him. He shoved it into the crack of the door, and it opened two inches. He bumped the door as he snatched the falling business card, and it opened farther.

Should I yell for him?

Feeling like an intruder, he'd started to pull it closed when he caught a whiff of a familiar scent.

Dread crawled up his spine, and he shoved open the door. *"Kaden?"*

He heard something. It sounded like a TV program in a back room.

He drew his weapon but didn't step inside the home as he yelled for the young man again. The odor was stronger now, and heat wafted out of the house. It was warmer inside than out, no doubt from the hot morning sun on the large front windows.

Call for backup and wait.

What if he needs immediate medical attention?

Mason placed a call, asking for local backup at the address, and then entered the house, clearing each room as he worked his way through the stifling home. The TV noise grew louder, and Mason continued to call Kaden's name, warning him that he was in the house. Like Gillian's, the home was identical to the Braswell home. He worked his way down the hall. Yelling sounded from the TV program.

The last door was open a few inches, and the TV noise grew louder as he moved closer. Mason shoved it open and his heart sank.

Kaden sat in a low gamer's chair, the warriors in his game shouting from the huge monitor in front of him.

He'd been shot in the head.

20

"It's got to be related," Nora said in a low voice to Mason as they watched the medical examiner look over Kaden's body. The young man was still in his gaming chair.

"Right across the street from another murder? I have no doubt," said Mason.

"But why?" murmured Nora.

"Number-one question on my list. Well—right after 'Who did it?'"

"Has to be the same person."

"Odds are likely."

"The father was gone overnight?" she asked.

"I assume so. Kaden said he was out of town when I talked to him yesterday." Mason didn't want to discover that the father had murdered his son. "I can't find a phone number for him."

Eliminate family as suspects first.

"You talked to the neighbors?" she asked.

"I sent two uniforms to knock on doors, but I talked with Gillian Wood," Mason said. "She couldn't help me contact the father. I told her to pack a bag and find a hotel or stay with family. It might not be safe here for her. She's the only other person on this street who was involved with Reuben Braswell in some way—as far as we know."

"We don't know that Kaden was involved with Reuben," Nora pointed out.

"No, but I did interview him, and he's the one who told me about the silver Mustang."

"Think he was holding back on you?"

Mason eyed the dead man as Dr. Gianna Trask bent the victim's arm, checking for rigor. It barely moved. "I suspect so. There's a good chance he knew more than he let on." He raised his voice. "What's the verdict, Doc?"

"Gunshot wound to the head," Dr. Trask said dryly. Nora made a small choking sound.

"But when?" asked Mason.

"Give me another minute." She raised a brow at Mason. "I'm not magic."

Mason struggled to wait. Patience wasn't his strong point.

"Detectives?" A tech looked into the gaming room. "I found something in a bedroom I'd like you to see."

Mason tensed, the tech's statement reminding him of how the courthouse bombing notes had been found.

He and Nora followed the tech into the bedroom across the hall. Mason had determined earlier that it was Kaden's room. It had an odor that reminded him of his son's dirty socks and sweaty shorts. The smell of a teen boy's room. An unzipped long, green duffel bag was on the floor next to the bed.

Several rifles were visible inside.

Mason blew out a breath and squatted next to the bag, opening it wider with the tip of his pen. He leaned over and sniffed several times. None of them had been fired recently.

"Five long guns," the tech said. "The bag was under the bed. Seemed an odd place to store them."

"Agreed." Someone who owned this many guns should have a gun safe or at least a rack. Not keep them dumped in a duffel bag and shoved under a bed.

"No ammo," said the tech. "At least not that I've found. Might be somewhere else."

Mason stared at the weapons for a long moment, a question growing in the back of his mind.

Are they from the ATF robbery, like the gun that Ava found?

"Do me a favor," Mason asked. "Send in the serial numbers before you do anything else, and have the results sent to me. Tell them I want to know if these are registered to Kaden . . . or his father." He stood and stretched his back.

This case is taking more turns than I can count.

"Where's Kaden's cell phone?" Nora asked.

"I saw it next to the monitor in the other room," said Mason.

Nora raised a brow. "I think we need to contact this boy's father ASAP. Especially after finding those." She pointed at the duffel.

"Agreed," Mason said. The two of them went back to the gaming room. Kaden's cell phone was still where Mason had seen it.

Dr. Trask looked up as they entered. "Based on his body temperature and the temperature in the room, I'd say he died between nine p.m. last night and two a.m. this morning."

"Thank you, Doctor." Mason looked at the game controller in Kaden's lap. "I wonder if there is a way to discover what time he stopped using the controller. That would help."

"I bet the RCFL would love to answer that," said Nora, referring to the FBI's computer forensics lab in Portland.

Mason nabbed a pair of gloves and a plastic baggie from the medical examiner's kit. He put on the gloves and carefully bagged the phone. Picking up Kaden's right hand, he pressed the thumb against the phone's Touch ID button through the plastic. Nothing happened.

"Shit."

"I hate it when you guys do that," said Dr. Trask as she watched. "I get the why . . . but it still disturbs me."

It bothered Mason a bit too.

"He has another thumb," said Nora.

The thumb of the left hand worked. Mason scrolled through the contacts to "Dad" and read the number to Nora, who dialed. She paused before connecting the call. "I think you should talk to him. You spoke with Kaden, not me."

His stomach tightening, Mason set Kaden's phone back where he had found it. The call would be a delicate situation. He had to inform a father of his son's death and ask about the weapons in the duffel in the same conversation. The gaming room suddenly grew airless and hot.

"I'm going out back to call," he said.

"Want me to come?" asked Nora.

"I do. I don't know how this is going to go."

Outside, Mason could breathe easier, and he immediately spotted fresh lumber in one section of the backyard's fence.

He helped my dad repair our fence.

Kaden's words rang in his mind. His father, Tony, had known Reuben Braswell well enough to ask him for help.

Mason cleared his head and mentally prepared himself, staring at the phone number Nora had tapped into the phone. A heavy weight settled on his heart.

How do I tell a father that his son has been murdered?

He touched the screen.

After three rings he heard a cautious "Hello?"

"This is Mason Callahan with the Oregon State Police. Is this Tony Schroeder?"

He purposefully left off his title, not wanting to alarm Tony beyond the normal worry that occurs when one is receiving a call from the police. People heard *Detective* and automatically thought the worst.

Although this case *was* the worst.

"Dammit. What did Kaden do? Is he all right?"

"Is this Tony?"

"Yes, I'm his father. Has he been arrested?"

"Are you in town, Mr. Schroeder?"

Tony paused. "No. I'm in Bend. I'm visiting my brother."

"Is your brother with you now?"

"Oh my God," Tony whispered hoarsely. "What happened?"

Mason took the plunge. "I'm very sorry, Mr. Schroeder, but Kaden died last night."

Silence.

"Mr. Schroeder?" Concern rocked through Mason.

A questioning voice sounded in the background of the call. Tony finally spoke, his mouth away from the receiver, his voice flat. "It's the police. Something happened to Kaden," he told whoever was with him. The voice grew louder with concern.

At least Tony is not alone.

"Mr. Schroeder?" Mason asked again. "I'm really sorry to tell you this way."

"What happened?" Tony asked in a broken tone. His voice fractured Mason's heart.

"I'm unhappy to tell you this, but Kaden died from a bullet wound . . . and it occurred in your home."

"Oh God!" Tony started to cry. *"Someone shot him?"*

"I'm so sorry." The words were fruitless, but he didn't know what else to say. He looked to Nora. She was watching and listening closely, biting her lip, uncertainty in her gaze. She gave him an encouraging nod.

"Mr. Schroeder. I hate to ask questions at this time, but we want to figure out who did this."

Tony sucked in air between wet, ragged sobs.

"Do you know who might want to harm your son?"

"No! No, I don't know! He's just an innocent kid who never hurt anyone!"

Questions were being asked in the background of the call. Mason couldn't make out the words, but it was clear the other person was upset and confused.

"He says someone shot Kaden," Tony said away from the phone. "Yes, he's *dead*." His voice cracked.

"We're doing everything we can to find who is responsible," Mason said, unsure if Tony was even listening to him. "But I wanted to ask you about the weapons we found in his bedroom."

There was a long pause. *"What?"*

"Kaden had a duffel bag with five long guns under his bed."

"Jesus Christ." Tony sounded shocked. "You're talking about rifles?"

"Yes. Three AR-15s. Two shotguns."

"He was shot with one of those?" Tony could barely speak.

"No. We haven't found the weapon he was killed with. It sounds like you were unaware of the guns under his bed?"

"This is the first I've heard about it. Where would he get those?"

"Do you know when you'll be back in town, Mr. Schroeder?"

"I'm leaving now." A voice in the background protested and then insisted on driving Tony to Portland.

Mason was relieved. He didn't want the man making the three-hour trip from Central Oregon on his own.

"I'll be there in a few hours," Tony told Mason, his voice flat.

Mason gave him his contact information and ended the call with promises to connect when Tony arrived.

He exhaled and ran a hand across his forehead. "Could have been worse," he told Nora.

"He didn't have any information?" Nora asked.

"No. Maybe once he has more time to think, he'll have something useful, but right now he's a wreck."

"You did good, Mason," she told him, an earnest look in her eye. "You handled it really well."

"Every parent's worst nightmare," Mason said, looking back at the house, unable to hold her gaze.

What if I got that call about Jake?

He shuddered.

It was too close. Jake was a good kid. Stayed out of trouble for the most part. But sometimes made poor decisions, like any young adult.

Did Kaden make a poor decision?

"Detective Callahan?" The tech who'd found the guns stood at the back door of the home. "The agent I spoke to at the ATF said to check your email."

"They traced them already?" he asked in shock.

"I knew exactly who to call to push it up the ladder," the tech said matter-of-factly. "We all know this is an important case. Everyone is making it a priority."

"They're all important cases," Nora said under her breath.

Mason opened his in-box, pleased to see that the first one was from the resident agent in charge at the Portland ATF office. He scanned her email.

All five weapons found in Kaden's room had gone missing during the ATF robbery—and she was sending an agent to the Schroeder home immediately.

"They're all from the robbery," he told Nora.

She tipped her head, her eyes thoughtful. "What in the hell does that imply?"

"I'm trying to process it too."

She touched the first finger on one hand, counting. "Did our shooter get his gun from Kaden or the other way around?"

Mason pulled out his notebook and wrote a note. *Check Kaden's financials for cash withdrawals/deposits. Check for Kaden's fingerprints in Reuben's home and vice versa.*

She touched the second finger. "Did the same person kill Reuben and Kaden?"

Mason considered. "One murder was physically brutal and mutilating, and the other was a single gunshot."

"They're on the same street and were killed within days of each other," Nora pointed out. "Even if the killers were two different people, I think we were correct earlier when we decided the deaths are related."

"What's Kaden's tie to Reuben is the third big question," said Mason. "Was Kaden involved in the courthouse shooting? Or supposed to be involved? Maybe he didn't do his part and was punished for it."

Too many questions to count.

Nora thought it over. "The most likely scenario is that he knew something he shouldn't about Reuben's murder, so the killer came back for him."

"If it's the same killer."

"My brain hurts."

"What if they just happened to buy their weapons from the same guy?" Mason said, going back to the guns.

"And Kaden just happened to have weapons from the same robbery and *just happens* to live across the street from the man our courthouse shooter murdered?" she asked skeptically.

"You're making the assumption the courthouse shooter murdered Reuben Braswell," Mason said. "I keep doing the same thing. It's not a given."

"Dammit! You're right." Nora turned away and paced in a small circle. "I can't do this on my fingers. We need to go back to the task force headquarters."

"And fill three whiteboards with our questions," added Mason, ignoring the fact that he wasn't officially part of the task force. He read the ATF email again, trying to recall what he'd heard about the weapons robbery in Nevada. "I feel like we're missing something . . . a very big piece to our puzzle."

"We're missing a lot of pieces," Nora stated as her phone rang. "Hawes," she answered. "Yes, sir." She frantically gestured for Mason's notebook and pencil. "Any damage, sir?" He handed them over, and she immediately wrote something down.

Mason tried to read what she'd scribbled. All he could make out was *airport*. And he wasn't positive that was the right word.

Years of deciphering Ray's chicken scratches punched him in the chest.

"Where is it being processed?" Nora asked. "Okay. Thank you, sir. I'll update you on Kaden Schroeder's murder when we return soon." She listened for a long moment, saying yes and no occasionally before ending the call.

"The sheriff," she told Mason. "Reuben Braswell's truck was found in the airport parking lot."

"Of course it was," said Mason. "When are people going to come up with a more original place to dump a vehicle? Did they get the driver on video when he entered? Or on the shuttle?"

"They're still looking."

"Now I want to find a silver Mustang."

"The sheriff says they're checking the lots at the airport for the Mustang. They were looking for both."

"You can go back to the task force. Kaden's father won't be here for several hours," said Mason. "The scene investigators still have a lot to do, but I know they're done with the body. It will be transported as soon as Dr. Trask is done."

"You're coming with me."

"I'm not part of the task force," he reminded her.

"That's ridiculous," Nora stated. "I'll have a word with the sheriff. You know more about this case than almost anyone."

"I'm only handling the Reuben Braswell part—and now Kaden Schroeder."

"I'm getting you on the task force. I'll get our boss's approval. Leave it to me. Let's go."

Mason had no doubts she could do it. She was right. Him working parallel to the courthouse investigation didn't make sense.

She started toward the house, determination in her step. "What's the latest on Ray?"

"No problems. Jill called me this morning." Mason checked the time as they passed through the house. "She said Ray wants to see me. I was going to head up there after I talked with Gillian." He grimaced. "Got a little sidetracked." He nodded at a crime scene tech working the front door.

"Ray's talking?"

"Yes, they aren't keeping him sedated anymore."

"A good sign."

"Very." Out in front of the house, he glanced across the road to Gillian's home. A vehicle still sat in her driveway. "I told her to leave."

"Maybe she's still packing."

Why hasn't she left?

Dread overwhelmed him, and he strode toward Gillian's house. Nora caught up to him, walking rapidly, scanning his face. "I'm sure she's fine," Nora told him.

"I don't want another surprise like the one I found at Kaden's," he muttered. He'd just stepped onto her driveway when Gillian came out the front door with a large suitcase.

Thank God.

Worry lit Gillian's face as she saw him and Nora approach.

"Is everything okay?" she asked, tugging the suitcase. She looked from one of them to the other.

"Yes," said Nora before Mason could speak. "We were checking to see if you'd left."

"I'll be gone in a minute—wait—did you think something had happened to me?" Her face went white.

"We're only checking on you." Mason reiterated Nora's words. "Did you find a place to go?"

"I'll be at my sister's in Seattle," she answered, still looking rattled. She popped the trunk of her car, and Mason stepped forward. He grabbed her suitcase—it was insanely heavy—and heaved it into the trunk.

"Thank you."

"We'll be in touch," Mason told her. She nodded, an unhappy expression in her eyes.

He didn't blame her. Anyone would want to distance themselves from what had happened in the last few days.

"What do you think of her?" asked Nora as they watched Gillian drive down the street.

"Two of her neighbors have been murdered. I think she's justifiably shaken."

"I thought you were going to throw your back out when you lifted her suitcase."

"I think she packed rocks."

Nora snorted. "Ready to go?"

Mason thought about Kaden Schroeder sitting in his gaming chair.

Too young.

"More than ready."

21

"This place is packed," Zander said to Ava.

"That's an understatement."

A city park had been offered for the officers' memorial. Weekly concerts were held there during the summer, so a stage was already set up at one end, and there was plenty of parking. Everywhere she looked, Ava saw different uniforms. It appeared as if every department in the state had sent representatives. And dozens more from out of state.

She and Zander stood near the park's edge under a tree as she kept an eye out for Mason. It was after 9:00 p.m., and the park was still warm even though the sun had gone down. Heat radiated from the parking lot and the hundreds of vehicles. Several food trucks were nearby, clearly popular with the crowd, but the shave ice cart had the longest line.

Ava wasn't hungry. She hadn't been since she'd learned that her twin was pregnant. Her thoughts vacillated between worry for the baby and worry for her sister.

Why hasn't she contacted me?

She was surprised Jayne hadn't shown up to brag about being pregnant.

"Do you think Brady Shurr knows about the pregnancy?" Zander asked, revealing she wasn't the only one pondering the puzzle that was Jayne.

"I think he would have told me," Ava said. "He seems like an open type of guy. He was really worried about Jayne, and I know he would be worried for a baby."

"Maybe it's not his."

The words sent a jolt through Ava's nerves.

Why am I surprised? When has Jayne ever stayed with one man in her life?

"Are you going to mention it when you tell him she was at the motel?"

"Heck no. I won't mention the pregnancy or the guy she was with. I'll tell Brady we saw her at the registration desk. That's all."

Zander was silent.

"Don't judge me." She was partly joking.

"I'm not. Just putting myself in your shoes and his. Can't put myself in Jayne's shoes because her thought patterns are irrational. But you're right. It's not your place to tell Brady about the baby. That's Jayne's responsibility."

Ava lost track of the conversation as a police uniform caught her eye. "Does that say San Antonio?"

"Yes," said Zander. "I saw one from Orlando too."

Her jaw tightened, and she pressed her lips together, emotion bubbling up in her chest. "That's amazing."

"It is. These are good people."

The Texas police officer blended into the crowd, and a Portland police officer wandered into her view, holding hands with a pregnant woman.

Suddenly Jayne was back on her brain again.

Is the baby healthy? Is Jayne taking prenatal vitamins? Is she seeing a doctor regularly?

Questions had been spinning in her mind since she saw Jayne glide her hand over the baby bump.

Is she faking?

Ava considered and then rejected the idea. Jayne had entered the motel room with a man. It was hard to fake a pregnancy with one's clothes off.

"Emily!"

The happiness in Zander's voice made Ava smile as Emily Mills joined them at the edge of the park and immediately gave Zander a hug and kiss. Ava sighed, wondering if outsiders saw Mason light up like that when he saw her.

I know they do.

Emily greeted Ava and then critically examined Ava's neck, evaluating the scars. Ava had been a passenger in Emily's car when she was shot last spring. "It looks good," Emily said, nodding in approval. "The marks are paler every time I see you."

"They are," Ava agreed. She liked Emily. She was blunt and direct and made Zander smile. All good things in Ava's book.

She spotted Mason cutting through a corner of the crowd, his cowboy hat making him stand out. "Be right back." He spotted her before she reached him. His eyes softened, and his tough-cop stride faltered.

Oh yeah. Zander's got nothing on Mason.

As he drew closer, she saw the strain around his mouth and in his gaze. He hated these gatherings. It wasn't the people or the venue he hated; it was the reason. He reached her and enveloped her in a hug, exhaling as he tightened his arms. "I've missed you today."

"Me too."

He pulled back and looked her in the eye. "What's wrong?"

Ava looked down at his boots against the grass. "Jayne showed up on a motel video from a week ago. She's pregnant."

Mason was silent, and Ava brought her gaze back to his. She was unsure of the emotion in his eyes, but it looked like concern . . . for her.

"Are you sure she's pregnant?"

Ava's lips quirked. Mason was almost as familiar with her twin's deceptions as she was. "Ninety-nine percent sure."

"Where is she now?"

"We don't know yet."

She took his hand and led him back to greet Zander and Emily.

"We're about ready to start." The Clackamas County sheriff stood at the microphone onstage, and the crowd immediately quieted.

"Feels like we just did this," Mason said quietly, looking over the crowd.

Ava squeezed his hand. He was right. They'd attended his friend Denny's service last fall, but it didn't feel like that long ago.

On the stage, officers brought out large photos of the murdered officers and placed them on stands. Ava had already memorized their faces. She knew each one's name and how many kids each had. Quiet murmurs rippled through the crowd.

We could be looking at a photo of Ray.

She glanced at Mason and found him watching her, his eyes red. He dropped her hand and slid an arm around her shoulders, and she leaned into him.

"I feel horrible that I'm happy Ray is okay," he whispered.

"It's the same for me too."

She scanned the crowd again, seeing tears and anger in the faces. The number of attendees was heartening, but—

Terror tightened her muscles. *So many officers. In one place.*

Her breathing labored as her hands grew icy.

"Hey." Mason gripped her shoulder. "I know what you're thinking. *Stop it*," he whispered.

"They're so exposed. We're exposed."

"I know. And every one of us knew that when we came, but we made a choice to be here. Dozens of officers are watching and patrolling the perimeter. There's no high ground. No one would dare try."

Ava doubted that.

It's not just officers attending. Their families are here.

It would be a bloodbath.

Light-headedness engulfed her.

"I need to go." Her voice was barely audible.

I'm having a panic attack.

Alarming energy and terror lit up her nerves. She needed to get away. Mason turned her to him and took her face in his hands, his dark eyes stern. "*Breathe.* Slowly in through your nose and slowly out."

Her gaze held on to his as if to a lifeline, but every muscle in her body screamed for her to leave and take Mason with her. Put as much distance between the gathering and them as possible.

"Breathe," he ordered again. "Focus on feeling the movements of your rib cage."

Faintly she heard Zander ask if she was okay. But her focus was locked on Mason's eyes. She continued to inhale and exhale, concentrating on the physical sensation in her lungs. She repeated each breath to a count of four in her mind. The panic eased.

"I'm all right."

"You will be in a few more seconds."

Exhaustion suddenly swamped her, and he pulled her close again. She pressed her face against his shirt; he smelled of heat and male skin. Soothing and comforting.

"I'm sorry," she murmured. "Stupid."

"Trust me. You aren't the only one having that experience right now."

She looked up. Sweat beaded his temples. It was hot. But not that hot. She wrapped her arms around his waist. *Ignoring himself to help me.*

The man was a rock.

Her rock.

"Thank you," she said.

"Anytime."

22

Mason could barely keep his eyes open as he turned onto his street. He'd left the memorial service before Ava, who was still talking with Emily, and she had promised she'd leave for home soon. He was waiting for a car to pass so he could turn into his driveway when taillights farther down his street caught his attention. The car had just pulled away from the curb, and its distinctive taillight shapes jolted him awake.

Three vertical rectangles on each side.

He'd grown up envying the people who drove the cars with the characteristic red pattern.

A Mustang.

He immediately pressed the accelerator, passing his home.

It's nothing. A coincidence. There are probably dozens in the area.

He swore at himself as he unsuccessfully tried to recall part of Shawn Braswell's license plate. He dialed Nora.

"What's wrong?" she asked sharply in lieu of hello.

"Nothing. I need the plate number for Braswell's Mustang."

"You've got one?"

"I'm following one that was parked on my street."

"It's silver?"

"It's a light color. I can't tell exactly in the dark."

"Hang on a second while I check."

The car took a left, and Mason continued to follow. He pulled closer for a few seconds, squinting at the plate. He rattled off the number to Nora and put more distance between the two vehicles.

"That doesn't match," she said.

Disappointment filled him. *I knew it.* "Wait," he said. "There were stolen plates on the vehicle Ava saw. Run the plate I just gave you."

"Hang on again."

The Mustang turned again. *He's heading toward the freeway.* The freeway entrance was still two turns away, but Mason felt it in his gut.

"That plate belongs to a Prius." Controlled excitement filled Nora's voice.

"It's definitely not a Prius."

Mason gave her the car's location and direction and asked her to call it in as he stayed on the line with her. He could make the call, but he wanted his complete focus on keeping track of the vehicle. The Mustang stopped at a red light, and Mason idled behind him, unable to see the driver.

Stay casual.

He wished he weren't driving his big truck. It had a powerful engine but lacked agility. Mason leaned to the left, trying to see the driver in the Mustang's side-view mirror. It was too dark. The light turned green, and the Mustang's tires spun as the car shot away.

"Shit!"

Mason floored the gas pedal and the truck's tires squealed. His pulse pounded in his head.

"What happened?" Nora asked.

"I think I've been made. He's still heading east but now going at least twice the speed limit." Mason was thankful the city streets were relatively deserted at the late hour, but that also meant the driver might be more reckless.

The driver turned sharply at the next right, his back end sliding far into the oncoming lane. Mason relayed the turn to Nora. "He's going to kill someone if he's not careful." Mason slowed down his big truck to take the same turn, his hands tight on the steering wheel. The taillights of the Mustang were much farther ahead than he'd expected. The lights vanished, but he still saw the silver car from the streetlights.

Mason accelerated again, his big engine roaring. "He turned off his lights. Where the fuck is patrol?"

"They've been notified . . . They're running a skeleton crew tonight because of the memorial service."

"He must have known we'd go to the service," Mason muttered. *Why was he on my street?* A chill went up his spine. "Dammit! Call Ava. Tell her not to enter the house. Get a couple officers over there to clear it first."

"On it."

Did he get inside our house? Their security system was top-notch. Mason should have received phone notifications if someone had entered. But he knew nothing was infallible.

"Shawn Braswell must have killed his brother," he told Nora. "That's the only explanation. Why else would he have stolen plates and be on my street?"

"And take off when he spotted you."

Mason was pushing seventy in a business area, and he wasn't getting any closer to the Mustang. "He's got to be headed toward the freeway."

"You should have a patrol vehicle joining you at any moment."

Mason checked his rearview mirror. Nothing. "Did you reach Ava?"

"I left her a voice mail. I'll send her a text too."

The Mustang's brake lights flashed, and the car took a hard left into a lot full of warehouses.

"He's cutting through the Robinson distribution complex."

Nora relayed the message to the dispatcher.

Mason slowed and took the turn, a back tire slamming against the curb, making his truck violently jerk. He ignored it. His need to stay on the Mustang was stronger than his need to take care of his vehicle.

The huge warehouse complex was well lit, and the Mustang shot straight ahead between two warehouses lined with dozens of loading dock doors. Mason followed, glad the businesses appeared to be shut down for the day. The Mustang's tires screeched as it turned at the end of the long warehouse and disappeared. Mason held his breath as he approached the turn, hating to have the vehicle out of sight.

He took the turn and didn't see the car. *"Where'd he go?"* Ahead of him was a road with a dozen warehouses lining each side. The car could have turned at any of them. He rolled down his window and listened.

The throaty roar of the Mustang's engine sounded from far away. *But where?*

Mason kept going forward, craning his neck to look right and left between the warehouses as he passed. Some of the warehouse alleys were lit, some not. *I'm going too slow.* At the far end of the warehouses on the right he faintly saw a tall concrete wall that separated the property from the freeway.

He glanced down a dark alley just as brake lights flashed at the far end and turned to drive parallel to the concrete wall. He yanked his wheel to the right and floored it down the alley, his truck rocking as he shot through sloped areas with drains. "He's on the south side of the complex!"

"Got it," said Nora.

Approaching the end, Mason decelerated to take the left turn and sped up as he came out of it. Up ahead the Mustang flashed in and out of sight as it sped through dark and lit areas.

Mason took a deep breath, his vision locked on the car. The Mustang was nearing the end of the complex. He was nearly past the warehouses on his left, and the concrete wall on his right stopped just beyond the last building. The Mustang turned left past the last warehouse, vanishing again.

"This is getting old," Mason stated. He took the same turn.

Too fast.

The back end of his truck seemed to float, and he tried to steer out of the slide.

Oil?

The truck continued to slide, and the right back end dropped. A horrific scraping sound vibrated through his seat and steering wheel before the truck slammed to a stop. Mason's head whipped forward, his body held in place by his seat belt.

Shit.

His back end was in a deep ditch. Frustrated, he punched the accelerator and rubber burned. The vehicle lurched but stayed in the ditch. He slammed his hands on the steering wheel.

Far ahead, the signature taillights flashed as the Mustang turned out of the complex.

"Mason?" asked Nora. "What was that?"

"That was me going into a ditch. He's headed west on the road in front of the complex."

"Are you okay?"

"I'm fine. My truck isn't."

Nora spoke into the other line, informing the dispatcher of the Mustang's direction and that Mason was in a ditch. "I'm getting you a tow truck," she told him. "I'll run you home."

"You don't need to do that. I can call Ava." He climbed out of the truck.

"She's waiting for officers outside the house. I can be there in fifteen minutes."

Mason scrutinized his truck, its back end several feet into the ditch.

Ava will give me a hard time for months about this.

He sighed and reluctantly agreed with Nora.

It was nearly midnight as Ava leaned against her car's door, waiting for the officers to finish clearing her house as Bingo barked nonstop from the backyard. The two officers had adamantly insisted she wait out front. She'd argued and then let them have their way. Clearly Bingo was fine, and that was all she truly cared about.

Mason had called, updating her on what exactly he had seen on their street and then admitting he'd put his truck in a ditch.

She'd wanted to tease him, but his frustrated tone made her hold back.

Headlights shone as a vehicle turned on her street, and a moment later she recognized Nora and Mason. Nora parked behind her at the curb, and Mason opened his door. Ava met him halfway, wrapping her arms around him. "You're sure you're okay?"

"Positive. Whipped my head a bit, but I've had worse."

"You sure it was Shawn Braswell?"

He grimaced. "I didn't see the driver. I could tell there was one male in the car, but that was it. Why else would he take off?"

"Because he had stolen plates?"

"Why worry that the person behind you in a pickup would know anything about stolen plates unless you recognize the truck as the personal vehicle of someone in law enforcement?"

Ava frowned. "You think he knows what you drive?"

"I think he knows a lot of things."

Ava turned to look at the house, her stomach tightening. "Mason . . . how does he know where you live?" she asked softly.

He said nothing.

Nora spoke up. "You think you've been followed?"

Fury burned in Ava's gut.

"That seems the most logical conclusion," said Mason.

Ava massaged the back of her neck, wanting to release its ache, which had hounded her all day. "We need to see if the cameras caught anything."

"I can do that on my phone."

Voices turned their attention. The two officers had stepped out of the home and were talking on the front porch. Ava was pleased that one had put a leash on Bingo and brought him out. She, Nora, and Mason crossed the street and met the officers as they came down the porch stairs.

"The house is clear," said the female officer. "We walked the yard too." She scratched Bingo's ears. "This guy wanted to come. I hope you don't mind that I brought him out."

"Not at all," said Ava, taking the leash. She squatted down and gave the dog a hug. "As long as he's safe, I don't care about the rest of the house."

"I care," said Mason. "We've got half our savings wrapped up in that money pit."

"The kitchen looks great," said the other officer. "My wife wants to do something similar in our house."

"Expect it to take thirty percent longer than estimated and cost twenty percent more," said Mason. "Nothing unusual inside?"

"No, all the doors were locked, as Agent McLane told us they should be. Windows intact and locked."

Bingo pulled on the leash, straining to go up the porch stairs.

"Sit," said Mason, who continued to speak with the officers.

Bingo sat, his dark gaze going from Mason to Ava and back. He gave a long whine.

Ava cocked her head as she studied the dog, and Mason stopped midsentence to look at Bingo. "What's-a-matter, boy?" he asked.

The dog whined again and pulled on the leash—while still sitting.

Ava looked to Mason, who lifted one shoulder. She loosened the leash. "Come on, Bingo," she said, taking a step toward the stairs. The dog bounded up in two leaps and stopped at an Adirondack chair near the door, making snorting sounds as he sniffed at it.

A small paper Starbucks bag was on the arm of the chair. "No," Ava told Bingo as she grabbed the bag a split second before he did. She glanced in the bag, expecting to find the remains of a scone or muffin.

It was a human finger.

"Ewww!" She stared, and then she held out the bag with two fingers, bile rising in the back of her throat.

"Mason, I think Bingo found Reuben's missing finger."

Minutes later the finger was in an evidence bag, and the three of them crowded around Mason's laptop to watch the camera coverage.

"There he is," Mason said under his breath. A man in shorts, cap, and T-shirt strolled to their front porch, took the stairs two at a time, pretended to knock, and casually left the Starbucks bag on the chair.

His face was hidden by his hat, but Ava knew that stride and physique. "That is the same guy who left the backpack in the dumpster. He knew exactly where our camera was. Look how he turns his face away at the right moment. The blond hair in the other video must have been a wig."

"Why didn't he use the same disguise here? Or maybe a different one?" asked Nora. "He appears to have short dark hair. That's what Shawn Braswell has, correct?"

"Don't know if it's currently short, but it is dark," said Ava. "Nothing here proves that it's not Shawn Braswell."

"Especially since he was driving a silver Mustang," said Mason. "I'll check with the neighbors tomorrow and see if anyone got his face on camera. Too bad it was so dark."

"I'm more disturbed that he knows where you live, Mason," said Nora.

The detective's face was blank, but Ava knew exactly what she was thinking.

Does he know where I live too?

"Please be careful, Nora," she said.

"I'm always careful, but this is unnerving. My condo building has good security."

"Watch when you park," added Mason.

"I don't like how personal this feels," said Ava.

"It was personal to start with," he said. "You knew the original victim."

"Not that well," she argued. Reuben Braswell had been low on her list of useful people. "But now Shawn has brought Reuben's finger specifically to *our* house, wanting to make a point. What is that point?"

The three of them were silent.

"I don't know," Mason said slowly. "Dr. Trask told me a middle finger was missing, so maybe it's a big fuck-you to us. But if I was Shawn, I'd be as far away from this town as possible."

Ava agreed. *Why was Shawn Braswell still in town?*

23

The next morning Mason strode down the office hallway to the detectives' area. He'd slept like crap. This frustrating case zigged every time he expected it to zag.

Someone was at my home.

Had he led danger to his own doorstep?

Last night he and Ava had lain awake for several hours, pretending to sleep. She'd finally drifted off, her breaths deepening and slowing. Mason had stayed awake for another hour, his thoughts wildly veering down every tangent in his case.

He set his hat on an extra chair near his desk. For the first time in days, he didn't feel ill when he looked at Ray's empty space. His partner was on the mend, and Jill hoped to have him out of the hospital by tomorrow. It gave Mason peace—a very small sliver of peace. He'd have more when he found the person who had pulled the trigger.

He logged in to his computer and looked up as Nora entered the big room. Last night they'd made plans to meet this morning to thoroughly review the case evidence. They needed to find Shawn Braswell's current location.

"Good morning," she said. Her eyes lacked their usual intensity, and she seemed pale.

Someone else didn't sleep well.

"Morning."

She sat heavily in Ray's chair. Her own desk was on a different floor due to the crowded office conditions. "With all the turmoil yesterday, I forgot to tell you that Kaden Schroeder's father never showed up at his home."

Mason went still. "And when you called him?"

"Line disconnected." Her gaze was flat.

"The same number I'd used with him yesterday?"

"Yep. I double- and triple-checked."

A dozen possibilities engulfed him. "What . . ." He couldn't sort his thoughts.

"I know. Believe me, I've been trying to figure out why he would vanish." She rubbed her eyes. "Did Tony disconnect his line, or did something happen to him?"

"If something happened to him, a call would still go to voice mail," said Mason.

"True. It's most likely he purposefully did it."

"Was he even in Bend?"

"Who knows? And I can't find any record that shows Tony Schroeder has a brother."

"Shit." Mason turned to his computer. "Tony sounded genuinely crushed when I told him about Kaden's death yesterday. Was it an act?"

"We don't know that you actually spoke with his father," Nora said dryly.

"What if someone also killed Kaden's father?" murmured Mason as he tapped on his keyboard. "What if Kaden *and* his father were targeted?"

"Before or after your phone call?"

Mason grimaced in frustration. The questions were coming too fast. "Just covering all the possibilities."

"I know." He focused on his screen, where he'd pulled up Tony Schroeder's driver's license. "Age forty-three, six-one, one-eighty-five. He has short, dark hair in this photo."

Nora raised her brows. "Who else fits that description?"

"Shawn Braswell." Mason stared at the photo, trying to mentally match the jawline to the only part of the man's face visible in the church videos and the one from his home last night. *Did we jump to the conclusion that Shawn Braswell was the man in those videos?*

"Was Kaden misleading me about the Mustang?"

"Shawn Braswell owns a silver Mustang. There's no doubt about that."

"What does Tony Schroeder drive?"

"A six-year-old Ford F-350. Kaden's Toyota pickup is in his father's name too."

"Put a—"

"I already put out a BOLO for the Ford."

"And the phone number?"

"Burner phone."

"Of course it was." Gillian Wood's voice rang in Mason's head as he recalled her statement that Reuben Braswell had been a burner-phone fan. "Doesn't anyone trust anymore?"

"Trust big companies with personal information? No."

"You saw all these priors for Tony Schroeder?" Mason scanned his screen. Tony had been arrested a number of times for breaking into vehicles and homes. Two DUIs. An assault. Possession of a stolen weapon.

"I did," said Nora. "They're all in Central Oregon counties. He hasn't been in trouble since he moved to this side of the Cascades. But that means we have prints on file for him."

"Which we can compare to any prints found at the Braswell murder."

"Tony and Reuben were neighbors. If Tony's prints show up in Reuben's home, it could mean nothing."

"Depends where the prints are found." Mason eyed Tony Schroeder's possession-of-a-stolen-weapon charge. It was three years old. "Your thoughts on the weapons charge?"

"Said he bought it from a friend . . . who conveniently moved to Mexico."

Of course. "On the phone Tony said he didn't know anything about the weapons in Kaden's room."

Nora held up her hands and shrugged. "Who knows what he lied about on that call."

"Or maybe he lied about nothing."

"And someone else didn't want him talking with us."

"Did the medical examiner say when they'd get to Kaden?" Mason wanted all the answers. Now.

"Sometime this morning," said Nora.

"We need to go back to the Schroeder home. I want to look it over again now that we know his father has vanished."

"What started as only the murder of Reuben Braswell grows in scope every day."

"Every hour, it feels like," said Mason. "First the courthouse murders and then Kaden's and now the question of what happened to his father." He consulted his little notepad. "Did we hear if there were any large transactions in Kaden's bank accounts?"

"No cash withdrawals of more than sixty dollars in the last six months."

"The ATF robbery was only a couple months ago." Mason tried to think of other ways Kaden could have purchased the weapons. "Maybe he traded something for them. He would have paid way more than sixty dollars for those five guns."

"Maybe they weren't his weapons," Nora said quietly.

"Maybe they were Reuben's . . . Maybe he stole them from Reuben . . . Could he have gone in the house after Reuben was killed and taken the weapons?"

"I don't think the window between Reuben's death and the arrival of the local police was long enough. There's a good chance Gillian scared off the killer when she banged on the back door."

"That's right." An icy thought occurred to him. "Would Tony kill his own son?" he asked quietly.

Nora was silent for a long moment. "We've seen it happen."

An image of Jake roughhousing with Bingo popped in his head. *I could never . . .*

"Where do you want to start?" Nora asked.

"I think we need to go back to the beginning. Reuben Braswell's home." Mason had a sinking feeling he'd missed something very important. "Then cross the street to the Schroeders'. Tell the lab to compare Tony Schroeder's prints to ones found in Reuben's home."

Nora nodded as she tapped out an email on her phone. "How's Ava holding up?"

"She's getting by. We'll definitely be ready for a couple weeks in Italy after the wedding."

"I'm still jealous." Nora had seen their plans to visit Florence, Capri, and Positano. "I'm sorry about the death of her father."

"It was a shock. A confusing event for her to process." Mason knew Ava still hadn't forgiven herself for not getting to know her father better.

"Ready to go?"

Mason stood and put on his hat.

Ava sighed as she eyed the *unknown caller* message on her screen. She never ignored the anonymous calls but always wanted to. She set her coffee cup in the kitchen sink and answered.

"Agent McLane."

"Ava?"

She caught her breath. "Jayne?" *She's alive.* "Where in the hell are you?"

"I don't know." Her sister sobbed as the connection cut in and out.

Every cell in Ava's body focused on the call. "What's wrong?"

"It's so awful! I didn't mean for this to happen," her sister wailed.

Ava pressed her cell tight to her ear as if that would improve the phone call's poor quality. "Where are you?" she repeated. "Are you safe?"

How many times have I promised myself to not get caught up in her problems?

Hang up.

She's pregnant.

"I don't know," Jayne moaned between sobs. "He wouldn't let me see when we drove here, and now I don't know what to do!"

"Who? Who's with you?"

"Quiet!" Jayne whispered loudly. Rustling sounded, as if Jayne was placing the phone under something.

Anger tightened Ava's grip on her cell. It was so typical. Jayne would call with a horrible emergency, begging for Ava's help, and then it would turn out to be nothing.

Hang up.

I don't need this right now.

"He's back," Jayne whispered between wet gasps. "I need to go."

"Who is back?" *If she doesn't give me a clear answer, I am done.*

"You've got to help me, Ava." Jayne was barely audible. "He killed David."

Ava couldn't breathe.

Did she say . . .

"He'll kill me next if I don't do what he says."

"Who?"

Jayne didn't answer, and Ava looked at her screen. The call had ended.

Icy shock raced through her.

He'll kill Jayne?

Jayne knows who murdered David?

Her hands shook as she called Zander. She needed to see Jayne's motel video again.

It has to be the man in the video.

24

Ava watched as Zander slowed down the video when the man came into view at the motel. They sat at her kitchen table, intently focused on Zander's laptop. He'd arrived fifteen minutes after she'd called, deep concern on his face.

Their original morning plan had been to return to the church where the weapon had been found and talk to Pat Arthur again, but Jayne's call had delayed that.

"We need to send this to the Clatsop County sheriff," Zander said, his gaze glued to the screen. "Maybe they'll recognize this guy."

"From his back?"

"Worth a try."

"They've gotten nowhere on my father's murder," Ava said. "The lead detective has emailed me status updates, and from the looks of things, they're being thorough, but nothing is panning out."

"Maybe the video will help."

Ava stared at the screen. It gave a clear shot of Jayne's pregnancy bulge. "She didn't say anything about being pregnant when she called."

"Sounds like she didn't have time."

"Maybe it is fake, and this guy is in on it . . . Maybe she does it to play up sympathy at the front desk to get away with paying in cash."

"You have a point." Zander ran the video again. "Any luck on finding where she called from?"

"The team is working on it. The reception was bad, so I have the feeling she's somewhere remote."

"Maybe she's still at the coast if this is the guy that killed David?"

Ava froze, her mind grasping at something just out of reach. *Jayne at the coast.* "I want to see the security footage from the bakery that the sheriff told us about. The one where a man hit a woman on the morning that David was shot."

Zander picked up his phone. "I'll call. And I'll tell him about this footage."

Exhaling, Ava sat back in her chair and rubbed her eyes. The bakery clerk had said the woman had been punched and then walked away with the man's arm around her shoulders.

Would Jayne put up with that?

She would if she believed he would kill her.

Jayne had genuinely sounded scared on the call.

But how many times has she lied to me before?

Ava had stopped counting decades ago. Jayne cared about one person: herself. She'd do and say anything if she believed she could benefit, no matter whom it hurt. Ava rose out of her chair, unable to meet Zander's questioning gaze, and headed for her formal dining room, needing space. The room was beautiful. Wide plank floors, white wainscoting, and a pale-teal paint—almost white. Tall windows let in tons of light.

Ava stopped in front of Jayne's painting and studied it as if it would give a clue to Jayne's location. The coastline watercolor was bleak and desolate, but Ava couldn't look away. The first time she'd seen it, she'd been immediately pulled in by its depth and color.

She saw pieces of Jayne in the painting. And herself.

What are you up to, Jayne?

Ava closed her eyes.

The spark was still there; it wouldn't go away. That damned spark simply wouldn't die no matter how much Ava ignored it or suffered from the consequences of Jayne's actions. A spark that made Ava give Jayne the benefit of the doubt. Every. Single. Time.

Call it a twin bond or sisterly bond or whatever. Ava hated that she couldn't sever it, but at the same time she appreciated its tenacity. If she gave up on Jayne, whom would her sister have left?

Brady Shurr?

Should I tell him I heard from Jayne?

Ava immediately decided against it. Brady didn't need to hear that Jayne was worried someone would kill her.

Still in the kitchen, Zander spoke into his phone. Ava couldn't make out the words but assumed he was talking with the sheriff or detective on David's case.

Ava wanted to see the bakery video. Now.

Why would Jayne be with someone who killed David?

She couldn't think of a reason.

David's death resembled an assassination. Why? Who would want to kill the man? Ava had thoroughly investigated David last fall when he'd first entered her life. If there were skeletons in his closet, she'd seen no hint of them.

"Ava?" Zander called.

She took one last look at Jayne's watercolor.

So much turmoil.

She joined Zander, who was opening his email. "I talked to the lead detective. He said he would immediately send the bakery video. He hadn't found it to be of any value in his investigation yet, but he is very interested to find out what we think. I emailed him the motel footage and gave him the name she's been traveling under."

Zander opened a link.

Ava watched. The angle of the video's view was high, looking down on the bakery's front porch and sidewalk. A few empty tables and chairs could be seen on one side. An arguing couple strolled into view.

That's her.

Ava had no doubt.

"There she is," Zander said quietly. It was apparent to him too.

Ava wished there were sound. Jayne was using her hands and arms to make a point. The man's back and jaw were stiff; he wasn't happy.

"Fucking hat again," said Zander.

The baseball cap hid most of the man's face due to the camera's angle. Jayne turned and walked backward, giving a clear view of her face. A gentle wind blew her sundress against her stomach.

"Still pregnant," Ava said, feeling oddly detached. She might have a niece or nephew. Why wasn't she more excited?

Because Jayne can't be trusted.

"I don't think I'll believe she's pregnant until I see a baby," she told Zander.

"I hear you."

The man halted. Jayne stopped, too, but continued with her hand gestures.

The blow was swift, and Ava gasped as Jayne dropped to her knees, shock in her face. But the man was immediately down and taking her hands in a pleading way, holding them to his heart.

His jaw moved, and Ava knew exactly what the asshole was saying. *I didn't mean it, baby. It was an accident. It won't happen again.*

He helped Jayne to her feet, but Jayne's face was blank. The animation from earlier, gone.

She knows he's trouble.

The man put an arm around her and pulled her to him. Jayne rested her head against his shoulder, and they continued to walk down the sidewalk and out of camera view.

"Wow." Zander sounded stunned. "Even though I knew it was coming, that punch surprised me. He's fast. What kind of asshole hits a pregnant woman?"

"The same kind of asshole that hits any woman."

"Touché."

"This was before David was shot?" Ava asked.

"They believe so. They're headed in the right direction to cross David's path too."

"Jayne would never shoot anyone." *I think.* "Jayne would never shoot David," she corrected. "She worshiped him."

"I have no doubt that the jerk who hit her is our shooter."

"She can't have been involved."

"I hope not," Zander agreed. "But she has a bad track record of picking the wrong man."

Ava couldn't disagree. Jayne's history proved she liked a bad boy. Many women did. But Jayne's bad boys were often violent felons or desperate drug addicts. Or both.

"I'll text the detective that we've identified her," said Zander. "I told him about your phone call and her claim that she knew who killed David. It's a start."

"A much bigger start than they've had," agreed Ava, checking her phone. Her heart skipped when she spotted an email from the agent she'd asked to find information on Jayne's call. She opened it. "Jayne called from a disposable phone."

"Not surprised."

"They traced the call to a cell tower near The Dalles."

Rural Columbia River area.

"Just one tower? I thought calls were usually picked up by a few and then went with the strongest signal."

"According to this, it only connected to one."

"So wherever she is, it's remote if there was only one tower within her phone's reach. Probably why it was choppy: it had no stronger choice."

Ava held Zander's gaze. "Now what?" She felt overloaded on adrenaline, a subtle buzz in all her muscles. She needed to act.

"We need to get back to finding Shawn Braswell." Sympathy lit his eyes. "I can tell you want to head to The Dalles, but that's not our priority."

"She claims she knows who killed David."

"And we passed that information to the investigators. You need to send them the email you just received too."

"I will." Frustration simmered under her skin. "I'll call Mercy. Maybe she can dig deeper."

"Good idea." He raised a brow at her. "Let *her* handle it," he said.

Mercy Kilpatrick was an agent at the Bend FBI office, a couple of hours south of The Dalles. On a map, The Dalles was closer to Portland, but its geographical region and rural community placed it in the Bend office's territory.

Mercy was one of Ava's top picks to be her wedding attendant.

The wedding isn't important now.

Ava touched Mercy's number in her phone and waited for the other agent to answer.

Zander was right; they had work to do.

Jayne was not her problem.

Maybe if I keep repeating that, I'll start believing it.

Mason paused in the doorway to Ray's hospital room. Ray's eyes were closed as he lay in a partially upright position. The room was very quiet. He'd called Ray an hour ago to let him know he'd be stopping by. Ray had said Jill and the kids would be running errands.

Ray looked thin, surprising Mason a bit. The man always had such a powerful physical presence, but now it was muted. He'd always had a bit of a Superman aura, seeming invincible. This week had proved that wrong.

He's going to be fine, showing he's still Superman.

But he looked a bit Clark Kent–ish at the moment.

Ray opened his eyes and a grin lit up his face. He pressed a button on the side of his bed and raised the head farther. Simply by smiling he lit up the room. He didn't need to be physically built to project his charisma. Ray was more than his strength.

Entering the room, Mason smiled back and then clapped him on the shoulder. "Looking good."

"I'll look better once I'm out of here. This afternoon looks promising. I'm so tired of green Jell-O."

"Green is the best flavor."

"Wrong. Strawberry is the best. And green isn't a flavor. Lime is the flavor."

Ray sounded like his old self, making the knot in Mason's chest ease.

"You could have waited and visited me at home," the patient said.

"I knew I had time this morning. Who knows what I'll be working on this afternoon?"

"True." Interest lit up Ray's eyes. "Catch me up."

Mason hesitated.

Ray pointed at a chair. "Sit. Talk. Everyone's being vague when I ask questions about the case, as if information will slow my recovery. I'm hungry for details."

Mason sat.

"What's this about a car wreck last night?" Ray asked.

"Who told you?"

Ray shrugged. "I hear things. Your truck okay?"

"It won't be the same, but it's repairable."

"What the hell were you doing?"

Mason told him about the Mustang, the stolen plates, and the chase that had ended in his accident.

"No one saw the vehicle after that?"

"No. A skeleton crew was working last night because—" Mason stopped.

"Because of the memorial service," Ray said bluntly. "I tried to finagle my way to it. Doctors wouldn't let me out even for an hour."

"Doing their job."

"How was it? Jill couldn't bring herself to go, and I know she feels guilty about not showing support."

"Not showing support? She's personally met with every spouse affected by the shooting. No one's going to fault her for not making a ceremony."

"You and I know that, but she still worries."

"The service was good," Mason said. His throat thickened, and he looked Ray in the eye. "I was thankful your picture wasn't on that stage."

"That would have sucked."

"That's putting it mildly." Mason looked at his hands, which were holding the side rail of Ray's bed. His fingers were white from gripping too hard. "I still feel nauseated when I think of it."

"It's past. It's over. I'm fine. I'll have a few new scars to show off," Ray joked.

Mason glanced away, struck by the memory of those bleeding injuries. "I'd rather not see them."

"I know," Ray said. "But I plan to use them as a reminder to not take every day for granted."

The men sat silently for a long moment. It was a comfortable silence. Mason didn't feel pressured to fill it with talk as he considered Ray's statement.

He needed to have the same attitude. Life had given him a second chance at happiness with Ava. He wouldn't take a day of it for granted.

"I heard the missing finger turned up at your place," Ray said, breaking the silence.

"Who told you all this?"

"I promised not to tell. Is it true?"

"There was definitely a finger, and I assume it's Reuben Braswell's missing middle digit. I hate to think that there're other people lacking fingers just to intimidate me."

"But why intimidate you?" Ray asked. "Why are you a target? Maybe it's Ava."

"True," Mason said. "Ava knew Reuben, but I'm the one looking for his killer—who most likely left the finger."

"There are a lot more people besides you working this case," Ray pointed out. "But to me the finger at your home feels very personal. Are you sure you've never encountered Shawn Braswell in the past?"

"He's never been in trouble. He doesn't have a record."

"What about in your personal life?"

Mason shook his head. "I'm old. You think I remember every person I've met?"

"Just because you're older than me doesn't mean you're old. You could kick the butt of any officer I know."

"That's doubtful."

"Maybe not through brute strength, but you're fast and sharp and conniving."

"Thank you, I think? Still doesn't mean I can remember if I've met Shawn Braswell. Maybe I cut him off on the way to the Starbucks drive-through. Maybe he's the type to hold a grudge."

Ray thought for a moment. "We can't assume Shawn was driving. Sure, it's a car like his, but with stolen plates, we can't say it was his for certain."

Mason noticed Ray's use of the word *we* but didn't correct him. "It'd be a big coincidence that I was following someone else's Mustang, but I won't rule it out."

"What about the missing dad . . . What's his name?"

"Tony Schroeder."

"Could he have killed Reuben?"

"It's possible."

"You're still considering that he killed his son, Kaden, right?"

"Yes. Gillian Wood says she saw a silver car in front of the Schroeder home the evening before Kaden was killed. We have no way of knowing who was there. Shawn Braswell seems most likely." Mason paused. "But Tony Schroeder has a record. Lot of little stuff."

"Could he have targeted you last night? Have you encountered him before?"

"Not that I'm aware of. He lived in the Central Oregon area for a long time, so I doubt it."

"You know what else has been bothering me?"

"The gunshot wound in your leg?"

Ray ignored him. "How did someone know we'd respond to the courthouse that day? What if the crime scene tech hadn't looked through those papers? How did the shooter know there'd be a large law enforcement response?"

"This question bothers everyone," Mason told him.

"Let me see the photos you took of the papers we found at Braswell's. The one that mentions the courthouse."

"You need to rest."

"I've been resting for days. My brain is starting to atrophy. Did you get a lab report on the papers?"

"Yes. Handwriting appears to all be from the same person. Blood on the papers matched the victim."

"Show me the pictures."

"Damn, you're pushy." Mason pulled out his phone and scrolled through the pictures. He found what he was looking for and handed the phone to Ray, who peered closely at the screen.

"What else did the report say?"

Mason thought. "Nothing jumped out at me. They didn't find any prints. Some of the smears indicated the killer was wearing gloves when he handled the documents. The blood was smeared over the ink, meaning they'd been written before our killer got blood on them."

"Over the ink," Ray mumbled as he looked at the photos. "What is the significance of that?"

"I don't see one," said Mason. "Reuben wrote it at some point, and then the killer smudged it with Reuben's blood that day. I imagine he was looking for Reuben's plans for the courthouse."

"He found them," Ray said.

"My question is, if they were originally working together to carry out the courthouse shooting, why kill your partner and then carry out the shooting?" Mason felt a spurt of energy. He'd missed brainstorming with Ray. The two of them always fed off each other's ideas, coming up with angles they would have missed on their own.

"Maybe they had a disagreement about it."

"That's quite the disagreement."

Ray enlarged a photo on Mason's phone. "Look at this."

Mason looked. It was the page with the sentences about the planned bombing at the courthouse. "What about it? Bloody paper. Same handwriting."

"You said the blood was over the ink, meaning it'd been written before the murder."

"Seems logical. I don't see any holes in that theory."

"But the part about the courthouse isn't smudged with blood. In fact, the first sentence about the courthouse skips down to the second line to avoid writing over a blood smear. Same with the other sentences about the bombing."

Mason stared. Ray was right. The writer had purposefully written around the blood as if it'd been already present when he wrote. None of the sentences about the courthouse and the time of the bombing had blood smeared over them. He quickly scanned the rest of the pages. The sentences filled the lines, with no odd spacing, as in the courthouse sentences.

"I think they were written after Gillian banged on the back door. The killer knew his time was suddenly short and the house would be crawling with police in minutes."

"But the killer didn't write this document. Reuben did. The handwriting matches other documents in the room."

"Look how shaky the letters are in the sentences about the detonation time of the bomb," Ray pointed out. "I don't know who analyzed the handwriting, but I could see this as someone trying to copy the rest of the writing."

"Maybe they didn't analyze each sentence. Maybe they looked at a sentence in every paragraph. This is on the last page, so they could have studied some of the above handwriting," Mason said as he mentally picked apart Ray's theory from every angle. "You're saying Reuben wrote the document, but the killer added the part about the courthouse."

"It would answer our question about how the killer knew there would be a law enforcement presence at the courthouse that day," said Ray. "He'd left the folder in plain sight. Closed, but readily available. The blood on the outside of the folder would call our attention to it."

"So say the killer hears Gillian making a racket, knows his time is up, so he takes off his gloves and adds the courthouse sentence to Reuben's rambling diatribe."

Ray nodded. "That means when he originally handled the document, his gloved hands were already bloody."

"But he came back to it . . . guaranteeing we'd react in full force to a bomb at the courthouse." Mason frowned. "Just how much time did he have to spare after Gillian banged on the back door?"

"Enough time to pull off his gloves, write the sentence, and get out."

"And somehow get out without Gillian seeing him when she came around to the front door."

"He could have gone out the back."

"The sliding glass door was locked from the inside."

"Right. And all the windows were closed and locked. The air-conditioning was running."

"He had to go out the front door."

"Do we need to talk to Gillian about her timeline again?" Ray asked.

"I'll call her," said Mason. "You're going to stay here, eat green Jell-O, and prove to them that you can go home today."

25

"Agent Kilpatrick." Mercy's voice was crisp in Ava's ear.

"Mercy, it's Ava."

"Hey! Nice to hear from you. I'm looking forward to your wedding."

"Me too. This is a work call. Sort of."

"What do you need?"

Ava explained about Jayne's phone call and the cell tower location. "She claimed the man she is with killed another man on the coast."

"What's the victim's name?" Mercy was immediately all business.

"David Dressler."

The line went silent. "Isn't that your father's name?" Mercy finally asked.

"It is." Ava swallowed hard. "He was shot the day before yesterday. Clatsop County sheriff has the case."

"Oh, Ava, I'm so sorry."

"Thank you. I'm okay." Ava glanced at Zander, who was listening carefully to her side of the phone call with sympathy in his eyes.

"Let me figure out exactly where this cell tower is. I should be able to plot its reach and see where no other tower's reach intersects. Maybe I'll be able to narrow down a location. Will you send me a picture of her? I'll send it to motels in the area."

"I'll email you video we have from a motel. It shows the man she's with, but only from the back."

"Ava . . ." Mercy seemed to be at a loss for words.

"Yes?"

"You've told me several stories about your sister, and I got the impression that you don't trust her that much. Is it—"

"I don't trust her at all," Ava said. "Not one bit."

"That's what I thought. Is it possible that the phone call was some sort of attention seeking?" Mercy asked delicately.

"It is. I don't want you sinking a lot of time into this. It could turn out to be nothing." Ava forced a laugh. "It probably will be nothing."

"You think she's lying."

Ava didn't know how to answer. "Yes and no and maybe."

"I understand," Mercy said. "I'll contact the sheriff and keep you updated on anything I find."

"One more thing." Nervous, she met Zander's gaze. "I don't have an attendant for my wedding yet."

Mercy was quiet.

Ava held her breath.

"Are you asking me?" Mercy finally said.

"I am."

"But Ava, it should be your sister."

"I know it *should* be, but my relationship with my sister isn't . . . normal."

"You waited until the last minute to ask me," Mercy said. "Is that because you hoped Jayne would come through for you?"

"She's supposed to be in Costa Rica." Ava didn't answer Mercy's question.

"Right. And now she might be in trouble. Tell you what. If Jayne is unable to do it, I will step in since I'll already be there. I'd love to be a part of your wedding."

A knot released in Ava's chest. "Thank you." She meant it. The question had been a burden for weeks.

"What color dress should I wear?"

"It doesn't matter."

"Yes, it does," Mercy said firmly. "I'm fully aware of how long you've waited to get married. What color?"

"Black."

"Really? It's summer."

"I guess white would also work."

"Even I know better than to wear that. Black it is. I'll find something that works. It's a black-and-white wedding?"

"No. I didn't pick a color scheme," Ava said.

"I've met Cheryl. She probably let you think that. I have no doubt she's planned something lovely."

"She did say she'd take care of the flower choices."

"I can't wait to be there. In the meantime, I'll make some stills from the video to send out and see if I can find a lead on your sister."

"Thank you." Ava hung up.

"Feel better?" Zander asked.

"Yes, she's got a plan to look for Jayne."

"You need to tell Mason about Jayne's call."

"That was next on my list, but we need to go to the church and interview Pat Arthur again. I can call while you drive."

She grabbed her bag and followed Zander out of her house.

Minutes later she had Mason on the phone, updating him on her conversation with Jayne.

"You understand why I'm cautious about taking her seriously," Mason said.

"I do. I feel the same way. But I can't not do anything."

"You were right to call Mercy. She knows that area, even though it's closer to Portland than Bend."

"She was the first person I thought of when I saw the call originated near The Dalles."

"I've got another call," said Mason. "It's the crime lab."

213

"Go. I'll talk to you later."

Ava ended the call and looked at Zander, intent on his driving. "I feel better now that I talked to Mercy. I don't know why I waited so long to ask her to be my attendant."

"Yes, you do. We all know."

"Mercy said if Jayne can't do it, then she will. She understood how I felt about wanting Jayne to be there if possible."

Ava pictured her twin standing beside her on one of the biggest days of her life. Pregnant. "It's got to be Brady Shurr's baby. Jayne hasn't been gone long enough for it to be anyone else's, judging by her size." Ava grimaced. "Assuming she was faithful to Brady." Jayne didn't know the meaning of the word.

"If there is a baby," Zander reminded her.

Ava's phone rang. Mason was calling her back. "That was fast," she answered.

"The call from the crime lab was about the ammunition used in Kaden Schroeder's murder." He sounded breathless.

"Are you all right?" Ava asked.

"The firearm examiner retrieving the ballistics information followed a hunch because the results felt familiar. He'd recently processed the bullets from another murder, and when he compared them to Kaden's, he discovered they matched."

"That's great. Do they have a suspect in the other murder?" Ava was thrilled for him. The bullets would have eventually been linked through a database, but the examiner had saved a lot of time.

"No suspect. But Ava." Mason paused. "The bullets he compared them to are from David's murder. The weapon used on Kaden Schroeder matches the one used on your father."

Ava went still.

"What does that mean?" she whispered into the phone as her mind raced.

"Your sister just told you she is with the man who killed David. If she's telling the truth about that, then he also killed Kaden or is connected in some way with the weapon that killed Kaden."

"How else would she know David was murdered unless she was there? It didn't make the news," Ava said, trying to keep her thoughts straight. "She must be telling the truth."

"You have to agree that we never know when Jayne is telling the truth. But either way, it was the same weapon."

Ava didn't know what to say.

"I'd like to know if this is tied to Reuben Braswell's murder," Mason said. "There's a strong possibility that Reuben's murder is related to Kaden's since they were across the street from one another."

"Are you saying Jayne could be with Shawn Braswell? The man we suspect killed law enforcement at the courthouse?" Nausea burned up her esophagus. "Jayne is connected to those deaths?"

Oh, Jayne. What have you done?

She faintly registered that Zander had pulled the vehicle to the side of the road and was watching her with concern.

"Shawn Braswell is a prime suspect for Reuben's death and those officers," said Mason. "I suspect he's involved in Kaden's death, and now that means he could have killed David too."

Ava's brain continued to spin, grasping at straws. "What about Tony Schroeder? He's a suspect in Kaden's death, right?"

"He is."

"He could be with Jayne and have shot David." Ava fought to keep the four incidents straight in her head. "But the stolen weapons found in Kaden's home are from the same theft as the weapon used at the courthouse. No matter how we look at it, Jayne is tied to the courthouse murders." Ava couldn't see a way Jayne wasn't indirectly involved. Unless she had lied about who had killed David.

"Ava . . . your name was in Reuben's notes about the bomb."

"Right. Your point?" Ava asked.

"That means that both you and Jayne are linked in *some* way to the courthouse deaths."

He's right.

"Why?" she breathed. "I don't understand. Jayne's supposed to be out of the country." She kept returning to that fact as if it proved Jayne couldn't be involved.

"She's here. Somewhere," Mason said.

"I need to go to The Dalles," Ava said. "I'll take this information to the task force and make them send me."

Zander cleared his throat.

"Me and Zander," Ava corrected.

"The lab is calling again. I cut our earlier conversation short because I wanted to tell you."

"Call me when you're done," Ava told Mason. She ended the call and stared out the windshield, feeling dizzy.

Jayne. David. Kaden. Reuben. Shawn.

She said the names out loud. "They're all connected," she told Zander.

"I gathered that."

"What is going on? How can Jayne be caught up in this?"

"You're asking me?"

She wasn't. "I'm thinking out loud."

"We both know Jayne has ended up in some insane situations," Zander said. "Several illegal. If Reuben Braswell was your informant and Jayne has a way of weaseling into every aspect of your life, then I'm not completely shocked to find out she might be with his brother."

"How could she possibly know about an informant of mine?"

"Maybe she followed you to a meeting. Maybe it was the other way around . . . Reuben or Shawn searched her out."

Ava gasped as the air left her lungs. "Reuben . . . he was attracted to me. He was upset when he saw my engagement ring. Tried to warn me that women can be physically hurt in marriage but said he would never do that to me."

"Jesus. Why didn't you say that before?"

"Because it wasn't relevant!"

"He could find all sorts of information about you on the internet. Especially with the trouble that Jayne has gotten into. It's possible he discovered you had a twin and went looking for her. And now she's with his brother somehow."

"That's ridiculous. We're making connections that don't make sense and jumping to conclusions." The car seemed to spin.

This can't be true.

"I'm not saying this is what happened, but it's possible." Zander restarted the car. "The task force will be very interested to know we've got a possible lead on Shawn Braswell's location. I have no doubt they'll send us to The Dalles."

26

Zander was wrong.

The sheriff wasn't impressed with Ava's report on Jayne's phone call. Especially when an officer standing nearby asked if Jayne was the same crazy sister who had stolen Ava's car and crashed it while drunk.

Ava stared daggers at the officer, stunned that the story was gossip among law enforcement. The officer got a concerned look on his face instead of crumbling under Ava's white rage. "Isn't she the one that tried to commit suicide?" he asked.

Zander placed a firm hand on Ava's arm. Her vision had tunneled on the officer, and she didn't know why he wasn't melting into the floor.

"That true?" asked the sheriff.

"What does it matter?" asked Zander in a rare tone that Ava recognized as a precursor to a high level of anger. "Do those stories mean her sister can't be in danger? That she isn't being held by a man who committed murder on the coast? It's very likely that she's talking about Shawn Braswell."

"Your evidence is a single phone call traced to somewhere in the gorge," said the sheriff. "You think this person killed David Dressler on the coast the day before yesterday, shot Kaden Schroeder yesterday, and now is in the Columbia Gorge somewhere with Agent McLane's sister."

"That's exactly what I think," said Ava. "At the very least, the man she is with did the shooting on the coast. The same weapon was used on Kaden Schroeder, but there's a chance it was in someone else's hands at that time. Either way we need someone in the area. I've already asked the Bend FBI office to get involved."

The sheriff looked at her for a long moment and then addressed Zander. "You go check in with the Clatsop County sheriff at the coast. Give them whatever help they need with the Dressler murder. Find out if Shawn Braswell has been in the area." His gaze went to Ava. "You go to The Dalles. Work with your counterparts. I want to know immediately if you find more leads on your sister or Braswell."

"Thank you, sir." Ava spun and headed toward the door before he could change his mind, Zander a step behind her. She sent a text to Mercy as she walked, informing her she would be on her way to The Dalles soon.

"At least I'll be working with Sheriff Greer again," said Zander when they stepped out into the late-morning sun.

"He likes you," Ava agreed. "Fewer hurdles to jump through." She reached her vehicle and opened the door. "I'll keep in touch."

"You're leaving now?" Zander asked.

"I need to go home and pack a bag in case I'm there a few days. Once I do, it'll take me about an hour and a half to get there. I want to get moving."

Her phone vibrated. Mercy replied that she was already on her way to The Dalles.

Good.

"Don't speed," said Zander.

"Hilarious." Ava sat in the driver's seat and slammed her door. Her nerves had been on edge since Jayne's phone call and now urged her to get to The Dalles as quickly as possible.

This is the right move.

She wasn't certain how she knew, but she'd never been more positive about anything in her life. Something was pulling her east.

Is that you, Jayne?

Back at the department, Mason sorted through his email on his computer. He wanted to thoroughly read the report from the firearms examiner and look at the photos on a decent-size screen instead of squinting at his phone.

The striations on the bullets found at David Dressler's murder and Kaden Schroeder's murder matched. The minuscule grooves were as specific to a gun as fingerprints were to a person.

Why these two men? What do David and Kaden have in common?

The questions had echoed in Mason's head during the entire drive back to work from the hospital. He didn't understand how Jayne fit in either. But no one understood anything Jayne did.

Her motivations were always self-centered; Mason was fully aware of that. But what would make her leave a cushy life in Costa Rica to come back to Oregon and stay under the radar?

She has something to hide.

Mason pushed a pencil into his electric sharpener and then examined the sharp tip as his thoughts wandered. Jayne's phone call to Ava was an enigma. Had her panic been real? Had she been attention seeking? Did Jayne really know who'd killed David? Why hadn't she given Ava a name?

He sharpened another pencil that didn't need it. All his pencils had perfect points, and he liked it that way. He didn't think he had OCD, but for some reason the sight of the perfect tips soothed him, and the sound and smell of the sharpener never failed to help him focus.

Ray hated the sound, but he knew that Mason was thinking hard when the sharpener started to grind. But today the answers weren't coming to him. Pieces of the puzzle were missing.

He abruptly remembered he needed to ask Gillian Wood about her timeline for the morning of Reuben's murder. Something had interrupted the abuse of Reuben's body, and it had to have been Gillian. But how had the killer left without her seeing him?

Mason looked up her number in his notes and dialed, hoping she'd made it safely to her sister's in Seattle. He opened the file of photos from the original crime scene. Specifically, Reuben Braswell's body in the bloody tub.

"Detective Callahan?" she answered.

He was pleased she'd entered his number in her contacts. "Yes, Gillian. Are you in Seattle?"

"Is everything all right?" Her voice went up an octave.

"Everything is fine," he soothed. "I have some follow-up questions for you." He clicked on a close-up of Reuben's damaged right hand.

Reuben isn't fine.

"Oh." She exhaled heavily. "I'm at my sister's house."

"Good. What I'm specifically calling about is how long you think you banged on the back door that morning after seeing the blood."

Gillian was quiet for a long second. "Why?"

"We're trying to tighten up the sequence of events that morning," Mason said smoothly. "When we first talked, you estimated you called his name and banged on the back door for thirty seconds."

"I think so."

"And then you did the same on some of the back windows."

"Yes. I couldn't see in any of them. The blinds were closed."

"What did you do after trying to get his attention through the windows?"

"I went around front and rang the bell."

"So maybe another thirty seconds between the windows and running out front?"

Gillian paused. "Was something wrong with that?"

"No, nothing's wrong. Like I said, we're working on a timeline."

She didn't say anything.

"Would you guess it was longer than thirty seconds?" Mason asked. "Shorter?"

"I didn't think it made any difference," she whispered.

Crap. What did she do?

"What difference?" he asked calmly.

"I ran back home first."

Mason briefly closed his eyes. "You didn't mention that." He continued to sound calm, though he wanted to reach through the line and shake her. "Why did you go home?"

No wonder she didn't see the killer leave.

"I knew from all that blood that something bad had happened. Reuben had told me that if something ever happened to him, I needed to get away."

"Get away where? How come?"

"I don't know. It was something he said one night . . . He was rambling on about safety. I didn't ask any questions. Most of the time I didn't understand what he was talking about."

"But you remembered that warning?"

"Yes. I didn't stay home very long that morning. I was freaked out and paced around, terrified of what could have happened. I wanted to call 911, but I was too nervous."

"But you finally did."

"I realized I should at least try the front door. If he was hurt, maybe I could help. I got up the nerve to go back and try the door. I rang the bell and then called 911."

Mason enlarged a picture of the loose fingers in the bathroom and then moved to Reuben's battered face.

How much of that abuse was he conscious for?

"How long would you estimate you were at home?"

"I know I finished a cigarette. It calmed me down."

Five minutes? Plenty of time for the killer to get out.

222

"I wish you would have told us that the first time."

"I was really nervous talking to you. I might have forgotten."

Mason doubted that. More likely she had been afraid she'd be in trouble.

He enlarged a photo of the Second Amendment and flag tattoo that filled most of Reuben's lower arm and remembered that Gillian had said he wouldn't tell her what his tattoos meant to him.

The meaning was obvious to Mason.

Tattoos. Plural.

Mason quickly clicked over to the medical examiner's report and opened the file of photos. He scanned each one, not seeing a second tattoo.

"Gillian, you told me you asked Reuben about his tattoos. What kind of tattoos did he have?"

"He had a lion's head on his shoulder and some sort of tribal tattoo that went around both his upper arms. You know . . . sorta geometric and badass looking."

In Mason's photos, Reuben's shoulders were clear.

His fingers grew icy. "No flag tattoo?"

"No. Not that I remember."

There's no way she forgot a tattoo that covers half of his arm.

"Thanks for answering my questions, I need to get back to work." His sentences ran together, his mind sprinting far ahead as he ended the call.

"The murdered man isn't Reuben Braswell," he stated out loud.

Holy shit. We fucked up.

He leaned back and stared at the ceiling as he mentally retraced their steps to identifying the body. Reuben didn't have any fingerprints on file.

The victim's face was severely damaged.

The victim's stats matched the license.

The victim's hair and eye color matched. Height and weight seemed about right.

Reuben's wallet had been in the bloody jeans. In his own home.

A forensic dental exam hadn't been done yet. The ME needed films from Reuben's dentist to compare.

I should have asked Gillian to visually identify him.

We made assumptions.

Mason dug his hands into his hair and pulled. *This isn't happening.* "Who the fuck was left in that bathtub?"

Tony Schroeder is missing.

"I talked to Schroeder on the phone," he muttered. "No, I talked to *someone* who answered his phone. *Dammit!*"

He abruptly sat up and tapped on his keyboard as he searched for Tony Schroeder's driver's license. He stared at the man's photo, comparing it to the battered face in the tub.

He couldn't rule it out. Hair, eyes, height, weight. All within reason. "Shit."

Where can I see if he has this flag tattoo?

His arrest records might mention a tattoo as an identifying mark, but it'd been years since Tony had been arrested. The tattoo could be new since then.

Facebook.

Mason grinned. The social media site had given him tons of information in past cases. He crossed his fingers in the hope that Tony had an account. Mason opened the site and immediately found him.

Tony hadn't bothered with privacy settings. Everything was visible to the public. Mason scrolled through photos until he found one of Tony and another man in swim trunks. They stood on a dock, a blue lake behind them, beers in their hands.

No tattoos.

The photo was two years old. Again, the tattoo could be recent. "Shit. Shit. Shit."

The other man in the photo had to be a brother or close relative of Tony's. They had the same posture, grin, and face shape.

A brother.

A light went on in his head.

Could the dead man be Shawn Braswell?

Nora had already checked Shawn's Facebook page to see if he'd done any recent check-ins or posts that would give a clue to his whereabouts. She had mentioned to Mason that the last post she could see was a year old and that he'd implemented privacy settings, severely limiting what was visible to the public.

Mason found Shawn's page. The only posts he could see were public ones Shawn had shared from other pages. Primarily from gun enthusiasts and Ford Mustang fans.

That fits.

No immediate photos showed his lower arms, so Mason opened up the photos page with the past profile pictures that were public and immediately zeroed in on one. Shawn sat in a lounge chair on a beach. Sunglasses, a tan, and a huge cooler. His lower right arm was covered with a flag tattoo.

Mason enlarged the photo, his heart pounding in his chest.

Bingo.

Shawn Braswell was dead. They'd been hunting for a dead man.

Where is Reuben?

He grabbed the phone to call Nora.

27

Ava barely noticed the scenery as she drove through the gorge. The Columbia River had carved it out and created some of the most stunning sights in Oregon. Mile after mile of lush landscapes and a blue river that reflected the sky. The highway threaded along the south side of the river, giving her views of Washington State across the water.

Her mind was preoccupied with Jayne. Twists and turns and questions and fear.

She almost craved the silence she'd experienced before Jayne had reappeared.

Almost. That silence was its own type of hell.

A phone call from Mason showed on her screen, and she jumped on the distraction. Earlier she'd texted him an update and her destination.

"You're not there yet, right?" Mason asked.

"No. Another fifteen minutes or so."

"You're not going to believe what I found out."

Her jaw hung open for the next sixty seconds as Mason told her about Shawn Braswell's tattoo.

"Reuben's alive," she stated. A twist of fear started in her stomach. "The courthouse shooting makes more sense now. According to the manifesto you found in his home, that shooting completely fits." The video coverage from the church popped in her mind. *That was him.*

"Mason, now I can see it was him throwing the rifle in the dumpster. His stride and bearing are completely familiar."

"We still don't know if he was working alone."

She hesitated, remembering how Zander had reacted to what she was about to tell Mason. "I told you about Reuben's flirting, but I played it down. When he saw my engagement ring, I swear he was shocked. He tried to insinuate that I was marrying the wrong man and he was the right one for me."

"You're telling me this now?"

"I thought he was dead. I didn't think it mattered."

"Ava . . . this means he was most likely the one who left the finger at our home, not Shawn. That wasn't a message to me—it was meant to intimidate *you*."

Her vision tunneled, the road ahead the only thing in her sight. "I thought he was dead," she repeated. "I had no idea . . ."

"None of us did," Mason said. "I'm furious with myself that I assumed the dead man was Reuben Braswell. I know better than that."

"I didn't question it. None of us did," Ava said. "This means he might have killed David? And Kaden? Oh my God—he's with Jayne." He'd only been on the motel and bakery videos for a few seconds, but Ava was suddenly positive she recognized him, as she had with the church video.

Or is my mind forcing the connection?

She couldn't make assumptions. There'd already been a huge one in this case.

"Would he hurt Jayne?" Mason asked.

The punch to Jayne's face played over and over in her mind. "I don't know."

"Why would he be with her? Is it to get at you somehow?"

She gripped the steering wheel, telling herself to focus on her driving. Her brain was trying to speed in a dozen different directions. "I can't guess at his motivation."

A nonanswer.

Reuben was a dangerous man. She'd felt it from the first time she'd met him, but she'd been confident it wouldn't be directed her way. She was a federal officer; he knew better than to mess with her.

Was I wrong?

He'd been upset at the end of the last meeting.

Did I trigger all this? The shootings . . . David's murder.

"Fuck that."

"What?" asked Mason.

"Nothing. Talking to myself."

"Are you all right?"

"Yes. Nothing has changed but the possible identity of who we're looking for. What does it matter if it was one brother or the other?" she lied.

I didn't know how Shawn thinks; I know how Reuben thinks.

And it wasn't good for Jayne.

"I'm going to head your way," Mason said. "The fact that we're now looking for Reuben Braswell, who might be fixated on you, makes it more likely that he is the man holding Jayne."

"Okay." *Mason is right.*

"I'll call when I'm nearly to The Dalles."

"I'll let Mercy know you're coming."

"I love you. *Be safe.*"

"I love you too. And the same goes for you."

Ava ended the call with a numb finger, stunned that Reuben was now her quarry.

Did I not take him seriously enough?

"He was wasting my time," she said out loud. It was true. She'd taken too long to decide that he had been playing with her and the FBI. She couldn't have guessed that part of the reason he'd met with her was personal. She'd believed he was just another guy who felt the need to hit on her. She'd believed it didn't mean anything; it happened all the time.

But this time it meant something.

Assuming Reuben was behind the murders.

It rang true in her gut, but she would keep her mind open to other possibilities. She'd been wrong before.

Her phone buzzed again. Mercy.

"I'm almost there," Ava said as a greeting.

"Ava, I'm already in The Dalles and was just notified that there is a man holding a woman hostage with a knife to her neck here."

Fear lit up her brain like a firework. *"What?"*

"Does this sound like something he'd do?"

Jayne collapsing to her knees flashed in Ava's memory. "Yes. He can be violent. And we know Jayne has been the recipient of that violence."

"That was my conclusion as well. We don't have any names yet. According to the officer I talked to, they're at an RV park across the river. Take the 197 bridge and it's on the west side, not far into Washington. I'll meet you there."

"I'll be there in fifteen minutes." Ava pressed the accelerator. "Sooner than that."

Eleven minutes later, Ava spotted a tall bridge with tan trusses. She took the exit and headed north toward Washington, crossing over the blue water. The lush landscape had turned a summer-toasted brown as she got closer to The Dalles. Now, as she drove on the Washington side, green trees were few and far between. Everything looked very, very dry.

Within a minute she saw flashing lights ahead on her left. A half dozen police cars were at the entrance to the RV park. As she pulled closer, she spotted Mercy. The tall, dark-haired woman in jeans and boots looked out of place among the uniformed deputies. She wore a ballistic vest with FBI emblazoned on the back and front.

Is this her day off?

Ava parked and grabbed her own vest as Mercy approached, a deputy walking beside her. She introduced him to Ava.

"Do you have an identification yet?" Ava asked, strapping on the vest. It was tight against her pounding heart.

"Not yet," said the deputy. "The manager says he doesn't recognize them and assumed they were visiting a friend. He called it in as a domestic dispute because the man was beating on the woman. By the time our first car arrived, he had a knife at her throat and yelled at them to leave."

"Where are they?" asked Ava, following the two toward the huddle of vehicles. A woman shouted in the distance, but Ava couldn't see her.

"Behind that second RV," Mercy said, pointing beyond the police vehicles. "I got a glimpse of him a few minutes ago. Tall. Dark hair. I couldn't see her."

"She's dark-haired too," the deputy added. "She's been screaming up a storm, calling him every name in the book. I don't think he's hurt her yet."

Ava didn't agree with the deputy's assessment. The woman had been hurt; it just hadn't stopped her shouts.

I can't tell if that's Jayne's voice.

"Has anyone communicated with him?" asked Ava. She eyed the group of officers, wondering if they'd had hostage-negotiation training.

"No. We've tried, but he's not responding. We've got two deputies around back with beanbag rounds and Tasers."

"Keep trying to talk to him before going that route."

"You okay?" Mercy asked in a low voice. "You look exhausted."

"It's been a long couple of days." Ava kept her gaze on the second trailer. "Mason called me with an interesting update." She told Mercy the details about Reuben Braswell not being dead.

"That's a big screwup on someone's part," Mercy said.

"Mason's blaming himself, but it does lend more strength to the idea that he's the one with Jayne."

Mercy narrowed her eyes. "Why?"

Ava explained about her dealings with Reuben.

"What an ass."

"Hold on, hold on!" Several shouts went up from the group of offi-cers. The dark-haired man had stumbled out from behind the RV and bent over in pain. He dropped a knife into the dust.

Who shot him?

His hands clasped his crotch, and he retched repeatedly.

He wasn't shot. She nailed him in the groin.

"Ouch," Mercy said as the deputy beside them flinched and looked away.

A woman appeared. Her T-shirt was torn, and red marks showed on her legs, but she stood tall, her gaze fastened on the man in pain.

Not Jayne.

The woman strode forward and shoved the man, pushing him to his knees. *"Fucking asshole,"* she shrieked at him. Six deputies immediately surrounded them.

Ava's heart dropped, glad that it wasn't Jayne who had been assaulted but also disappointed it wasn't her. "That's not her," she whispered to Mercy.

Ava turned away, frustration burning in her veins. *Now what?*

Back to their original plan. Starting with showing Jayne's photo at motels in the area.

How long will this take?

"I'm sorry, Ava," said Mercy. "We'll find her." The two women walked to their vehicles. "Let's get some food and regroup. There's a good place east of town. We can map out our strategy there."

Ava forced a smile. The letdown of the last minutes had obliterated any hunger. "You're on."

28

At the diner, Ava paid the check. She'd snatched it out from under Mercy's hand as the server set it on the table.

"You're right," she said to Mercy. "I needed that."

"Comfort food."

The women had divided up a list of local hotels. They had flyers featuring Jayne's pregnant image from one of the videos and the picture from her driver's license—revoked driver's license. Jayne had lost it years ago for drunk driving. The photo was older, but at least her hair was the right color. Ava had suggested a photo of herself, but Mercy said that the driver's license photo would do. Ava didn't have photos of Jayne on her phone.

When would I have taken a picture?

Her sister had been always in motion, moving from one town to the next, one boyfriend to the next. They didn't have family get-togethers where everyone posed on the stairs. No birthday parties with goofy selfies and big smiles.

That had never been Ava's life.

The two women were leaving the diner when Ava's phone rang. She halted. "It's Jayne." Ava stared at the screen. The call was from Jayne's phone. The one Ava had checked on her locator app multiple times since she first knew Jayne was missing. The app had never been able to locate her, and Ava's calls went to voice mail.

Jayne had turned her phone back on.

"Jayne?" Ava answered, her heart in her throat. "Where are you?"

"Ava?" Jayne whispered. "I don't know where I am." Her voice quivered.

"Hang on a second." Ava put the call on speaker and opened the locator app. She held her breath as it searched for Jayne.

It found her. Six miles away.

Ava showed the screen to Mercy, who nodded and gestured to her car. Both women broke into a run. "Are you okay?" Ava asked.

"I'm scared," Jayne whispered. "He's furious right now—but not with me this time."

"Jayne, I'm coming to get you. I'm only a couple miles away. Are you in a house?" Ava slid into the passenger seat of Mercy's SUV. Gravel scattered as Mercy flew out of the parking lot.

"Yes, it's a house."

Ava zoomed in on her screen. The satellite imagery showed only trees where Jayne was located. *Shit. Is it wrong?* She tapped her screen to give directions to Jayne's location.

"Can you get outside?" Ava asked.

"No. One of my hands is tied to a post inside."

Jesus.

"He's yelling at another guy. I think he hit him."

"If you can get out, is there another home you can run to?"

"No. There's nothing else here but trees. It's more like a cabin."

That made sense, given the trees Ava had seen on the map. "Take the next right," she told Mercy. "Jayne, who tied you up?"

"Cliff did."

Cliff?

"Is Reuben Braswell there?"

"Who? Is that the other guy?"

Maybe.

It didn't matter who she was with—he was a threat.

233

"Ava, if he learns I found my phone and—"

"I want you to hang up and call 911," Ava ordered. "They'll lock on to your location. Tell them everything—"

"No! No police!"

Mercy swore under her breath and used her console to dial 911.

"Jayne," Ava said firmly, "you are with a dangerous man. We need the police."

"He'll kill me," she whispered.

"Do it now. I'm hanging up, Jayne. I've got directions to your location, so I want you to dial 911 from your phone right now. We're calling them too. I'll make sure they send plenty of help so you're safe."

The call abruptly ended.

"Dammit!" *Did he find her?*

Ava clutched her phone in her hand, staring at the location showing Jayne's icon, willing it not to disappear. If the icon vanished, it would mean someone had turned off her phone, and it probably wouldn't have been Jayne.

Carefully setting her phone on the dashboard, Ava half listened to Mercy tell the 911 dispatcher that Jayne was being held by someone who was armed and very dangerous. She removed her Glock from her bag's special pouch and slid an extra magazine in her pants pocket.

What are we walking into?

The dispatcher stated someone else was currently taking Jayne's call and that they had her location.

Good.

"Jayne said he's arguing with someone," Ava told Mercy and the dispatcher. "Another man. I got the impression that no one else is there, but I can't be positive." She glanced at Mercy. "She said the man holding her is Cliff."

"What? It's not Reuben Braswell?"

"She didn't recognize that name. He could be lying to her."

"Shit."

"Whoever it is has harmed her, and she's terrified. Our plan is still the same." She told Mercy to take another turn, and they headed up a steep hill. "I think we need to park down the road from her location and go in on foot."

"We'll wait for backup."

"Yes, but I want to get within visual. I think we'll have good cover with the trees."

"Agreed."

Ava studied the map and told Mercy to pull over. The road had turned to dirt after the first mile, but they were nearly upon Jayne's icon. Mercy parked at the edge of the gravel road, and Jayne's icon vanished. Ava gasped, her lungs suddenly tight.

"She's gone!"

"What do you mean?" Mercy asked.

"Her phone turned off. I doubt she did it herself. Dammit!"

"We're close, though, right?"

"I think it's just up this road." She hopped out of the SUV. "Do you have another vest?" She'd left the one she'd worn earlier in her vehicle.

Mercy blanched. "I don't. Take mine."

"No. You wear it. We don't have time to argue about it."

Mercy clearly wanted to argue but didn't. She opened the back of her SUV and pulled on her vest. "Wear my jacket. At least it will tell our backup who you are."

Ava slipped on the light windbreaker and instantly started to sweat. It was nearing ninety and there was no breeze.

"Jayne would never go through this sort of effort for you," Mercy stated.

"I know. It doesn't matter."

"You're risking your life for someone who could care less about you."

"It doesn't matter," Ava repeated. She knew her twin cared about her on some level, and although Mercy was correct that Jayne would never lift a finger to help her, it made no difference to Ava.

This is who I am.

The area was silent and smelled like sunbaked dirt. Mercy checked her weapon, and the women jogged up the road. Mercy informed the dispatcher of their movements and intent to get a visual on the cabin.

"There," whispered Ava. A section of pine-needle-covered roof showed through the trees. The women immediately moved off the road. It wasn't a heavily wooded area with huge firs. Most of the trees were smaller pines, too thin to completely hide behind, but the scrub brush was thick and dense.

They froze as yelling filled the air.

Two men. Just as Jayne had said.

They exchanged a look of resolve and continued to move closer, their weapons ready. Ava keenly felt the loss of her vest, but their plan was to stay back at a safe distance.

More of the cabin came into view. A Dodge Durango truck was parked in front along with the silver Mustang, its dark-tinted windows covered with a fine layer of road dust.

Reuben has to be here.

Between the Mustang and the cabin, two men were brawling. Full-fledged punches to the face and powerful kicks to the legs. One lunged and caught the other in a headlock, and both fell to the ground, blocked from Ava's view by the silver car. The men swore and cursed at each other.

Ava and Mercy carefully moved left among the trees to try to see around the car as Ava scanned the cabin area for any sign of Jayne.

Where are you?

A dust cloud formed where the men wrestled on the ground, shoving each other's faces into the dirt and still flinging punches. One lurched to his feet and kicked the other. Ava got a clear view of the kicker's face over the hood of the car.

Reuben Braswell.

The Mustang's driver's door was wide open, the seat tipped forward toward the steering wheel as if someone had recently climbed out. Reuben slammed the other man's head against the front fender. The man moaned and disappeared behind the car as he sank to the ground. Reuben staggered backward a few steps and then veered toward the open door.

He's leaving.

Ava took three steps closer, ignoring Mercy's hiss to stay back.

"No! I'm not going!" Jayne's shout filled the clearing, and she lunged out from the back seat of the car. Ava halted, stunned at her sister's sudden appearance.

Jayne's hands were tied at the wrists, and blood ran from a cut near her eye. Ava couldn't see lower than her chest because of the car, but her movements indicated her legs weren't tied. She plowed into Reuben, pushing him aside, but he neatly caught her with an arm around her waist.

"Back in the car!"

Jayne shrieked and bucked against his arm. He bent into the Mustang near the driver's seat, Jayne still trapped against him. As he straightened, Ava caught a glimpse of a pistol in his other hand.

It was in the car.

Ava raised her weapon another inch, but the Mustang was in the way, and Jayne was thrashing in his arms.

No shot.

Reuben turned toward the front of his car, his upper arm moved forward, and the crack of his shot filled the air.

The man on the ground screamed, and Jayne's shriek erupted a split second later. Ava looked to Mercy, who had moved ten feet forward and to her left, but the woman shook her head. Neither had a shot with Jayne tight against Reuben's torso.

Jayne swung her bound hands over her shoulder at Reuben's face as she continued to kick and scream. He slammed the butt of the pistol against her head, but she didn't stop fighting.

Ava stepped closer. *I have to do something.*

Jayne suddenly went limp, using her weight to throw him off-balance. Reuben floundered forward a step and wrapped his other arm around her.

Another shot cracked, and Jayne's howl of pain turned Ava's blood to ice.

She's shot!

Reuben flung her into the back seat and shoved the driver's seat back into position.

"Stop!" Ava shouted. "Federal agents."

He glanced her way and dropped into the front seat, slamming the door closed and starting the engine. The tires spun as he floored the gas pedal, and the car leaped forward. It turned onto the road, speeding away in the opposite direction from where Ava and Mercy had just come.

Fury rushed through Ava. She could shoot at the rear window, but Jayne was in there somewhere, still screaming at the top of her lungs.

No shot.

The throaty roar of the engine sounded, and the car disappeared around a bend.

"Let's go," she shouted at Mercy. *Her vehicle, now.*

But Mercy knelt by the man on the ground, pressing her hands against his bleeding chest. "Give me your jacket!"

I've got to go after Jayne.

Ava froze, torn between running to their vehicle and helping. "Dammit!" She ripped off the windbreaker, balled it up, and pressed it against the wound, kneeling beside Mercy.

"I've got a kit in my vehicle." Mercy pushed to her feet and dashed toward the road.

Ava pressed harder and the man moaned.

Reuben's getting away. How badly was Jayne hurt?

"Hey!" She caught the man's painful gaze. "You're going to be okay. What's your name?"

"Fuck off." He groaned and tried to roll to his side.

A large exit wound high on his back, near his shoulder, bled freely. She pushed him flat on his back.

"You've been shot, you idiot. Hold still."

"I'm going to kill him!"

Not if he killed you first.

The FBI windbreaker wasn't absorbent, and the blood soaked Ava's hands. *Hurry up, Mercy.* She took the man's fury and fight to be good signs, but there was still too much blood.

Far-off sirens sounded.

Thank God.

"What's your name?" she asked again.

"Tony," he said through gritted teeth.

Tony Schroeder?

"Are you Kaden's dad?"

Surprise flared in his eyes, and Ava took that as a yes.

"Why were you fighting with Reuben Braswell?"

His eyes clenched shut, and he groaned. "That fucker."

"Did he shoot your son?"

Tony's eyes startled open. "You knew?" He shuddered, and his face contorted in agony.

"We suspected. Why'd he do it?"

"I hadn't gotten him his money yet," Tony slurred, his voice heavy with pain.

"Money for what?"

The man screwed his eyes closed as his legs convulsed. "Guns."

Ava remembered the stash of weapons under Kaden's bed. *Reuben killed a boy because of his father's debt?*

"How'd you find Reuben?"

"My cabin," Tony forced out between clenched teeth. "Loaned it to him a few times. Thought he might hide here."

Mercy's SUV stopped a few feet away from Tony's head. She leaped out and dashed to the rear, where she grabbed a large kit. Dropping to her knees beside Ava, she lifted the windbreaker and peered at the wound. Blood seeped steadily from the small hole but didn't spurt.

"Exit wound?" she asked.

Ava indicated the back side of his shoulder. Mercy took a quick look. "Shit," she murmured, "I called 911. Told them about the Mustang and asked for an ambulance." She turned to dig in her kit, and Ava watched her work. Mercy had field talents that no other agents had. She had been raised in a survivalist and prepper family, and there wasn't much that Mercy didn't know how to do. Emergency medical care was the tip of the iceberg.

Mercy ripped open a silver package to reveal a large syringe that appeared to be full of small tablets. "Roll him to his side." Ava supported him as Mercy pushed the wide tip into the exit wound and pressed the plunger.

Tony screamed.

"What is that?" Ava asked.

"Sterile sponges made from crustacean shells. They'll expand and clot."

"I've heard of that," Ava said. Mercy layered gauze packs over the wound and secured it with tape. Then she ripped open another and did the same thing on the entrance wound.

The sirens were nearly on top of them. Two vehicles came to a rapid stop, and car doors slammed.

"The Mustang?" Ava asked as one of the deputies slipped on vinyl gloves and then checked Mercy's dressing. Ava sat hard on the ground, out of the deputy's way, her adrenaline rush gone.

"Two other units en route. They'll intercept him at the other end of the road."

"Good." Drenched in sweat, she wiped her forehead on her shoulder, and something on the ground far to her left caught her eye. Blood, a lot of blood.

She looked at Tony, trying to understand how his blood had landed five feet away.

It's Jayne's.

"Mercy." Ava pointed at the blood, unable to speak. Mercy scowled at it, and then her face cleared.

"That has to be Jayne's blood."

"She's pregnant," Ava whispered, her adrenaline spiking again.

Sympathy flowed from Mercy's gaze. "I know. Don't worry. We'll find her in time."

I hope so.

29

Mason was ten minutes from The Dalles exit off the highway when Ava called.

"We found Jayne." Ava's speech was high and fast. "But Reuben got away with her. He shot her, Mason. I don't know how bad, but she left a lot of blood behind."

"Slow down," Mason ordered. "What happened?"

Ava's story made his jaw drop several times.

"They haven't caught up with him yet?"

"They lost him." Anger rang in her voice. "They've got every Wasco County deputy hunting for the Mustang, and I'm searching on the highway west of The Dalles. Jayne didn't look good, Mason. He'd tied her hands together, and she had a big cut on her face, and now who knows how bad she's wounded?"

"I'm so sorry, Ava. I'm sure they'll spot him." He crossed his fingers in the hope that Jayne wasn't badly hurt. He didn't know how Ava would handle it if Jayne was killed when she had been so close to getting her twin away from Reuben.

Ava would blame herself.

"Reuben killed Kaden," she said. "Tony owed him money for guns. I assume the ones you found."

"Reuben murdered Kaden because of a few guns?" Mason nearly steered into another car.

"I know. *It's horrible.* Tony said he's lent this cabin to Reuben before and decided to check if he was hiding here. I think these men were originally friends."

"That's a twisted friendship when you murder your friend's son over a debt."

"There has to be more to it than that. Reuben returned to the scene of the original crime when he killed Kaden. He had to have a powerful motivation to do that."

"Maybe Kaden knew something about the courthouse shooting," Mason said.

"That seems most likely."

His phone beeped. "I've got another call. I'll see you in ten minutes or so."

"Love you."

"Love you too." Mason switched over to the other call. "Callahan."

"Detective Callahan?" a female voice whispered.

He frowned. "Yes. Who's this?"

"Veronica Lloyd."

Mason's pulse stuttered. *Reuben's sister.*

Moaning and sobbing sounded in the call's background.

"What happened?"

"Reuben's not dead." Her voice cracked. "He just showed up at my house, and he's got a gun." Terror filled her tone. "I don't know what he's going to do."

"I just passed your exit!" Mason slowed on the busy four-lane high-way. A concrete divider kept him from pulling a U-turn, and The Dalles was the next exit, which was miles away. "Did you call 911?"

"Yes, we're covered by the county sheriff's department here. Sometimes it can take twenty minutes for them to arrive." Her voice quivered. "He brought a woman with him and she's hurt. She's bleeding all over the place." More moans rumbled.

Jayne.

"Are your kids there?" An image of Veronica's two young girls popped into his head.

"Yes. I shut them in the playroom and ordered them not to open the door. They're petrified. Reuben thinks they're at a friend's."

Ahead, Mason spotted a gap in the concrete divider, probably for police and emergency services to reverse direction. He pulled onto the shoulder and steered through the gap, his speed far too high for safety. He merged onto the highway, stomped on his accelerator, and received an angry horn blast from a semi.

"I'm headed back your way. Where is Reuben now?"

"He's upstairs grabbing towels. This woman is really bleeding. *I think he shot her!*" she exclaimed in a hushed voice.

"Are you in danger? Did he threaten you?" His knuckles turned white as he gripped the steering wheel.

"I don't know. He said he needs my minivan, but he's trying to stop her bleeding first."

"She's inside your house?"

"On the floor in the kitchen. I'm putting pressure on her thigh. She looks really bad—there's blood everywhere." Veronica gasped. "Are you pregnant?" she asked in a surprised voice.

Mason couldn't hear Jayne's answer. He took the Mosier exit, thankful there wasn't a light or stop sign to deal with. *How badly is Jayne injured?*

"He's coming back!"

The call ended, but Mason was less than a half mile from Veronica's house. Long seconds later he slowly drove by the home. A burgundy minivan was parked under the attached carport on the east side of the home, and once he'd passed the home, he spotted the tail end of the Mustang behind the house. It'd been driven over the grass and around to the back.

Reuben is still here.

Mason turned around and parked at the curb across the street. He sent Ava a text with an update and Veronica's address. He took a picture of the home and sent that too.

The return text was three letters.

OMW

On my way.

If Ava was already on the highway, she might arrive sooner than the Wasco County deputies.

How long can Jayne wait?

"Dammit!" He stepped out of his vehicle, dashed across the street, and ducked behind a large rhododendron outside the white picket fence. Jayne was in the kitchen, so Reuben must be too. He tried to remember the layout of the home. The kitchen was in the back with large windows overlooking the yard.

Wait for backup.

He checked his weapon. "What if she's bleeding out?" he muttered. No sirens could be heard; backup might be crucial minutes away. He was on his own for now.

Staying low, he followed the white fence until he was closer to the home. He awkwardly stepped over the fence and was jabbed in the thigh by its pointed pickets. Darting to the west wall of the home, he kept his head down, avoiding the few windows. He guessed they were bedrooms since the kitchen and main living area were on the other end of the house, but he wasn't taking any chances. His goal was the back side of the house, where he hoped to find a protected view of the kitchen.

Immediately ahead were three narrow concrete steps that led up to a single door with a half window.

He couldn't guess what was on the other side of the older house's door. *A utility room? A family room?* He stopped, his back to the siding as he contemplated the best way to avoid being seen from the door's window. While he thought, the door opened a few inches and he froze, holding his breath.

"Don't go out!" a child said from inside.

The door slammed shut and little-girl voices argued.

The girls. Veronica hid them in a playroom.

Mason holstered his weapon and removed his badge. *Will they trust me?*

He had to try. He crept toward the door and tapped softly on it, holding his badge up to the window first, keeping his face out of sight. The arguing voices went silent.

"I'm a policeman," he said quietly, his mouth close to the door. "I know there's a bad man in your house, and I've come to get you out. I talked to your mom on the phone."

The lock on the door clicked into place.

Smart girls, but that's not helping at the moment.

"Two days ago I was talking to your dad in the front yard when you came home. I had a white cowboy hat in my hand." He crossed his fingers, hoping the hat was enough to trigger a memory. "I'm going to show you my face now, okay?"

Keeping his badge still at the window, he raised his head and looked through the glass. The playroom was small, and the girls were huddled together behind a play kitchen, watching the window. The oldest scowled at him. He guessed she was about eight, the other around six.

Faint yelling sounded from inside the home.

The younger slapped her hands over her ears.

"You can trust me." *Exactly what every predator says to a child.* "Do you remember me?"

The oldest nodded, her eyes still wary.

"Good. Let's get you to a safe place. Is there a friend's house close by you can go to?"

The older said something to her little sister, who shook her head. The first girl pointed at Mason and said something else to the younger girl, who shot him a cautious glance.

It appeared he'd convinced one.

Come on.

The bigger girl stood, pulled the younger out from behind the kitchen, and moved toward the door.

Thank God.

The lock clicked, and Mason backed away, giving them space. The oldest stepped out, suspicion in her gaze. "How do I know you're a policeman? Badges can be fake."

"You're right."

"You're not wearing a uniform."

"I'm a detective. We don't wear uniforms." He was running out of ideas to persuade her. "I talked on the phone with your mom a few minutes ago. She said she'd told you to lock the door in the playroom."

The younger girl pushed her way past the older and faced him. "What's happening? Is he going to hurt Mommy?" Her eyes were terrified.

Mason held his hand out to her. "I hope not. I'm going to stop him, but first I need you two in a safe place. Let's go." He held his breath.

The youngest took his hand and came down the steps. The older hesitated.

"I need you to show me the house of a neighbor you know," he said to the older girl.

Indecision flickered, but she closed the door and came down, though she didn't take his other hand. She grabbed her sister's.

"Let's go," said Mason, relief flooding his veins. The girls led him to a gate that blended perfectly into the picket fence, and the three of them quietly sneaked out to the road. "Which house?" he asked.

"Madeline lives there." The older girl pointed across the street and two houses down. A sedan was in the driveway.

The three of them jogged toward the home. *I need to get back to Jayne.* "When you get inside, tell them the police are at your house but to stay away, okay? Have Madeline's mom call 911 again. But *do not go back to your house.*" He gave his best authoritative-father look. "I'll come get you when it's safe. Okay?"

The girls nodded, and he watched impatiently from the road until they rang the doorbell and the door opened. A woman smiled at the girls but glanced up as she realized Mason was in the street. He held up his badge for her to see, pointed at the girls, and ran back to the house, hoping the mother would clue in quickly.

Now to get Jayne and Veronica to safety.

30

Ava ended the 911 call as she sped toward Mosier.

The operator already knew that Reuben Braswell was in his sister's home and that several units from the sheriff's department were on the scene. Ava had tried Mason's number, but it had eventually dumped her into voice mail.

Is his phone on silent? Is he unable to answer?

Praying it was the first, she took the Mosier exit. As she crossed over the highway, she spotted more county patrol units not far behind her.

It'd been ten minutes since she'd talked to Mason. A lot could happen in ten minutes.

She turned onto Veronica Lloyd's street. A hundred yards in, it was blocked by Wasco County patrol cars.

Good. Where's Mason?

Ava parked and got out, scanning for him. She put on her ballistic vest, her hands stinking of bleach from the Clorox wipes she'd used to clean off Tony Schroeder's blood.

Mason's vehicle was inside the blocked-off zone. He was nowhere to be seen.

She checked her phone. Nothing from him. "Shit." She approached the deputies standing behind their cars, recognizing a deputy and a sergeant who had responded to the Braswell incident an hour ago. "Have you seen Detective Callahan?"

The men looked at one another.

"OSP detective. Cowboy boots." She pointed. "That's his car."

"We haven't seen anyone else," said the sergeant, frowning. "What's he doing here?"

"The homeowner called him. Reuben Braswell is her brother. Detective Callahan was investigating him in Portland."

"We understand Braswell is inside with an injured hostage from the shooting in The Dalles," the sergeant replied.

"I believe so. Who's your hostage negotiator?"

"She's on her way. Same with SWAT. We're trying to get Braswell on a phone to start talking."

Ava sent a text to Mason asking where he was.

A shot cracked. Ava and the deputies dropped to the ground behind the cars.

Her heartbeat pounding in her head, Ava held her breath, waiting for another shot.

"That was fired in the air to get your attention," Reuben yelled from the house. "I want safe passage out of here, or next time I will shoot both of these women!"

Jayne's okay?

"How far out is your negotiator?" she asked the sergeant as they continued to crouch behind the cars.

"Too far."

Ava considered her options. "I've done negotiating in situations like this. I've had a lot of training on it, but I'm not one officially." *Will Reuben respond negatively to me?* She suspected he could be a loose cannon. Clearly he was angry, and currently he was surrounded by the very people he hated and claimed only existed to control people like him.

She decided it was worth the chance. He'd always had a strong interest in talking to her.

"You think you can reason with him?"

"I can listen to what he has to say. That's a start."

Getting hostages to safety is always the priority in negotiations. The fact that Jayne is one won't make a difference in how I handle this.

The sergeant asked a deputy to get a bullhorn out of his car.

He handed it to Ava. She took a deep breath and stood. No one could be seen in the house. "Reuben," she started, "is Jayne okay? I know she's been injured."

There was a long pause. *Will he answer?*

"Special Agent McLane," he yelled. "I thought that was you back at the cabin."

"You know him?" asked the sergeant.

"I thought I did," said Ava.

"Are you the right person to be doing this?"

"Yes," Ava said firmly. She knew more about Reuben than anyone else there.

"Yes, that was me," she said through the bullhorn. "Is Jayne all right?"

Reuben didn't answer.

"Who else is in the house with you?" Ava asked.

"My sister."

The sergeant touched her shoulder. "911 is reporting that his sister's children are at a neighbor's. I'll send a deputy to check on them."

Ava nodded and lifted the bullhorn to her mouth. "What can we do to end things safely for Jayne and your sister?"

"Move the fuck back!"

"We can do that for you, Reuben, but I'd like you to do something for me. Jayne needs medical attention. It will look good for you if you release her so we can get her to a hospital."

"You say that as if a judge will hear about it," he yelled. "I have no intention of ever being brought before a fucking judge."

"Shit," muttered the sergeant. "He's got a death wish."

"Can you move everyone back a hundred feet or so?" Ava asked. "It'll make him feel he has some control over what is happening. Also, it will be better if he decides to shoot."

The sergeant studied the scene. "Yeah. We'll still have the house in sight."

"Reuben, we're going to move back," Ava told him. "I'd appreciate it if you let Jayne go after we do that for you."

Silence.

"Back it up," ordered the sergeant. The sheriff department's vehicles slowly moved away. Ava went with them, hating to put more distance between herself and Jayne.

A deputy approached the sergeant. "The Lloyd daughters are just fine. Shaken up, but okay. The neighbor is keeping them distracted."

"Do they know what's going on?" Ava asked.

"They do," said the deputy. "Their mother ordered them to lock themselves in a playroom and not come out. Said they could hear a man yelling and someone crying. But then a policeman in cowboy boots got them out the back door."

Mason.

"That's Detective Callahan," said Ava, tension and relief battling for control of her limbs. She checked her phone. He hadn't responded to her text. "Where'd he go?"

"The neighbor said he ran back to the house. This was before any squad cars arrived."

"I suspect he's unwilling to leave his location," Ava said. "Either he can't, or he's got good eyes on the situation. Get his description to everyone. Let them know there's a plainclothes officer on the scene. Tall, salt-and-pepper hair, jeans, cowboy boots."

"No white hat?" asked the sergeant in a joking manner.

"Not in a situation like this," Ava replied in all seriousness. She lifted the bullhorn again. "Okay, Reuben, we've given you some space. Let Jayne go so we can help her."

Her eyes continually scanned the home, looking for any movement.

"Stay back," yelled Reuben. "I don't want to see anyone walking toward the house!"

Will he let her go?

"There!" said the sergeant a long moment later. "The door in the carport."

Ava stared, willing Jayne to appear.

A dark-haired woman stepped out. Her shorts and hands were bloody.

Ava's knees weakened.

Not Jayne.

"That's the sister," she told the sergeant.

Veronica Lloyd was barefoot. She walked a few steps, looked at the house over her shoulder, and stopped. She turned her back to the police and appeared to be talking to someone.

Come on. Don't stop.

Veronica took a few backward steps and then spun around and ran toward the police-car blockade. Her eyes were wide, her face wet.

"My kids," she cried as the sergeant stepped out to her. "My girls are still in the house."

"We got them out," the sergeant told her. "They're at a neighbor's."

Veronica quaked and nearly collapsed, but the sergeant grabbed her. "Are you sure? I need to see them. Right now." Her legs continued to shake. A deputy brought a thin silver blanket and wrapped it around her shoulders.

"Are you hurt?" he asked.

She shook her head. "Not my blood."

"I'm going to let this deputy get you cleaned up," the sergeant told her. "And then he'll take you to your girls."

"Wait," said Ava, grabbing Veronica's arm. "Is Jayne okay? Why didn't he send her out?"

Veronica studied her for a split second. "You're the twin."

"What's she talking about?" asked the sergeant. He looked from Veronica to Ava, suspicion dawning in his eyes.

"Jayne is my twin." She calmly held his gaze.

"*He's holding your twin hostage?* Why didn't you mention that?" He turned to a deputy. "Get an ETA on our hostage negotiator."

"I've formed a connection with Reuben," said Ava. "I got him to let Veronica out. Even your own negotiator will tell you to stick with me."

Indecision flashed on his face.

"I know what I'm doing," she told him.

"Let's hope so. Anything else you need to tell me in addition to knowing both people inside?"

"Detective Callahan is my fiancé."

The sergeant was shocked. "And has disappeared," he said.

Ava refused to worry about Mason. *He's a good cop. He can handle himself.*

"Reuben only mentioned two women," replied Ava. "If he's unaware of Detective Callahan, he must be somewhere safe." She turned to Veronica. "Why didn't he send out Jayne too?"

"He seems fixated on her," Veronica said slowly. She eyed Ava. "And you."

Shit.

"Is she all right?"

"The bleeding slowed down. She's in a lot of pain. It can't be good for the baby."

"She's pregnant?" muttered the sergeant.

"Is he worried about her medical condition at all?" Ava asked.

"Very worried," said Veronica.

"Why won't he let us help her, then?" *There really is a baby.* She kept her thoughts calm. This information didn't change the current situation. *But a baby does give me something to pressure him with.*

"I think he believes he can handle it. He's going to try to get her in the minivan," Veronica added.

"She'll slow him down. That doesn't make sense."

"As if this guy is thinking logically," the sergeant pointed out.

"Ava!" Mercy jogged up. "What a mess."

Ava quickly gave her an update and then lifted the bullhorn. "Reuben. Thank you for letting Veronica out," Ava said. "Would you let Jayne out now? We have concerns about the baby."

No answer.

"Will you be able to get Jayne medical care?" she asked him. "Let us help her, and then I'll see what can be done for you."

"I know you had me followed after our meetings," Reuben yelled. "Why should I trust you?"

"I'm sorry you felt that way," said Ava, "but I didn't. When a meeting ended, it was over. I went back to work, and no one else was there to follow you."

"You cops are all talk. You say you'll help and then you don't."

"I'll see that Jayne gets help," Ava told him. "She's my sister."

"She's told me how you've ignored her and pushed her away over the years."

Ava bit her tongue. *He's trying to get a reaction out of me.* "Right now I'll do anything to help her and my niece or nephew. Let me see her at least."

I'm going to be an aunt.

It didn't feel real.

"I'll let her go, but you have to come get her. She can't walk on her own," Reuben hollered. "And it has to be you, Ava. No one else."

"No," said the sergeant. "Absolutely not."

"Why me?" Ava asked Reuben.

"Because that's the deal. Leave your gun behind."

Is it a trap?

She didn't think he would hurt her. He'd portrayed her in a good light while raining anger on all other law enforcement in his notes. He hadn't purposefully injured Jayne, and according to Veronica was very concerned about her twin's condition.

But she'd been wrong before.

She went with her gut.

"Okay. I'll come get her."

Ava set down the bullhorn and handed her weapon to Mercy.

"Are you crazy?" Mercy whispered. "He's going to kill you."

"I don't think so," said Ava. "His sister says he's worried about Jayne. I think that extends to me."

Or is it vice versa?

"Wait," said the sergeant.

Ava ignored him and worked her way around the police cars. The house seemed miles away.

I can do this.

31

Mason flinched as Reuben demanded Ava come get Jayne.

She knows better than that. Nice try.

He crouched under a kitchen window in the backyard. It was a sort of mini greenhouse that extended outside beyond the home's wall. It was stocked with herbs on glass shelves and provided good cover from above. None of the windows on the back of the house were useful for viewing the situation inside, but several were open, and he could hear most of the conversations.

Reuben had asked about his nieces, and Veronica had lied, saying that they were at a friend's home. His reply had been, "Good. They shouldn't see this."

Mason estimated Veronica had been reunited with her girls by now.

Reuben was stressed. He had yelled at his sister before letting her go and constantly complained about the police presence outside. Over and over he'd said he needed to leave the state, and he paced nonstop in the kitchen. He sounded exactly like the antigovernment websites. He believed the cops outside were there to dominate and control a working man like him. The only good thing Mason heard was that he was troubled by Jayne's injuries. Veronica had pleaded with him to let Jayne get medical help, but he kept repeating that he could handle it.

His tone didn't sound so certain.

Reuben was falling apart. If the police could just wait him out, Mason thought it could end without violence.

Through the bullhorn, Ava announced she'd come get Jayne.

Shock filled him. *Is she crazy?*

He checked his phone. He had missed texts and calls from Ava. His sound was off because he'd worried someone inside would hear. He replied to her texts, telling her he was at the back of the house and could hear Reuben talking and to not come get Jayne.

He waited. She didn't respond.

No. No. No.

Inside, Reuben told Jayne that Ava was in for a surprise if she tried to trick him. Jayne didn't reply. She'd been quiet for several minutes, making Mason wonder if she had lost too much blood.

"Get up," Reuben ordered.

Jayne's answering moan made the hair on Mason's neck stand up. *She's in bad shape.*

Some grunts and scuffles told him that Reuben was helping her to her feet.

How will she walk?

Mason crept to the sliding glass door and risked a look inside. Reuben's back was to him as he supported Jayne against his front with an arm around her chest. He had a pistol tucked in the back of his jeans. Mason could do nothing until Jayne was out of the way.

Maybe once he lets her go?

If he truly plans to let her go.

Ava knew a half dozen officers' rifles were trained on the house as she approached. If Reuben stepped out, there was a good chance the cop killer would be shot.

He must know this.

She walked up the drive toward the carport, holding her arms away from her body, so Reuben could see she wasn't armed. An odd calm had taken over her senses. She was highly aware of every movement before her, but her heartbeat had slowed, and her tension was gone.

Her head was clear, focused on her goal of getting Jayne safely away.

Reuben might shoot me. The alarming thought tumbled into her brain, and she smoothly pushed it away.

Calm.

Something moved at the door inside the carport. The door had cracked open, but she couldn't tell if it was Reuben or Jayne standing at the gap.

The door fully opened.

Jayne.

Blood covered her twin's leg, and it pasted her short sundress to her skin, highlighting the small bump of her abdomen. Reuben's arm clasped her to the front of his body, and he watched Ava over Jayne's shoulder as they awkwardly stepped from the home.

No one has a shot with Jayne in front of him.

The cinder-block back wall of the carport obstructed any view of Reuben from behind.

Ava halted twenty feet from the couple, her ballistic vest hot and heavy in the sun. The vest gave her no confidence. At this distance Reuben could easily shoot her in the head.

"No, Ava." Jayne shook her head at her. "Go back. Don't do this."

Does she know his plan?

"Can you walk?" she asked Jayne.

"Sort of. Not far."

Ava took another step closer, concentrating on Reuben's eyes and hands, hoping he'd project any sudden moves before he took them.

"Let her go," she told him.

His gaze bored into hers. "I was nice to you, but you just used me at our meetings," he spit out.

Isn't that what a confidential informant signs on for? "I'm sorry you feel that way."

"We had a connection."

Speak carefully. "I was trying to help you—help your friend with the domestic abuse situation. Anyone would have been concerned."

Resentment shone in his eyes. "Now you're like everyone else. Especially them." He jerked his head toward the show of police down the street. "They have no intention of letting me pass, do they?"

"I don't know the exact plan. But turning yourself—"

"Don't even say it!"

"Can you let Jayne go now? She needs medical help."

"Don't tell me what to do!"

Ava stayed silent.

Jayne was pale, nervously licking her lips over and over, and her injured leg quivered from her weight. Ava sent a silent message of support through her eyes.

I'll get you out of this.

Reuben dropped his arm from Jayne's chest and shoved her at Ava. Jayne stumbled forward several steps, whimpering, her legs shaking. Ava rushed to grab her, and she clutched her twin chest to chest, planting her feet as Jayne's weight threatened to knock her over.

Ava glanced over Jayne's shoulder. Reuben stood in the doorway, his expression vacillating between yearning and anger and indecision.

She shifted to Jayne's side and tucked her shoulder under Jayne's, drawing her sister's arm over her shoulders and keeping her upright. "It's not far," she promised as Jayne struggled to balance.

They took a few steps, Ava bearing most of Jayne's weight. Panting, Jayne stopped and looked back at Reuben. Her entire body tensed.

"Ava, get down!" she shrieked.

Jayne lurched into Ava and shoved her aside as a shot cracked.

Her twin's body jerked, and a warm spray covered Ava's face. *She's shot.* Jayne collapsed, pulling Ava to the concrete with her weight.

He'd barely stepped inside the house when Mason saw Reuben lift his arm toward Ava and Jayne. Time slowed, and Reuben seemed to move frame by frame, the pistol in his hand coming into clear view. Mason stilled as he aimed in Reuben's direction.

The women are in my line of fire.

Reuben fired, and the women went down.

Now!

Mason smoothly pulled his trigger three times. The blows knocked Reuben onto his stomach. Beyond him, Jayne and Ava thrashed on the carport floor, blood covering both of them.

I'm too late.

He ran through the kitchen but stepped cautiously around Reuben's prone figure, kicking the unmoving man's weapon across the carport.

Ava had flung herself over Jayne and was frantically running her hands over her sister's body, trying to find the source of the blood.

Jayne shuddered. "I'm so sorry. I'm so sorry." Tears flowed from her eyes.

"Shut up," Ava ordered. *"I need a medic!"* she shouted at the roadblock.

Mason knelt beside Ava and removed his shirt, wadding it into a ball. "Use this." Blood oozed from an exit wound near Jayne's collarbone.

Ava pressed the shirt against the blood. "She pushed me out of the way," Ava told him, panic garbling her words. "Reuben aimed at me, and *she stepped in front of it.*"

"I saw," said Mason. "The two of you fell and gave me a clear shot. I wouldn't have been able to shoot until that moment without possibly hitting one of you."

"You're going to be okay," Ava said fiercely to her sister. "I swear it."

Jayne smiled faintly. "You always take care of me."

"You did it this time."

Jayne closed her eyes. "It hurts," she whispered.

Ava's face went white. "You're going to be okay," she repeated.

Mason prayed she was right.

Three days later

The luxury home was familiar to Ava. Brady Shurr's parents' home was on Pete's Mountain, south of Portland. It sat on a five-acre lot that overlooked a vineyard and had a perfect view of the Cascades. She leaned closer to Mason. "This house was in the Street of Dreams a few years ago," Ava said, remembering the big local event that featured a tour of new luxury homes.

"Hard to forget that infinity pool," Mason replied.

They sat in a high-ceilinged family room, waiting for Jayne and Brady to return from the kitchen. Jayne had spent two nights in the hospital, and now she and Brady were staying in his parents' home while his mom and dad were in Germany for a month.

Reuben Braswell was dead. Mason was on leave, waiting to have his shooting reviewed. Ava had no doubts about the outcome. Reuben had shot Jayne and would have shot more if Mason hadn't sneaked into the home behind him.

Ava had picked up bits and pieces of the days leading up to the shooting as she talked with Jayne in the hospital. Jayne had tearfully confessed that Reuben made her call and cancel the winery wedding venue. The more Jayne had talked, the more Ava had realized that she had been correct that Reuben had harbored a fixation on her. And it had extended to her twin as well.

Jayne and Brady entered. Jayne on crutches and Brady carrying a tray with coffee. He set the tray on an end table near Ava and immediately helped Jayne get settled, sliding an ottoman under her injured leg. Jayne's baby bump seemed to have grown in the last few days. She had told Ava she was five months along.

The tender look on Brady's face made Ava's heart melt. *He really does love her.* Jayne's smile and eyes returned the affection.

Ava wondered how long it would last. Reuben Braswell had turned Jayne's head in Costa Rica, persuading her to take a trip with him.

How Brady had forgiven Jayne was beyond Ava's understanding.

But how many times have I forgiven her?

She's my twin. He can walk away. Something won't let me.

Ava handed a cup of coffee to Mason, who cleared his throat before speaking. "I don't know if you want to be around for this conversation, Brady." He, too, had been baffled by the young man's acceptance of Jayne's behavior.

"I've already heard it all," Brady said. "Jayne's told me everything. There is no chance that she would leave again."

Ava wanted to shake him.

Mason sighed. "If you say so." He turned to Jayne. "When did you first meet Reuben?"

"I knew him as Cliff, but it was a few weeks ago. He came up and talked to me at a local bar." She glanced at Ava. "He first mistook me for you. He told me he knew you."

Ava had already heard this from Jayne and had decided Reuben had said it as a ruse to approach her twin. No doubt it had been easy for Reuben to discover she had a twin. Jayne had been arrested several times in the past, and there were plenty of articles online about the crimes. Once Reuben discovered her twin, Jayne's Instagram account made her easy to find. She'd created the account to showcase her art, but Jayne also posted pictures of the gorgeous scenery, frequently linking the photos to her location.

That Reuben had decided Jayne was worth a trip to Costa Rica didn't seem logical, but Ava figured Jayne's arrests indicated a person who made reckless decisions. And the recent Instagram images of Jayne had shown they were identical twins.

If Reuben had been obsessed with Ava, the idea of meeting her twin must have been very tempting.

"After we met, I bumped into him all the time in our little town."

He stalked her.

"He was a big flirt." Jayne looked at her hands in her lap. "I'm sorry, Brady," she whispered.

Brady took one of her hands. "It's okay. You were lonely. I shouldn't have been gone so much."

"You had been flying back and forth to Portland?" Mason asked.

"Yes. Mom and Dad are cutting back how much time they put into the dealerships. I've been trying to pick up the slack and get ready for a bigger role in the business. Jayne and I had planned to move back this coming fall."

"He was gone for weeks at a time," Jayne added. "Reuben showered me with the attention I was missing."

"You were pregnant," Ava pointed out.

"He didn't mind."

Ava hid a shudder. "Were you going to leave Brady?"

"No, it was just a fling. Both Reuben and I knew that."

She's so matter-of-fact about it.

"We flew into San Diego and drove up the coast."

Ava decided not to ask where she'd gotten the fake passport.

"I'd told Reuben about David's birthday party at the coast. He convinced me I shouldn't tell them I was coming and make a surprise entrance."

Reuben figured out how to appeal to her ego.

"Why use the stolen driver's license?" Mason asked. "Why didn't Reuben put the rooms under his name?"

A thoughtful look crossed Jayne's face. "He said he didn't want any trace of us being together in case Brady came looking for me. That made sense at the time, but now it seems kinda lame. I think I was too excited to really care."

Brady's throat moved as he swallowed. Ava ached for the young man.

"Before David's birthday, we stayed in a little house in Seaside for a few days. Reuben got phone call after phone call from his brother. All they did was argue. I knew Shawn didn't want him to go through with something, but I didn't know what it was . . . I guess I do now."

The courthouse shooting.

"Reuben said he had to go to Portland for a little bit to meet with his brother. I stayed at the beach. He promised he'd be back in time to go to David's party."

"He was going with you?" Ava asked, shocked that Jayne would show off her fling to that family.

"Oh no. He would just drive me."

"So Reuben left for Portland," Mason said to get Jayne's story back on track.

"Yes. He was stressed. He told me that Shawn had changed his mind about something and Reuben was determined to change it back."

"Shawn stuck to his guns," Ava said. "Reuben killed him for it. Shawn must have threatened to go to the police."

"Reuben was furious with Shawn," Jayne said. "He told me he'd always hated his brother, but the two of them did see eye to eye on the role of police." She glanced nervously at Ava. "He alluded to a plan to make a statement to the leaders of our country. I thought he was all talk. I ignored it."

The same way Gillian did.

"How long was Reuben gone when he went to Portland?" asked Mason.

"One night. He came back late the next evening."

"Shawn was killed that first night," said Mason. "Reuben disfigured the body and left his driver's license behind to make us assume it was him. We wouldn't search for a dead man."

"That's why he used the mallet on the jaw and cut off the fingers," Ava said. "Didn't want us to quickly figure out it was Shawn."

"Shawn's fingerprints aren't on file. He's never been arrested," Mason said. "I guess Reuben didn't know that about his brother. I don't know what it would take to make me cut off my brother's fingers."

"There was some deep hatred on both brothers' parts," Ava said. "But why leave the fingers and teeth behind?"

"My guess is he panicked when he heard Gillian freaking out at his back door."

"He knew she'd call the police," Ava surmised. "He had to act fast to write the statement to lead the police to the courthouse. I wonder if he and Shawn had actually planned a different day for the attack? But Shawn's refusal to follow through changed the plan?"

"We'll never know," said Mason. "Two dead brothers."

Ava studied Jayne. *What does it take to kill a sibling?* She'd lost patience and been angry with Jayne more times than she could count. She had never considered killing her. Not literally, anyway.

"Reuben wasn't right in the head," Ava said. It wasn't a medical diagnosis or definition, but something had definitely been off.

"I think he may have killed his father," Mason said slowly.

"What?" Ava was startled. Brady and Jayne both turned their attention to Mason.

"I gathered from his sister and her husband that the festering anger was present in their father. It was possibly passed to Reuben through genetics or simply a brutal childhood. The report on his father's suicide doesn't read like a suicide to me. Reuben may have acted on pent-up anger. Anger for his father's treatment of his mother and of her children. The police were called several times to his childhood home. From the reports I read, they talked to the parents, but no one would press charges. They noted they saw bruises on his mother."

Ava stilled as something clicked into place in her brain. "The police never helped his mother?"

"It doesn't appear so. But she has to want the help. It wouldn't surprise me if she turned them away. It happens a lot with violence in families."

"Reuben questioned me on how to handle a domestic violence situation for a 'friend,'" Ava said. "His friend wasn't getting the help expected from the authorities. It's odd that he brought it up years after his parents died. He must have still carried resentment about the situation." She grimaced. "I think my answers and unexpected sympathy are part of what made him see me as different from other law enforcement. I listened and offered solutions. As a child, he probably saw the police come and leave, but nothing ever changed. He witnessed his father do brutal things to his mother and possibly transferred a lot of his anger to the police," said Ava. "Those poor kids."

"Veronica has her head on straight," said Mason. "I think." He took a deep breath. "Where were we? Oh. What Reuben did after the courthouse shooting. At some point he dumped his truck at the airport and was driving Shawn's car, but he used a rental car to get away from the courthouse shooting."

"He was driving the Mustang when he came back to the beach," said Jayne. "The rental car we picked up in San Diego."

"And he stole plates for it in Medford," Ava added. "He was planning ahead."

"We did stop in Medford," Jayne said. "I went shopping while he watched a baseball game at a bar."

And stole license plates.

"We saw security footage of him hitting you in Cannon Beach the morning after the courthouse shooting."

"We had been arguing for most of the night by then. He had been stressed out of his head when he came back the evening after the shooting happened. I asked how it went with his brother, and he got angry with me. I'd seen the news about the courthouse and brought it up." Jayne shrugged. "I thought it was just a topic of conversation, but he absolutely lost it. That's when he first hit me. I accused him of being the shooter—I didn't mean it. It just came out. But when I saw his face after my accusation, I knew he'd done it." She took a deep breath. "I told him I wanted to go home, and it went downhill from there.

"By morning he said he had something to show me, and we went to Cannon Beach. I was a wreck." Her voice cracked. "That's when he killed David right in front of me. He said that if I told the police anything about the courthouse, he'd do the same to Brady and Ava." She wiped her eyes and sniffed. "I believed him." Brady tightened his grip on her hand, sympathy on his face.

"How did he know where to find David?" Ava asked.

"We knew where they were staying because of the party invitation. I don't know how he found out that David ran on the beach every morning."

"Then what happened?" Mason asked gently.

"I did whatever he said. We went from the coast to that cabin that day. He didn't trust me anymore and kept me tied up for two days. Sometimes he'd be gone for hours."

"He killed Kaden during one of those times," Ava said.

"Reuben had also been arguing on the phone with someone else," Jayne said, rubbing tears from her cheeks. "Someone owed him money. And then the man showed up at the cabin."

"Tony Schroeder," said Mason. "He's lucky he's going to live. I asked him where Reuben got the guns I found under Kaden's bed, but Tony didn't know. He told me Reuben thought Kaden had seen something when he killed Shawn. He told Tony he was cleaning up."

"He shot Kaden in the head and said that to his father?" Ava was stunned. "His paranoia was out of control. What does it take to do that *and* to kill your own brother?"

"Tony's appearance caught Reuben off guard, and he only tied me by one hand," said Jayne. "That's when I called you." Tearful eyes looked at Ava. "I made huge mistakes. Tons of them."

Surprise filled Ava. Jayne never admitted to mistakes. "What about the baby?" she asked.

"What about it?" Jayne looked confused.

"I've asked her to marry me," Brady said.

Jayne turned to him. "You know I'm not quite ready for that yet. Especially after what I just did to you," she said earnestly.

But you're ready for a baby?

"We're going to live here for a while," said Jayne. "After the baby comes, we'll look for our own place. I think it'd be too much to do during my last trimester."

She almost sounds responsible. Maybe the months off drugs and alcohol have helped.

"I agree with you," said Mason. "But it will also be hard after the baby comes. Those first few months are a blur." He caught Ava's eye but didn't say anything.

She frowned at him, unsure of what he was trying to tell her.

He took her hand and rubbed his thumb over her engagement ring.

Oh. My wedding attendant.

She considered Jayne as her twin spoke quietly with Brady about where they wanted to look for a home.

What have I got to lose?

"Jayne." Ava struggled for words. *Just say it.* "I want you to be in our wedding."

Jayne's lips formed an O. "Are you sure? I've been so awful. And I can't promise I won't do anything stupid ever again."

"You're still my sister." Ava hesitated. "But you have to promise to not make a scene. It's *my* day," she said firmly. She gestured at Jayne's stomach. "Your day is coming."

Jayne clapped her hands together. "I'm so excited. What will I wear?" She laid both hands on her belly. "I saw the most awesome formal maternity dress the other day. It was a deep red."

Ava pictured a red dress next to her gown's unusual shade. "No. We need to look for black."

"Black?" Jayne grimaced. "That's depressing. I think the dress came in purple too."

"I'm positive it has to be black. Remember—it's *my* day."

Her twin pressed her lips together, the need to argue clear on her face. "It's your day," she finally admitted.

Ava took a moment to appreciate the sensation of her sister giving in. She caught Mason's amused gaze. He knew it was a foreign feeling.

Progress.

32

"You look amazing."

Cheryl handed her a bouquet of white flowers, and Ava smiled at the wedding planner. The two of them were in a large airy room near the back of the winery. Sunshine spilled in through tall windows. Ava couldn't have asked for better weather. Even the blue skies were happy on her wedding day.

It was almost time.

Family and friends were seated in rows of white chairs on the winery's large patio, overlooking acres of grapevines and stunning views of the coast range. The winery was more beautiful than she'd dreamed it would be when she first visited the charming French château and grounds in the fall. It was a storybook setting.

"Nervous?" Cheryl asked.

Ava considered. "Not at all. Am I supposed to be?"

"Most brides are. But you are not most brides." Cheryl raised a brow as she pointedly looked at the dress.

"I absolutely am not." It had been impossible to find the color of dress she wanted. Wedding gowns came in almost every color, but none of them had been right. She'd finally had a dress professionally dyed. It was perfect.

"Still don't know what to call that shade," Cheryl said. "Silvery teal blue? Pale stormy ocean? Icy aqua sea mist?"

Ava didn't care. It was a dreamy shade and made her happy.

She ran a hand over the bodice of the strapless gown. It was a heavily beaded corset with a peplum that flared several inches over the tulle skirt. Cheryl bent and swished the long skirt at the hem, making it lift and float into place. Dozens of layers of tulle gently draped and flowed behind her. It was ethereal, and Ava reveled in the confidence that came from wearing an incredible dress.

"Ready?"

Ava nodded.

"I got a look at Mason. He should definitely wear a suit more often. Made me second-guess my singlehood."

"Let's go."

Ava followed Cheryl down a hall and into the beautiful tasting room, which was set for the wedding dinner. Large windows lined an entire wall, and Ava saw her guests patiently waiting outside. Cheryl paused at the winery's large iron-and-wood doors, which belonged on a regal home in France. She winked at Ava and pushed them open. Sunshine streamed in and Ava stepped out.

Her gaze went straight to Mason, standing with Ray, the pastor, and Jayne on a slightly raised platform at the edge of the patio, beautifully framed by the mountain range behind them.

Mason's dark-brown eyes locked with hers. Ray elbowed Mason and leaned close to whisper something. Both men broke into grins, but Mason didn't drop his eye contact.

It'd been less than two years, but she felt as if she'd known him forever. Somehow he'd always been a part of her, but that piece had been hidden until they met in person.

I sound sappy.

But it was true.

She moved down the aisle between the rows of chairs. It wasn't a large group, and she knew every single person. A loud sigh caught her attention, and she spotted Henley, the young daughter of Mason's ex-wife. The girl's wide-eyed gaze said she was in love with the gown. Henley's kidnapping had brought Mason and Ava together.

A horrible episode.

But happy results.

Mason's son, Jake, stood by Henley. He was looking more and more like his father every day.

So many friends had come to share their day. Michael Brody and his wife, Jamie. Gianna Trask, the medical examiner, her husband, Chris, and her daughter, Violet. Chief Medical Examiner Seth Rutledge and his wife, Victoria Peres. The forensic odontologist Lacey Harper and her husband, Jack. Mercy and Truman.

Ava gave Zander a deep smile, delighted to see him happily standing next to Emily. He deserved love.

And then there was her new family. Her father, David's, two children, their spouses, and their four children. At David's funeral, Ava had made the decision to involve them in her life. Life was too short and too precious. Her father's death had taught her that.

Jayne's near-death experience had reinforced the belief. She looked to her twin, and Ava knew she'd made the right decision—to have Jayne stand up with her today.

She reached Mason, and he took her hand. "About time," he said.

"I love you too." She did. Wholeheartedly.

"You take my breath away," he told her.

"I don't think my feet are touching the ground," she said. "I can't believe we're finally standing here."

"I knew we'd make it. All of us." Mason glanced at Ray and Jayne.

Both of them could be gone.

Ray coughed. "Didn't know being shot was required to be an attendant today," he whispered.

Jayne slapped a hand over her mouth, stifling her laugh.

At least we can laugh about it now.

Mason squeezed her hand. "Ready?"

273

"I've been ready for months."

"Me too."

Ava's heart swelled, and she remembered her discussion with Cheryl a few weeks ago. Ava hadn't believed a ceremony would change the love between her and Mason, but now she knew Cheryl had been absolutely right.

As the two of them stood before their friends and family, proclaiming their vows, she felt their love expand and deepen. It wasn't logical, what she experienced around him; the happiness resonated in every cell, every nerve, every vessel in her body.

He kissed her. It was done.

Mason enveloped her in a deep hug as everyone applauded and whistled.

"Not letting you ever get away, Special Agent McLane," he whispered.

"Never."

Acknowledgments

I've known for a few years that I'd left unanswered questions about Mason, Ava, and Jayne. I'd intended to return to them after I wrote a few Mercy Kilpatrick books. I had no idea that I would write six Mercy books. It felt good to write about these people again. Mason Callahan has been an important character in my books since my debut novel, *Hidden*, came out in 2012. Don't be surprised if he and Ava pop up in future books. I love returning to old characters, and according to the emails I receive, my readers do too.

Thank you to my team at Montlake, who give me free rein to write about my favorite characters. They are amazing people, and every day I am grateful to work with them. Thank you to Charlotte Herscher, who has edited every book I've ever written. I've learned a lot over seventeen novels. Thank you to Meg Ruley, my amazing agent and number one cheerleader.

Thank you to Melinda Leigh, who always gets my butt in gear when I need it. Our friendship means the world to me. If you haven't read her books, do it!

Thank you to my readers, who come back for more and write me kind notes. They make my day.

Thank you to my girls for being patient with a very distracted mom.

ABOUT THE AUTHOR

Photo © 2016 Rebekah Jule Photography

Kendra Elliot has landed on the *Wall Street Journal* bestseller list multiple times and is the award-winning author of the Bone Secrets and Callahan & McLane series, as well as the Mercy Kilpatrick novels. Kendra is a three-time winner of the Daphne du Maurier Award, an International Thriller Writers Award finalist, and an RT Award finalist. She has always been a voracious reader, cutting her teeth on classic female heroines such as Nancy Drew, Trixie Belden, and Laura Ingalls. She was born, raised, and still lives in the rainy Pacific Northwest with her family, but she looks forward to the day she can live in flip-flops. Visit her at www.kendraelliot.com.